UNSEEN UNKNOWN UNIMAGINABLE
THE WORLD OF DARKNESS IS
ALL AROUND US
JOIN US THERE

Keith "Doc" Herber
Scott Ciencin
John H. Steele
S. P. Somtow
Ray Winninger
Thomas Kane
Scott H. Urban
Sam Chupp
Richard Lee Byers
Phil Brucato
R. S. Martin
Lawrence Watt-Evans
Bill Bridges
Don Bassingthwaite

THE WORLD OF DARKNESS

WEREWOLF
Wyrm Wolf
Conspicuous Consumption

VAMPIRE
Dark Prince
Netherworld

MAGE
Such Pain

WRAITH
Sins of the Fathers

Published by HarperPrism

Strange City

ANTHOLOGY

Edited by

Staley Krause and Stewart Wieck

HarperPrism
An Imprint of HarperPaperbacks

This is a work of fiction. The characters, incidents, and dialogues are products of the author's imagination and are not to be construed as real. Any resemblance to actual events or persons, living or dead, is entirely coincidental.

HarperPaperbacks *A Division of* HarperCollins*Publishers*
10 East 53rd Street, New York, N.Y. 10022

First printing: February 1996

Printed in the United States of America

HarperPrism is an imprint of HarperPaperbacks.
HarperPaperbacks, HarperPrism, and colophon are trademarks of HarperCollins*Publishers*.

❖ 10 9 8 7 6 5 4 3 2 1

Contents

Introduction vii

Dancing with the Devil 1
Keith "Doc" Herber

Hunter's Blues 23
Scott Ciencin

Glimpses of Before 49
John H. Steele

The Voice of the Hummingbird 67
S. P. Somtow

The Bye-Bye Club 111
Ray Winninger

The Way It Goes 125
Thomas Kane

The Scarlet Letters 143
Scott H. Urban

Descent 163
Sam Chupp

Wolf Trap 191
Richard Lee Byers

Shards 215
Phil Brucato

Rootbound 227
R. S. Martin

The Art of Dying 253
Lawrence Watt-Evans

The Waters of Lethe 269
Bill Bridges

Power 285
Don Bassingthwaite

Introduction

Critics of so-called "game fiction"—that is novels or stories that are set in a world originally created for use in a storytelling game—like to point out how clique-ish such work appears to be. Such stories are supposedly meant to be read only by readers "in the know"—those who are already familiar with the fictional setting. The same argument has been leveled against stories set in any licensed universe, such as the future depicted in *Star Trek* or the investigations in the X-*Files* novels.

The challenge is often valid. Books using such worlds as a background can be created with that specific audience of those "in the know" in mind. In some cases, critics point out, the stories suffer because this built-in audience will buy the book simply as a fan of the world and not necessarily as a discriminating reader looking for a good story.

Therein lies the difference between stories set in White Wolf's World of Darkness and stories based in many of the countless other fictional worlds.It has always been the goal of the creators of the World of Darkness to share this rich setting by reaching many different people in many different ways.Gamers can interact with the world through storytelling games; computer games exist (or soon will) that allow the player to access the World of Darkness in another way. And fiction, like the short stories collected here, allow the general reader to also explore the World of Darkness.

Newcomers to the World of Darkness, as well as those who have entered the world before, will find a rich selection of stories here.The World of Darkness is a complex setting harboring many creations that will be new and unfamiliar to the general reader of horror or dark fantasy, but that doesn't stop these stories from succeeding for all readers.

Certain stories ("The Art of Dying," "Wolf Trap," and "Rootbound") make very definite use of the unique lexicon of the setting, and may indeed take some warming to, but the richness of the World of Darkness is such that these excellent stories work within or without the World of Darkness. The fact that they are set within the world adds depth to the setting and demonstrates that readers who simply enjoy fine stories can find something to their taste in the World of Darkness as well.

But if you do find you need some help getting up to speed on the three main aspects of the World of Darkness covered in this collection, then I recommend the following stories: for *Vampire: The Masquerade* try "The Scarlet Letters"; for *Werewolf: The Apocalypse* try "The Waters of Lethe," and for *Wraith: The Oblivion* try "Glimpses of Before." Those should whet your appetite and again prove that the stories set in the World of Darkness are not, in fact, restricted to those "in the know."

Stewart Wieck
October 1995

Dancing with the Devil

by Keith "Doc" Herber

Delfonso awoke late. He had overslept again; he could feel it.

He stretched in his coffin, felt his joints creak, then sat up. He was awake.

Gaining his feet, he groped the old adobe wall for the light switch. Overhead, a bare bulb sprung to life, splashing the ancient corridor with yellow light.

Delfonso stretched again, rolled his head around, working the stiffness out of his neck. He was an old vampire, among the oldest in San Francisco. And if not the oldest, certainly the longest resident undead.

He felt as though he'd been asleep a long time and wondered if he had not slept through a whole night, failing to wake altogether. It had happened before—only a few times—but enough to raise Delfonso's concerns. As vampires grew older, he had learned, they often slept longer, more deeply, and through almost anything. Delfonso had been undead nearly five hundred years. Perhaps it was catching up with him.

With a pale-white hand he brushed the dust from his black trousers, his fingers finding the small rip where he had snagged them the night before on the seat of his limousine. He had ordered Juan to fix the broken spring first thing the next day.

Looking into the small mirror hanging on the wall across from the alcove containing his coffin, Delfonso smoothed his black dress coat, straightened his collar and white tie, and, with delicate fingertips, brushed smooth his narrow, closely trimmed mustache and tiny, pointed beard.

He must appear respectable.

He felt the urge to go out tonight. Hunger gnawed. How long since he had last fed? A week? Ten days? He couldn't remember. All he knew was that as he grew older the Hunger seemed to wane. Oh, it was still as demanding, but it came less often, forcing Delfonso to kill less often.

He would have to call Juan from the upstairs phone, he thought to himself, get him over right away. What time *was* it?

To his right, the corridor led to a narrow wooden stairway that reached the house above; at the other end stood a heavy, rough-timber door, mounted with black iron hinges and lock. It was to this door he now walked. Pulling an antique key from his pocket, he unlocked it and pushed it open, revealing a midnight-black chamber beyond. He snapped a wall switch and light sprang up. The room was filled with ancient instruments of torture: the rack, strappadoes, and other examples of the Spanish Inquisition's trade shipped here centuries ago from Mexico City. Delfonso had them installed in this underground chamber—a chamber once connected to the adobe mission built here in 1776 by the Franciscan father Junipero Serra. Serra had disapproved of the chamber, but Delfonso had then been posing as an agent of the Inquisition sent from Mexico City. Fear kept the father from protesting too much.

Delfonso had made good use of the chamber, encouraging recalcitrant Indians to accept the word of God, and occasionally chastising a Spanish soldier from the Presidio who had strayed from the righteous path. Originally a scheme hatched by the vampire to afford him a steady source of food, it was while torturing one of his victims that he had at last, finally realized the role he was meant to play in this world. He was to be an avenger sent from heaven to save the most desperate of lost souls. Many had found God while writhing on his rack. Delfonso, watching their agonized throes, eventually found God too. After hundreds of years "lost in the wilderness," he had come to discover *why* he was. He returned to the warm embrace of his Catholic religion, once more assured of his salvation in the hereafter.

Gently, with a loving hand, Delfonso stroked the dark-stained timbers of the rack. So many had died on this machine—in immense pain and suffering—but how many souls had Delfonso saved? How many had he, at the last minute, saved from Eternal Damnation and sent winging to heaven?

Delfonso had lost count.

Turning to a small niche in the wall, he struck a match and lit a small votive candle within. Light filled the opening, revealing a statue of the Virgin Mary. Delfonso genuflected, quickly muttered a Hail Mary, then made the sign of the cross. Before extinguishing the candle, he drew out a small, silver crucifix from inside his shirt, kissed it, then touched it to the even colder lips of the statue.

Tonight, he had promised the Virgin, he would save another soul.

Once upstairs, Delfonso telephoned his Filipino chauffeur and told him to bring the car around. They would be going out tonight. Putting a CD on his large stereo system, he listened to the opening strains of *La Bohème* while waiting for Juan to appear. The chauffeur lived a few blocks away, and it would be a few minutes before he arrived.

While he listened to the music, Delfonso's eyes roamed over the souvenirs, trophies, and other memorabilia crowding the house's small living room: a large, antique globe; a bookshelf crowded with old volumes and binders full of maps and charts; a pair of antique Spanish lances and a shield mounted over the fireplace. Delfonso noticed the dust thickly coating everything and made a mental note to have Juan come in and clean sometime soon.

His eyes came to rest on the old Spanish helmet sitting on a walnut end table. Looking at it, he was taken back to his early days in the New World whence he had come, the poor third son of a Spanish nobleman, desperate to make his own fortune. Carrying banners, Delfonso and four hundred other Spaniards had marched inland in search of gold and Indian souls to save. They discovered the Aztec civilization, its gold, and worse, its infernal rites. Delfonso could still remember the endless lines of captives marched up the broad temple steps to where the priest Nezahualcoyotl would carve their living hearts from their bodies and offer them to the sun god. The Spaniards had been horrified by the spectacle and soon after overthrew Moctezuma II, ending the savage worship.

But before that would happen Delfonso himself was to die in this horrible manner. Captured by the savages one evening while separated from his troops, Delfonso was carried to a secret temple outside the Aztec city. Here, the Indians threw him on his back across the sacrificial altar, holding him fast while a priest raised a jagged obsidian blade high in the air, then plunged it down through Delfonso's chest, hacking away the Spaniard's still-beating heart.

Delfonso winced at the pain of the memory.

He had awakened some time later, near midnight, choking on a vile fluid being poured down his throat. Surprised to find himself alive, Delfonso listened as the Aztec priest explained what had been done: how Delfonso had been killed then resurrected with the living blood of a secret and eternal race. The priest was aware that the coming of the conquistadors meant the doom of his people—as had been prophesied for so long—and, knowing that he would die, the priest intended the lineage of Nezahualcoyotl to continue. Delfonso recalled having the distinct impression that Nezahualcoyotl himself was not aware of the "favor" the priest was doing him.

After the Aztecs had fallen to the Spaniards, Delfonso found himself alone in the wilderness, an untrained vampire Childe whose mentor had been slain, and who knew little of himself other than he was no longer of his own kind. Years he had spent in the jungle, dwelling on the outskirts of the slowly expanding Spanish settlements, preying on pagan Indians and the occasional Spaniard. He thought of those years spent alone, his very soul in mortal jeopardy . . .

A soft knock at the front door brought him out of his reverie. Juan had arrived.

Rising from his chair, Delfonso grabbed his cape and hat hanging on the wall and, opening the door, stepped out into the damp, heavy air of the city's Mission District.

Expertly, the young Filipino driver maneuvered the black stretch Continental through the Friday late evening traffic.

"I think Domingo is probably down around Twenty-fourth Street," Juan said, glancing over his shoulder to where Delfonso lounged in the back seat.

"Head down that way, then," ordered Delfonso. "He should accompany us on our foray this evening."

The Filipino smiled and nodded. A ghoul now working for Delfonso nearly six years, Juan hoped that someday Delfonso would adopt him as Childe. Delfonso found Juan properly subservient and respectful, but not the sort he would consider raising to vampire—although he never indicated this to Juan.

The limo made its way steadily south down teeming

Mission Street alive with excitement and action on a weekend night. Lower middle class at best, the Mission district is a sprawling flatland nearly surrounded by hills and mountains, its streets a never-ending series of wall-to-wall cheap stucco or frame houses now inhabited mainly by Hispanics. Located south of the city proper, the district was built up during the late nineteenth century, a blue-collar neighborhood successively inhabited by Scandinavians and Germans, then Irish, then Italians, and now Mexicans and other Latino groups. Even the small enclave of Chinese hail mostly from Peru and speak fluent Spanish.

Louder, noisier than ever, its streets plied by low-riders booming salsa and with Mexican restaurants on every corner, the Mission District seemed to Delfonso fated to be home to a never-ending string of ill-educated, uncultured immigrants. He had lived here since 1906, after losing his suite and nearly all his belongings in the Palace Hotel fire following the great quake. Uninsured, and finances dwindling, he'd moved to his present home in a part of the Mission untouched by the holocaust. He had lived here ever since. Hardly a day went by that he had not had occasion to regret it.

He scanned the streets, filled with pedestrians, lingerers, girls in low-cut dresses too tight and too short. Sinners, he thought to himself.

Sinners—every one of them. Would they someday be redeemed?

"I think I see Domingo," Juan said over the back of the seat. "Over there, in that crowd."

Delfonso sat forward, looking through the windshield at the corner where Juan pointed. He easily spotted Domingo.

A squat, hefty Mexican, Domingo had been Delfonso's Childe for almost forty years now. Born in Los Angeles, the man had come to San Francisco in

1943, one step ahead of the draft board, and soon after met fatefully with a hungry Delfonso. A dope-peddling zoot-suiter back in L.A., Domingo had proven useful to Delfonso. Domingo had a street presence Delfonso lacked, and did a much better job of controlling the local area than the elder Spaniard could ever hope to. True, he could terrorize in a way that Domingo couldn't, but Delfonso felt he could not—perhaps would not—meet and mingle with this half-breed crowd of Indians and Spanish.

"Pull over and blow the horn," Delfonso told Juan.

At the sound of the horn, Domingo looked up and saw the limo waiting at the curb. A quick knocking together of fists with the gang members he was talking to, then he was walking toward the limo. Delfonso watched Domingo's strut. Just slow enough to impress his friends, but not so slow as to anger his master. Domingo could play the line.

"Good evening, Mr. Delfonso," said Domingo, sticking his head through the opened window, grinning, showing his gold tooth.

"Hop inside," Delfonso told him. "We go hunting tonight."

Domingo waved his friends off then clambered into the front seat, next to Juan.

"Hey-y-y," he drawled. "It is a good night for hunting, eh, amigo." He smiled at Juan.

Juan grinned back, and winked.

"Head downtown," Delfonso ordered the driver, then settled back into the deep-red velvet seat while Domingo filled him in on street happenings.

While the limo crept steadily north, Domingo described current conditions in the Mission, moneys collected, and suspected infringements by "poachers"—vampires from other parts of town—hunting and feeding in the Mission District. Vannevar Thomas, reigning Prince of the city, kept a sharp eye on the boundaries between provinces, and violations were dealt with harshly.

But Delfonso soon found the talk growing stale. The two had really very little in common aside from a similarity of native language. The older Spaniard found himself growing bored.

"I require privacy," Delfonso finally said. "Notify me if you spot a likely prospect."

Pushing a button in the armrest he watched Domingo's scowling, thick-headed face disappear behind the opaque screen rising up out of the back of the front seat. The passenger compartment was now sealed and although he could still hear the muffled conversation of Domingo and Juan, Delfonso chose to ignore it.

Delfonso relaxed back into his seat, letting his mind wander. His idle fingers again found the tear in his trouser leg and he thought of the broken wire in the limo seat. He bent forward to see if Juan had repaired it as he had asked him to and was appalled to find that, although the wire was now safely clipped, the chauffeur had patched the fabric with nothing more than a piece of red cloth tape that *almost* matched the red of the velvet upholstery.

"Damn," Delfonso told himself. Was there no one he could trust to do a proper job anymore? Then, taking a good look at the limo's interior, realized how worn and threadbare the whole vehicle was getting to be. Even the exterior—as polished as Juan might keep it—on closer inspection showed numerous chips and dents inexpertly filled and repainted. Delfonso realized the car was getting old and a little care-worn.

Much like himself, he thought.

They reached broad, busy Market street, and Juan turned right, heading northwest; the Moorish-styled clock tower of the old Ferry building stood proudly at the end of the street. Built in 1898, it was one of the few major structures in this part of town to survive the great earthquake. Ahead, on the right, a few blocks this side of the Ferry building, was the spot where once stood the grand and resplendent Palace Hotel, Delfonso's home from 1876 until his forced move to the Mission in 1906. Dwelling on the top, seventh floor, he was one of many permanent residents that lived in the luxurious place. From the gallery outside his apartments he could gaze down upon the Grand Court far below, watching the coming and going of guests riding in carriages that entered and exited via the circle drive in the hotel's interior.

Posing as the Spanish Count Delafonsa, the ex-conquistador had spent the best evenings of his existence there. Famous and distinguished guests from all over the world stayed at the Palace which, with eight hundred rooms, was the largest hotel on the West Coast and one of the largest in the world. Surpassed by none for service, food, and elegance, its furniture was special ordered, as was the solid-gold place setting for one hundred. The hotel's restaurants were unsurpassed, the owner going so far as to lure away the chef from New York's famed Delmonico restaurant. Delfonso, over the years, had spent many a wonderful evening with the likes of such people as Oscar Wilde, Edwin Booth, and even—on the night before the great earthquake—the incomparable Caruso.

Delfonso had attended the grand balls staged there, the lavish parties, and even the funerals of a few distinguished guests. In those days Delfonso had moved with the best society San Francisco could offer, mingling with Floods, McKays, Hopkinses, Stanfords, and Crockers. He had, with Englishman Ned Greenway, helped establish the city's first social register, and because of his noble descent, was often consulted on matters of etiquette and protocol. Inside tips from his Nob Hill acquaintances helped him to amass a fortune in the silver market, and this money he poured back into theaters and operas, raising the social status of the city. San Francisco had been truly great then, he told himself.

A knock on the opaque glass panel startled him. He jabbed at the button in the armrest, dropping the screen ten or twelve inches.

"The usual route?" asked Domingo.

"Yes, yes," Delfonso answered impatiently. "Up through North Beach." Then he closed the screen again.

Juan turned north on Kearney, moving up through the dark and nearly deserted Financial District.

Unlike most of the vampires in the city, Delfonso, by dint of his long-time residence here, had been granted extended hunting privileges, allowing him to seek prey outside his usual Mission District boundaries. Others complained, but because he was so discreet, and because of his dwindling need for food, Vannevar had so far refused to revoke the privilege. Only Chinatown was off-limits to him, and even that not officially. But Delfonso stayed clear of the area, regardless. The mysterious and grotesque thing that dwelled in an underground warren somewhere beneath that crowded and evil-smelling quarter of town was jealous of its territory. Although Delfonso feared little in San Francisco, he had learned to honor the wishes of that thing known only as "Grandfather."

They crept north along Kearney, skirting the southern border of Chinatown, heading toward Broadway and the old Italian section beyond. This was the first inhabited part of the city, back when it was known as Yerba Buena, and not San Francisco. The street they were on, now blocks from the waterfront, was once nearly the edge of the cove that once stood here. Since filled in with rubbish, abandoned ships, and goods whose prices on the market had fallen below reasonable level, it now supported some of the largest skyscrapers on the West Coast, including the strangely pyramidal Transamerica building.

A few blocks further brought them to Pacific Avenue: the old Barbary Coast, once roamed by the worst sorts of thieves, murderers, and prostitutes. It had provided Delfonso with some of the most degraded sinners he'd ever attempted to save, but was now given over to antique shops, graphic design firms, and light industries.

Crossing Broadway and Columbus the air was suddenly filled with light and sound. Traffic was heavy and the sidewalks crowded with people: singles, career-types, yuppies dressed in expensive leather coats haunting cafes and bistros, drinking cappuccinos, chattering brightly, desperately trying to score.

They swung back toward Grant, then north again, past the crowds in front of the Saloon, Grant-Green, and other music clubs along this strip. Although prospects seemed numerous, Delfonso saw nothing to catch his eye. He ordered Juan to keep driving.

They swung west, moving slowly along Fisherman's Wharf, even at this hour still flush with tourists. He saw a few possibilities, but nothing that urged him to stop the car and "invite" one in. Some of them, on some other night, might have tempted him—but not tonight. Tonight, he had decided, he would need a *real* sinner, someone truly deserving of the fate he had in store for them. A fallen and disgraced soul that Delfonso might raise to momentary glory before doing them in.

He dropped the screen a few inches. "Juan!" he ordered sharply. "Take us to the Tenderloin."

A few minutes later found the black limousine prowling that part of San Francisco long known as the Tenderloin. Searching carefully, they worked their way back and forth across the face of Lower Nob Hill, tracing the one-way streets back and forth. First Post, then

Geary, Eddy, and Ellis, working their way downhill, deeper and deeper into the seediest part of the city. The type of woman Delfonso looked for—a prostitute—was plentiful, as were drug pushers, addicts, thieves, and others. But to take a working prostitute right off the streets might lead to trouble. He would have to make a deal with the local pimp, the vampire in charge of running the Tenderloin, an Irishman named Sullivan.

They finally located Sullivan down on O'Farrell Street, near the gaudy and tasteless Mitchell Brothers Adult Theater. The vampire leaned against the wall of the building, partially lit by the glow of the neon sign. His pale skin stood out in the darkness, exaggerated by his Levi's, dark shirt, and pea-jacket, and the knit watch cap he habitually wore.

Sullivan spotted the limo as it pulled near, and stood up straight, watching its approach.

Juan parked the Continental at the curb, and Sullivan, unbidden, approached, glancing up and down the street as he drew near. Delfonso powered down the rear window, and the screen separating him from Juan and Domingo, as well.

"What do you want?" said Sullivan, charmlessly, leaning through the rear window. Once a sailor out of Massachusetts, his thirty-year-old face was rough and lined. Badly trimmed red hair stuck out from under his cap, and his beard, also red, was short and stubbly.

Domingo turned sharply around in his seat. "Hey, gringo! Have some respect, you know? My man here is no street punk, eh?"

Sullivan shot Domingo a glance that might have killed, but Domingo didn't bat an eye.

There was no love lost between these two; Delfonso moved to interrupt.

"Now, now, there's no need of all this. After all, Domingo, we are in Mr. Sullivan's territory and we should behave as proper guests."

Domingo never took his eyes off Sullivan, but he said no more.

"Mr. Sullivan?" Delfonso said.

Sullivan looked back toward Delfonso, ignoring Domingo still boring holes into him with mean, slitted eyes.

"We would like to make a purchase tonight."

This had happened before. Sullivan knew what the old vampire wanted.

"How much you lookin' to spend?"

"About a thousand dollars, I would think."

"That's not very much. I don't even know if I got anything that cheap," said Sullivan.

"I don't require quality," Delfonso explained, smiling. "In fact, the lower the quality, the better."

Sullivan hesitated—looked up and down the street again.

"No. Not for a grand," he finally said. "You're asking me to take a perfectly good whore off the street—permanently. Even the worst of the junkies can turn in that much in three or four days."

"How about twelve-fifty?" offered Delfonso.

"Make it fifteen," countered Sullivan.

"Fourteen hundred?" asked the Spaniard.

"Deal." Sullivan stuck out his hand.

"Pay the man, Domingo," said Delfonso.

"Now," he asked, "who is it we are looking for?"

Domingo fished out a handful of wrinkled bills, counted out the proper amount, and stuffed it in Sullivan's hands. The Irishman, fanning the bills, made a quick count then shoved them in the front pocket of his jeans.

"Her name is Christy," Sullivan said. "Or Christine. I forget. Anyway, bleached blonde hair, kinda frizzed. Real skinny. You can spot her for a junkie a block away. She should be working down around Turk or Golden Gate somewhere. Just prowl around down there. You won't miss her."

"Thank you, my good man," smiled Delfonso. "A pleasure doing business with you, I'm sure."

Sullivan grunted something affirmative and stood back up. Juan waited for a break in traffic then pulled smoothly away, leaving the tall, lean Irishman standing on the sidewalk.

Down on Turk they were in the darkest and lowest part of the Tenderloin. Sandwiched between housing projects and the ornate, expansive Civic Center Plaza, the area was roamed by the worst elements of the city—veritable predators and prey. Pondering this, Delfonso found he did not like the comparison with himself and his business here. But his was a different mission than that of some others. Tonight he would save a soul, perhaps.

They spotted Christine on the corner of Turk and Polk—as Sullivan had said, from nearly a block away. Thin to the point of emaciation, she watched warily as the lone, black limousine rolled toward her down the street. When it stopped in front of her and the rear door opened, she sauntered over, doing the best she could to wiggle what little hips she had left.

"What can I do for you, mister," she piped, trying to sound casual, seductive.

"Step in," said Delfonso, his eyes glowing a bright red from the darkness within.

Without a word the hapless woman stepped into the limo. Now under the power of the vampire, her will was no longer her own.

At the last moment Delfonso decided they would go for a drive rather than go straight back home to the fate awaiting Christine in the secret underground chamber.

"Take us through the park, Juan," he asked. "I feel like a moonlight drive."

Indeed, the moon had risen throughout the evening, up over the Bay to stand at almost zenith in the sky above. Nearly full, its cold, pale light shone down on the city, glowing off the fog rolling in from the Pacific.

Juan's route through Golden Gate Park carried them past the glass-paneled Conservatory and the California Academy of Sciences building built in 1916. Nearby stood the old Music Pavilion, one of the few remnants of San Francisco's Mid-Winter Exposition of 1894. Delfonso had spent many a lovely evening at that fair, more often than not in the company of a lovely young lady or two. In those day he had made the perfect escort: sophisticated, charming, elegant, European, and completely honorable. Never once in all those years, Delfonso thought with a smile, did anyone ever accuse him of attempting liberties with a lady. No, the sort of liberties that Delfonso took were with ladies of an entirely different caste; and they were the sort of liberties that few of his Nob Hill friends would ever guess.

"Do you see, dear," Delfonso asked, pointing out the window as they passed. "I once listened to night-time concerts at that Pavilion, enraptured by the music, with the beautiful Emma Flood on my arm. Yes, those were wonderful evenings. And here . . . here stood the Tower of Electricity with its thousand lights and bright beacon on the top. Electricity was a new and marvelous invention in those days, you know."

Christine did not respond. She sat silent, stupefied, in her seat.

"I'm sorry, my dear," he apologized. "I chatter on when you're not really in the mood for talk. I apologize."

He studied the woman's face, silhouetted by moonlight. Although her skin was coarse and pocked from drug abuse, her features were finely made, and delicate. She had blue eyes much like Emma Flood's, although a bit cloudy. Her forearms were covered with needle scars.

"Perhaps some fresh ocean air will restore your spirits," he said, cheerfully. "Juan?" He dropped the screen a couple inches. "To Ocean Beach please. The lady wishes a drive along the water."

Christine, sitting motionless, said nothing.

The limo wound its way through the park, past ornamental lakes, cultivated gardens, and stands of exotic flora: Australian tree ferns, rhododendron, eucalyptus. At the end of the park they swung out onto the Great Highway and began coasting south, along the broad, gray expanse of Ocean Beach. The wind, as usual, blew in from the sea, the fog bank rising from the waters to drift over the western portions of the city, shrouding it in damp, gray cloud. The breakers rolled up to shore, the surf pounding the beach. Behind them, the Cliff House stood brightly lit atop the bluff overlooking Seal Rock.

"I have a fondness for the salt air," Delfonso told Christine. "It reminds me of times long ago."

Christine again said nothing.

For a time they road in silence, Delfonso gazing out the window wistfully, Christine silent. Delfonso ordered Juan up Twin Peaks Boulevard, running along the city's three central mountains. From this vantage point the city's distant spires and towers sparkled as though dressed in thousands of jewels: a veritable Oz on the water.

"A city of light and life," Delfonso observed. "So much life."

"You know," he said, turning toward the still-silent Christine. "Years ago they dug up all the cemeteries in the city. They moved all the dead out of town in order to make more room for the living. All my old friends, kicked out like so many vagrants. What do you think of that?"

Christine didn't respond.

"They live in Colma, now—south of the city."

The small town of Colma, in the center of the peninsula, is home to San Francisco's dead. Thousands of acres are covered by numerous cemeteries—Russian, Chinese, Catholic, Jewish, and others. The few living residents of Colma community are employed caring for these cemeteries. It was to Colma the limousine now headed. Delfonso had decided to pay his old friends a visit.

Parked at the entrance to Wood Glen Cemetery, Delfonso told Domingo and Juan to wait with the car while he and Christine wandered out into the well-groomed graveyard on foot. The moon was now past overhead, sinking slowly toward the ocean hidden beyond the ridge of the Santa Cruz Mountains running along the coast. Over these mountains the ocean fog crept slowly inland—ghostly, ragged fingers pouring slowly down the slopes.

"Look," he said, gesturing with his arm at the acres of tombstones glistening white under the bright moonlight. "Here lie the fairest of the city's fair, the greatest of its great!"

Pulling the unresisting Christine along by the arm they walked along the rows of endless graves, Delfonso reading names aloud, telling her their stories, their triumphs, and defeats.

"Here's a Crocker grave," he said. "You remember Charles Crocker, don't you? One of the Big Four railroad tycoons? He built the huge mansion on Nob Hill near the Hopkinses and Stanfords."

Christine showed no sign of recognition.

"Certainly you can't forget the famous Crocker spite fence?" he asked.

Crocker had tried to buy the entire block but one stubborn homeowner refused to sell the modest home he'd built on the corner of the lot. Crocker went ahead and built his mansion anyway, then, in an attempt to force the poor man to move, constructed a thirty-foot-high fence of concrete surrounding the shabby little home, virtually shutting out all the man's windows save those facing the street.

"Crocker never was one to take 'No' for an answer," Delfonso chuckled.

"And here's Barnard's tomb," Delfonso cried, half-dragging the girl toward a white-marble mausoleum set atop a slight rise. "One of the city's shining examples of civic responsibility—at least until he got caught in bed with a wife other than his own," Delfonso chuckled. "Shot dead by a jealous husband, but nothing that would keep San Francisco from throwing him one of the best funeral parades ever."

And so it went on, Delfonso half-escorting, half-pulling the bewildered woman through the moonlit cemetery, pointing out names familiar to him, some he'd even forgotten until now.

A tombstone made him pause. He read the name aloud: "Flood. The Bonanza King."

James Flood and his three partners—McKay, Fair, and O'Brien—had early on cornered the Nevada silver mines and cashed in big on the Comstock Lode. His mansion, of Italianate design and built of brownstone, still stands on the corner of California and Mason Streets, the only millionaire's edifice to survive the fire of 1906.

Gazing on the name carved in marble, Delfonso was again reminded of those grand and wonderful days living in the Palace Hotel: the potted palms, the uniformed help, the grand restaurant in the court.

He looked at the girl next to him staring without comprehension at the tombstone. No longer did he see the emaciated prostitute he had picked up on the streets. He saw instead Emma Flood, the silver baron's beautiful, young niece from Sacramento. Young, vivacious, Emma had been a favorite of Delfonso's, and he one of hers.

A sudden thought struck him.

"Mademoiselle?" he asked coyly. "Would you honor me with the next dance?" He made a slight bow in Christine's direction.

Not bothering to wait for an answer, the vampire lifted Christine's arms and, humming Strauss, began waltzing the woman across the cemetery, their forms spinning lightly under the cold and silky moonlight.

Faster and faster they whirled, Delfonso's voice lifted in song, ringing across the deserted cemetery. As they danced, the tombs and grave stones melted away, becoming the white-linen-draped tables of the Palace Ballroom during the Friday night Cotillion. Crowds watched from the sidelines as Delfonso and the lovely Emma Flood tripped lightly across the floor. Other dancers gave way, retiring to the sidelines to watch, relinquishing the entire dance floor to the lovely couple. Emma laughed gaily, giddy from the dance, and Delfonso caught the envious looks cast at him by the younger men attending the ball. Let them envy us, he thought. Smiling widely he spun the light-footed Emma through a series of fast spins that left the gaping crowd speechless. They then applauded while Delfonso and Emma beamed back at them, radiant in the moment.

At the end of the song, to the sounds of more applause, Delfonso politely bowed to the young woman.

"Perhaps you should return to your beau," he said. "I think we have made him a bit jealous. Perhaps you should put his fears to rest . . ."

Emma said nothing—only smiled then turned and walked away, back to the young men waiting impatiently on the sidelines.

Delfonso sat down on the nearest chair, resting,

looking over the faces of the crowd. He could see them all clearly: the friends, the rivals, even a few that had eventually fallen to Delfonso's Hunger. They were all here.

The sound of a woman's scream shook him awake. The crowds of people melted away into nothing, the tables and chairs became tombstones once again. A second scream—suddenly choked off—brought him to his feet. Alert, he realized he'd been lost in a daydream.

Up the rise, a short distance off, stood the limousine. Two dark figures—Juan and Domingo—huddled nearby. Shocked, Delfonso could see them sharing the corpse of Christine in feast.

"Stop!" he shouted, sprinting back to the limo. "God! Don't do that!"

But it was too late. Christine was dead, already a good portion of her blood drained away. Juan had jumped up at the sound of Delfonso's voice, but Domingo remained where he was, crouched over the corpse.

"We thought you gave her to us," the Mexican said. "You sent her over to us."

Regaining his composure, Delfonso realized Domingo was right.

"Yes, yes, of course," he corrected himself. "By all means . . ."

The two immediately fell back upon the corpse.

Delfonso chose not to watch, instead waiting patiently in the backseat of the car for the two to finish their meal. A few minutes later Juan and Domingo got back in.

"Where to, sir?" Juan asked.

"Take us home," Delfonso said quietly.

"We are finished tonight?"

"Yes," Delfonso answered. "I'm afraid I no longer have an appetite."

Hunter's Blues

by Scott Ciencin

They had to shout to make themselves heard over the sound of the chopper's blades and their own weapons fire. Larry and Joe didn't mind. Getting used to the noise had been no more difficult than acclimating themselves to the freezing cold temperatures and hostile living conditions in northern Alaska. Both men were used to making changes. In their business, they were constantly reminded of the old adage: adapt or perish. Younger, stronger, and faster competitors came out of the woodwork on a daily basis, yet Larry and Joe were survivors.

They were *professionals*.

"You remember Sienkevitch?" Larry asked as he switched to a scope rifle and took aim at a fleeing form below. "That asshole from Corpus Christi? Said he was the best hitter in the Lone Star state."

Joe nodded. "That one."

"Hang on," Larry said. It had taken him a little while to get used to the harness that allowed him to sit with his feet dangling out of the helicopter's passenger side. His first few shots this way had been misses, but he quickly got the hang of it. He was 6'2", with blocky features and pockmarked skin. His black hair was slicked back and held in a ponytail. Joe teased him that he was trying to look like Steven Seagal. Larry didn't care. "Got me some easy money down here."

Below, the glaring, white carpet of snow was not enough to hide the frantic movements of a light-gray wolf and the animal's nightmare-black companion. Larry squeezed the trigger and the head of the gray wolf exploded. The black wolf that had been running beside the fallen creature stopped suddenly and let out a howl that cut through the screaming winds and the monotonous sounds of the helicopter.

"What did you load that thing with?" Joe asked. He was a little shorter than his companion, with a shock of red hair, doughy features, and an honest-to-God dimple. His professional name was "The Choirboy." Larry was known as "The Pilot" for a job early in his career. Both men were in their mid-forties.

"I tried out some hollow points."

"Damn. Well, there's the last one. Big son of a bitch. He's all mine."

"Have at it, partner." Larry settled back in his harness and allowed Joe to get comfortable. Beneath them, the black wolf obligingly padded around the body of its dead companion in aimless circles. The chopper pilot held their position. "Anyway, like I was starting to say, this guy, Sienkevitch."

"Right. The asshole from Corpus Christi."

"He's like, what, twenty-three years old. Thinks he knows everything. Going on and on about how crisp and clean he makes his kills, how he gets to know them so well, even bought his last one a drink in some bar an hour before he ran him down on the street."

"Gotcha." Joe readied his automatic weapon. He wanted to wait until the black wolf looked up. Then he was going to turn the creature into pulp, just as they had the other seven members of the pack they had stalked this morning. Their agent, Old Lou the Repairman, said the boys needed to get away from it all. He suggested they take a *rest cure* somewhere, try to unwind. Their last couple of assignments had been performed with such enthusiasm that even Old Lou was taken aback. Larry and Joe said they were just doing their jobs. Old Lou changed his tune a little, said he respected that and wanted to reward them. So here they were in Alaska, doing for fun what they normally did for $100,000 a head:

Spilling blood.

"I told this snot he didn't have to be so anal. Most times, you got to take someone out; they pretty much help you do it. People are idiots."

"Got that right," Joe said, waiting patiently for the wolf to look up at him.

"I made a bet with this dick. I told him, I had this guy to get rid of the next day. Simple job, no big deal. Seven or eight sticks of dynamite rigged up to his ignition. Start her up, *bam*, it's all over folks, one less moron eating oxygen."

"Sure."

"I told him, this guy's car looks like it hasn't been washed for six months. A black car, foreign. Doesn't take care of it at all. I said, before I plant the stuff, I'm gonna hot wire the car, take it through a car wash, then put it back and see if this guy notices anything different."

"I love it."

"Well, our pal Sienkevitch, he says, of course the guy's going to notice. No one could be that dumb. So we go out there together. I show him the car. It looks almost gray, there's so much muck on it. We take it out, put it through a car wash, even get one of those lemon scent things to spray around inside. Sienkevitch is like, gimme a break. Even if the guy's so stupid he doesn't notice the way his car's all black and shining after this wash and wax, he's gonna smell the scent and know something's up. I tell him, he's got to have a little faith in human nature."

On the ground below, the wolf looked up. Its green eyes sparkled in the intense sunlight. Joe opened up on the wolf as it bolted. Impossibly, not one of his shots connected.

"Follow that piece of shit!" Joe commanded. The helicopter pilot was already tracking the wolf, giving the assassins a clear shot at all times. "Sorry. What happened? Who won the bet?"

"Let's just say, when our buddy Sienkevitch went to pay the rent that month, he was a little short."

"You sent that asshole packing."

"To the moon, Alice. To the moon."

Joe grinned. The black wolf was still in view. He went to single shots and started firing. This time he was certain he tagged the animal at least twice. The creature flinched, but didn't stop running.

"Better get him now," Larry said. "Son of a bitch is making for the woods."

"I see that." Joe fired until his clip was gone. He reached out and Larry handed him the rifle filled with hollow points. Joe grabbed it and kept shooting.

One of the shots connected. A geyser of blood blew out of the creature's side, but it kept running. Joe blinked, wondered if he was going snow blind, despite the special polarized lenses he wore. The wolf seemed to be growing, changing into something less like an animal, more like a man.

Crazy. Not only crazy, irrelevant. He had that thing's head in his sights. The chopper came to a dead stop as he squeezed the trigger and his shot went wild. The wolf bolted into a copse of trees and was gone.

"What the fuck you do that for?" Joe screamed to the pilot.

"Chill out," Larry said. "We can't go any farther. Look up!"

Joe saw that they were on the edge of a forest. If they tried to get any closer, the chopper would crash.

"Don't worry about it, partner. There's plenty more where that came from. Besides, the way your last shot ripped open that thing, it won't last long."

Joe was silent as the chopper pilot took them away. He kept staring at where the wolf had disappeared. An instant before the woods went out of view, he thought he saw movement, something stumbling their way. He couldn't tell if it was an animal or a man.

"Bothers me," Joe said. "I hate leaving a job half-finished."

"We're here to have fun," Larry said. "Relax!"

Joe nodded, but somehow he sensed that for the rest of their vacation, and for some time after that, the shape at the mouth of the woods was going to bring him nightmares.

One year later.

Desmond Willits was surprised to see the large figure framed in the cold, white morning light filtering in from the open doorway. He wondered if *he* had been the fool who left the club's front door unlocked. "Sorry, man, the Blue Note Cafe won't be open again until seven. You come back then, we'll serve you up something right, like some homemade jambalaya and a little music to soothe the soul."

The figure did not retreat. There was something familiar in his shape. Desmond studied the fall of his wild hair and the manner in which the intruder carried himself—shoulders pushed forward, head down a little, like a fighter about to take someone on. Desmond had been a fighter once, when he was younger. Now that he was in his seventies, the only thing he fought was his arthritis.

"It's me," the man in the doorway said.

Desmond Willits felt his entire body stiffen. He hadn't heard that raspy voice in ten years. Desmond tried not to think about the past. Too much pain waited back there.

When he was young, he had won several title bouts. Some men in fancy suits told him to take a fall during the fight that would have made him a champion. If he didn't, his wife, Bobbi, would find out what life was like when you didn't have any arms or legs. The money he earned allowed him to open the Blue Note, which had gone on to become the oldest blues cafe in San Francisco. Ten years ago, when he had last heard this man's voice, his Bobbi had just died. Too much pain.

The man stepped forward, into the light. He had blazing emerald eyes, swarthy skin, and proud, noble features. The man's chin and cheekbones were elegantly sculpted, his Cupid's lips vulnerable. Steel-tipped alligator boots glinted in the light, along with turquoise rings and bracelets. A flak vest revealed a host of tattoos along his solid biceps. Above his button-fly jeans a black fishnet T-shirt covered a washboard stomach and a male model's chest.

"It's me, Old Paw. Donovan McKinley."

Desmond tried his best to be nonchalant. "I got eyes. You think someday you'll tell me why you call me that?"

"Call you what?"

"Old Paw."

"Habit."

The old man shook his head. "Didn't think you were ever coming back."

"Me either. I need work, a place to stay."

"Come right to the point, don't ya?"

Donovan shrugged.

"Ever wonder which side you got to thank for that?" Desmond asked. "Indian or Irish?"

"Don't think about it much."

"No, I imagine you don't." Desmond looked over to the stage. A set of instruments lay around in their cases. "You want some work, you got to show me what you can do."

"Have you forgotten?"

"Time messes with everyone," Desmond said. "I got to know if you still have the old magic."

"Fair enough." Donovan leaped onto the stage with a single, effortless stride. He took an electric guitar from its case, turned on an amp, and plugged in. After checking to see that the instrument was tuned, Donovan loosed a heavy metal riff that would have made Eddie Van Halen duck and cover.

Desmond frowned. "What was that?"

The guitarist smiled. "You said times change. I wondered if maybe you had changed with them."

"You wondered wrong. Now gimme some sugar, baby."

Shaking his head, Donovan took a step back and allowed himself to feel the old rhythms. A moment later his fingers touched the frets and the sounds that came out were so mournful they reminded Desmond of a dead man weeping at midnight.

The old man closed his eyes and let the haunting sounds wash over him for several minutes before he allowed a smile to spider across his deep brown, wrinkled face. "That's nice, old son. Like a butterfly looking for its dead love."

Donovan finished the tune. "Do I have the job?"

With a half-laugh, Desmond said, "Not everyone can play the blues. You got to have hurt way down deep in your soul."

"So nothing's changed?" Donovan asked, only a little unsure of himself.

"I didn't say that. You're not bad. Not like you used to be, but not bad. I remember when you first came back from 'Nam. You played like that. But you got better."

"I'm overwhelmed."

"You want coddling, you go somewhere else. Always been the deal."

"I need work," Donovan said.

"You got that," the old man said. "It's the old magic you're lacking. Don't worry. Time wears on us all. You'll get it back."

"Thanks."

"Thing is, you couldn't have picked a better time to come back. Guy I had playing with us disappeared last night. Asian kid, coaxed the notes out of that guitar like he was kissing his lover's neck. Cleaned out his room. Didn't leave a forwarding. Damn deadbeat. You want the gig?"

"I do."

"It's yours."

The images came in a jumble, a chaotic mix of darkness and light. One ripped from the other as if they were being reflected on the blade of an overworked scythe. He was in the wilderness, with the pack. They were on the hunt, playing, making love, singing, and dancing in the moonlight.

A chainsaw cut to the next scene.

The sun baked him and explosions came from above. One by one the wolves fell. Strange thoughts started to wake in his animal skull. Horrid, unwanted thoughts.

Human thoughts.

A painful tearing and suddenly it was just a little later. He was running beside one that might have been his brother. A final crack of thunder came from above. A torrent of blood, brains, and fangs spilled upwards.

Assault rifles, helicopters, two-leggers, laughter, speech—all the myriad shades of damnation. He didn't want to change again and become a man. More than anything, he wanted to stay in the wild, needed to stop the process dead in its tracks, stay pure, regain what had been lost, but it was too late, his human brain was waking after its long slumber, and it was turning his heavenly dream of peace into a nightmare!

Torture! *Intolerable*!

A knock came at the door. Donovan vaulted awake, thankful that the nightmare was at an end. He raised his trembling, human hand before him, and saw that he was wrong. The nightmare of human existence was his again, and this time seemed never-ending.

"Coming," he said as he hopped off the bed and slipped into a pair of blue jeans. The room Desmond had given him was small and poorly furnished, but it was all he needed. He went to the door and breathed in a familiar scent. Steeling himself, he opened the door.

A beautiful, dark-haired woman stood before him. She wore sunglasses, a white shirt, a black vest, and jeans ripped at the knees. Her lips were blood red. She pursed them indecisively and leaned against the door frame.

"Want me to come in?" she asked in a husky voice.

Donovan stood back and allowed Melinda to enter the small bedroom. The window was lacking a curtain. Crossing the room, she stood before the fiery light of the sun and stretched, raising her arms high over her head. The vest fell back, allowing the full, sensuous curves of her breasts to be revealed by the light.

Donovan was unashamed by the animal desire that rose within him. Melinda caught the way he looked at her and grinned. She would have been offended only if he was not aroused.

"Thank you for coming," Donovan said haltingly.

"Leitch called," Melinda said as she threw herself to the bed on her belly. Rising to her elbows, she looked up at him, certain to give him a perfect view of her ample cleavage. "I figured he was crazy. I didn't think you were ever coming back, not after what happened with Calle Ann and your son."

Donovan looked away.

"What is it?" she asked. "The harano get you?"

"The suffering of Gaia plagues us all."

"Come on," she said. "Don't give me the company line. You haven't been active in the cause for a long time. Besides, this is me you're talking to. You know what I am. I see past the shadows."

Donovan watched as Melinda rolled onto her back and looked at him upside down. She reminded him of a cat as she slowly and sensuously writhed.

"Long drive," she said. "Could use some rest. Want to lie with me?"

"Maybe later."

Melinda rested her open hand on her forehead. "This is serious."

"Yes."

She rose to a sitting position, slipping off her sunglasses and depositing them on the bed. "Did you take out Jimmy Wang, the guitarist? I hear he was a good kid. Hope you didn't hurt him. I mean, you used to be a healer, at least in the army. Hate to think you've gone the other way."

"Made some calls. Got him a better gig with a band in Seattle."

"That's my *Wakiza*. No innocent blood on your hands."

Donovan flinched. "Please. Don't call me that. Wakiza's dead. He died with my wife and child."

Melinda reached out and caught Donovan's hands. She was determined to remain quiet until his gaze met hers. The last time she had seen Donovan, he claimed that he was never coming back to the human world. Killian Cross was dead. Donovan had been cheated out of his revenge on the murderer of his wife and child by yet another Black Spiral Dancer, one that Cross had betrayed.

Finally, Donovan looked into Melinda's ruby eyes.

"What made you change your mind?" she asked. "Why are you here?"

A ragged breath escaped him. The first time he had seen Melinda's eyes, he worried that she was an Enticer, a human seductress who served the Wyrm, a fomora, the enemy.

The truth had been far stranger. Their friendship stranger still. He remembered what she told him when he confronted her about her origins: "You know what they say: I was Snow White, but I drifted."

Donovan shrugged. "I had what I needed: peace. That was taken away. I've come here to get it back."

"There's going to be blood, isn't there? With you, there always is."

The dark-haired man said nothing. He lowered his head and looked away. "You didn't bring my guitar—Blue Light."

"You're the only person I know who would give a name to a guitar."

"It meant a lot to me. That's why I entrusted it to you before I went into the wild."

"It's safe. I wasn't sure it was really you. I'll bring it next time."

Donovan nodded, his gaze averted.

Melinda released his hands. "What do you want me to do?"

In his low, raspy voice, Donovan told her. Waiting for her reply, he went to the window and stared out at San Francisco. It was the last Saturday before Halloween. A full moon was due. That was not his auspice. His was the Galliard, the gibbous moon. No matter, it would do.

"Will you?" he asked, breaking the silence.

"Gee, I don't know. I might be busy. AMC's running

The Princess Comes Across tonight. Carole Lombard, Fred MacMurray. 1930s innocence. Hard to pass up. Though, I'll tell ya, I always thought that title sounded a little like a porn film, you know what I mean?"

Donovan was unmoved by her attempt to lighten the mood.

"What do you think?" Melinda said with a sigh. "You know me. I'll do anything for old times' sake."

"Yeah, I know you." He waited a few more seconds, then glanced back at her. The room was empty. He didn't even hear her leave. The brief flickering of a smile touched his face. He whispered, "You've gotten good since I left."

From somewhere below, in the main chamber of the club, he thought he heard a woman's appreciative laughter.

Donovan was lost to the music. The Saturday night crowd was always the best. He had forgotten how sweet the release had been when he had played the circuit, traveling from city to city, playing a live gig here, a studio set there. Always moving. Calle Ann had changed all that. She wanted a stable environment in which to raise their son. He gave her that.

It cost him everything.

"Man, you make that thing weep," one of the other musicians whispered to him as he continued to play. The band had accepted him without reservation. The evening was passing in a haze of soft, sensual music, pierced by the haunting wail of his anguished guitar.

The club was about three-quarters filled. Only a few tables were empty. Donovan waited patiently for his visitors to arrive. They would be cautious, on the lookout for any kind of trap. Only when they were assured that no danger waited inside the Blue Note Cafe would the pair of men enter the club and find the table that had been reserved for them.

Another hour passed, and finally they arrived. Donovan did not miss a note. He played two more blues standards and a scorching rendition of "Hellhound on My Trail" before he bothered to glance their way. His senses had not betrayed him. The two men seated at a table in the far corner were indeed the ones he had been hunting for close to a year.

The Choirboy and the Pilot.

The killers of his pack, the monsters who had shattered the sanctuary he had found, and all for a few hours of amusement. He had used all his talents, all his Gifts, to learn their names and how to contact them. Returning to the world of man had been jarring, but Donovan knew there was no other way.

His friend Leitch, a man with money and contacts, had made all the arrangements. The assassins didn't like the idea of meeting their "client" face-to-face. Leitch had insisted. If they wanted the job, which paid a million dollars, ten times their usual fee, they would arrive on the Saturday before Halloween, at the Blue Note Cafe in San Francisco.

Despite their misgivings, the killers had made their appearance. A sizable wire transfer of funds from one of Leitch's dummy corporations had ensured their cooperation. Whoever said Glass Walkers were good for nothing had never met Archibald Leitch.

An odd sensation came over Donovan—a strange longing for the life he once led. After turning his back on his friends for ten years, Donovan had worried that they would want nothing to do with him. Instead, they welcomed him back and agreed to help. Explanations were unnecessary and unwanted.

It was Calle Ann they all loved, he tried to tell himself. *They're doing it out of respect to her memory.*

The velvet notes he coaxed from his guitar told another story.

Donovan looked over to his guests, Joe Entwhistle and Larry Santos. The set ended and he put down his guitar, smiled perfunctorily as the crowd applauded, and stepped off the stage. On his way to the men's room he walked past them. Once inside, he reveled in the foul scents he had taken from each of the men. The redhead, the Choirboy, smelled like embalming fluid. The black-haired one, the Pilot, bore the odor of copper-tainted blood. He had them now. They could run to the ends of the earth and never escape him.

Soon, the hunt would begin.

He left the men's room, took a longer route around the men, and was pleased to see them fidgeting nervously. Their "client" had already shown, only they would never know that.

Donovan picked up a snippet of their conversation. The redhead was bothered by some people he had seen on the street. A few had a single red eye, always the left one. He had never seen anything like it. Bunny eyes, he called them. Weird.

"You ain't seen nothin' yet," Donovan whispered as he walked back to the stage.

Another hour passed. The assassins were getting ready to leave. Before they could rise from their table, Melinda appeared. She wore a sexy red dress that revealed her hourglass figure. Contacts covered her crimson eyes, making them look bluish black. It wasn't much effort for her to talk them both into a night of fun in her hotel room. They negotiated what they believed was a fair price, took one more look around for their absentee client, and left the club with Melinda.

Donovan's second set was almost finished. The last chord was played and he set down his instrument.

There was no reason to hurry. He knew exactly where Melinda was taking them:

Straight into the jaws of hell.

Donovan stood outside the door. He had been worried that the floor would be teeming with people. Instead, it was deserted. Gaia was smiling on him tonight. He knew that even if a few humans stumbled by at an inopportune moment, the delirium would take care of them. Nevertheless, he wanted to be a nightmare solely reserved for the two men waiting in the room beyond this door.

He waited a few moments, choosing to give Melinda a little time with them. That way they would be all nice and comfortable. Completely relaxed. That was how the first of his pack had been when the assassins had blown his guts out. The wolf had looked down stupidly, unable to comprehend what had been done to him, why his steaming entrails had sprung out of his belly, when death overtook him and came charging after the other members of the pack. In the beginning, the killers had been on foot. If Donovan had remembered who he was, what he was, just a little sooner, he might have saved at least a few of his wolf-brothers. That had not been the case. It had not been until the hunters were airborne that his human mind had resurfaced, and by then it was too late.

Now all he had to look forward to was paying these bastards back for the blood and terror they had delivered onto their victims. He thought he would be looking forward to their screams, but all he wanted was to get this over with so that he could go back to the wild where he belonged. Perhaps he wouldn't chase them into the streets after all. It might be best to end it quick and clean. Not for their sakes, but for his own.

He had dressed himself in a long, leather raincoat

and his favorite boots. Nothing else. He kicked off the boots and set them beside the door. Shrugging off the raincoat, he folded it neatly and set it beside his footwear.

Closing his eyes, he willed the change to come over him. A fire raged through his soul, boiled his blood, and consumed his flesh. Hair sprouted on his skin in great gouts, and his bones quickly unfolded and grew into shapes no longer meant for human flesh. His skin bubbled and changed, crawling and expanding. Donovan's ears yanked back and drew long, while his jaws extended and filled with razor-sharp teeth. His forehead became hooded and his snout itched. He touched the doorknob and began to turn it. As they had agreed, Melinda had left it unlocked. In seconds his hands would become sharpened talons and the human part of him, which told him that doorknobs were meant to be turned, not ripped from the wood that housed them, would begin to retreat. He pulled his lips back and could not resist a snarl as he started to push the door open.

A bright light and a sound like the world's end came to him as the door exploded outward. Splinters and fiery shards of metal slammed into him, sending him back against the opposite wall. His mind scrambled to reach beyond the surge of agony that had torn through his chest.

A gunshot! Someone had opened up on him with a shotgun!

He didn't have to wait long to learn the identity of his assailant. What was left of the door swung inward and the Choirboy stood before him, gun leveled.

From deep in the room, he heard a cry that could only be Melinda. Stupid, he thought. Walked into it, just like my wolf-brother. Stupid.

Shuddering, he tried to cover the gaping wound in

his chest and willed the change to continue, but the convulsions ripping through him had other ideas.

Melinda felt the cold metal of the gun pressed against her skull. She had been shocked when her victims had so easily slipped out of her spell. Were they fomori? Is that why her power hadn't worked against them? No, judging from the way the delirium was beginning to affect the redhead, the one who had shot Wakiza, that was not the case. A more simple explanation came to her: The killers had no souls, nothing for her to manipulate and tempt. She should have guessed that when she had looked into their flat, dead eyes.

Even more surprising had been Wakiza's dulled instincts. She was certain that he would have sensed the trap waiting for him on the other side of the door. He would have found another way in, some other means to take out this trash that had performed some deep and unforgivable hurt on him. Instead, he had acted like a human in wolf's clothing, forgetting his many Gifts. His sloppiness had damned them both.

Ahead, the red-haired assassin advanced on Donovan's shuddering form. The man's limited, human mind was shutting down at the sight of the werewolf in transformation. His partner, who could only see a vague, black shape, was far more in control of himself. Melinda saw that Donovan was still changing, but now the changes were coming very slowly. Given time, his wounds would heal. If the killers had their way, Donovan would be dead in a few seconds.

Not enough time.

"What is he?" the redhead asked.

"Who cares, just finish him off!" The black-haired murderer couldn't understand the reason for his partner's hesitation. He tightened his grip on Melinda and hissed in her ear. "Christ, what did you fuckers think you were dealing with here? Amateurs? This is the oldest goddamned lure on record."

Joe Entwhistle, the Choirboy, pointed his gun at the werewolf's head. A sudden calm descended on him. For a moment, he had seen the man on the floor as some kind of animal, a creature from a horror show when he was a kid. Fear like only his father could provoke—before he sliced off the old man's hands, feet, and dick, and left him chained to the sink to die screaming—had washed over him, engulfing him, drowning him. He felt a wet stain by his crotch and knew that he had peed himself. Christ, how embarrassing. Maybe the bitch had slipped something into their drinks.

Right now, he could see his victim for what he was: a mark, a bleeding, spasming human being who had come willingly to his own personal end of the world party.

"Yeah, pal, only it's your world that's ending."

He had no idea that his will was so great, his denial so encompassing, that his mind had created this fantasy of a human being at his feet. When the dying man rose to his knees, Joe did not blow his head off, though his partner was hollering for him to do just that.

"What, he's naked, he got no weapons, what's he gonna do, swat me to death?" Joe asked, cutting a look back to the Pilot. He had phrased it this way because a second before he looked away from his victim, the man pulled his hand back, as if to swat an insect. The image had amused Joe.

He looked back, about to say, "Fuck it, let's do this asshole," when he saw a blur of motion and felt the shotgun drop from his arms. He looked down and saw that his hand was gone. Blood spurted from the ragged stump.

"Hey," Joe said, his voice high and strained, like that of a confused little boy.

Donovan roared like an engine out of hell's lowest pit as he sprang up and gutted the man with his other claw. Snarling, he yanked back his hand, unraveling the killer's insides. Joe Entwhistle, the Choirboy, dropped to the floor, jerked a few times, then died.

The werewolf entered the room, its fur matted with blood. Melinda stared at the creature, wondering if the crimson stain on its pure black pelt had come from his own wound or the flow of his victim. Not that it mattered. One look into the creature's glowing green eyes told her that it would be all right. Wakiza was going to make everything all right.

The Pilot quaked with fear as the werewolf came closer. "Stay back! I'll shoot the slut, I swear I'll do it!"

Melinda's fear returned. The way the assassin was shaking, he might discharge his weapon by accident as easily as by design. She had no idea what he was seeing. Wakiza was very strong, he could use his power to allow the killer to see him in his true form. One way or the other, the situation was again becoming untenable. If Donovan's rage outweighed his reason, he might ignore the gunman's threat and she could end up very dead.

There was only one thing for her to do. She was actually grateful that she had worn heels tonight, though they were uncomfortable as hell. She brought her foot up then jammed it down on the killer's instep. He hollered and fell back, squeezing the trigger. Melinda darted forward, certain that she would be out of his line of fire.

She was wrong.

As Wakiza moved forward, a black, inhuman blur advancing on his prey, the bullet cut through her neck, entering on the left side and exiting on the right. She felt as if she had been slapped, but there was no real pain. Only, she couldn't breathe. Shuddering, she grabbed her throat and dropped to her knees. She felt the ragged holes in her flesh and slumped back, quivering, gasping for a breath that would not come.

For Donovan, it all happened so quickly that he also believed Melinda to be out of danger. He reached out and tore the Pilot's head from his shoulders with one clean swipe of his claw. The severed head struck the ceiling, ricocheted off a lamp, and fell neatly onto a recliner, its jaws quivering as it tried to form a word. The werewolf looked at his dying victim in satisfaction, howling as life fled from the killer's eyes.

His satisfaction was short-lived. He looked down and saw Melinda's bloodied, twitching form. At first, he couldn't believe that she had been hit, then his old training, acquired over a two year stint in the army as a medic, kicked in. Picking her up, he was relieved to note that the wound had only grazed her arteries. She had to breathe. He saw a can of soda with a straw nearby. Somehow he summoned enough presence of mind to snatch the straw as he looked to the window and launched himself, with Melinda in tow, at the glass.

Donovan landed three stories below, the impact hurting his ankles, but not shattering them. The street before the hotel was filled with traffic. A car was stopped before him, waiting for a light to change. Donovan reached out, tore the passenger door from the vehicle, and stuck his head inside as he let out a terrible roar. The driver scrambled out of his seatbelt as Donovan slammed the gearshift into Park. The man was in tears as he fled the vehicle, almost running into an oncoming car. Donovan was beyond caring about anyone except Melinda. It was happening all over again. He had been careless and because of that, someone he cared about was dying.

Forcing himself to concentrate, he willed the

change to reverse. As his body slowly lost some of its bestial aspects, Donovan gently set Melinda down on the car's backseat. People were watching, but he didn't care. The delirium would keep the Veil from being pierced. He tore a section of fabric from her dress and wound it around her neck, cutting off the flow of blood. Then he took one of his sharp nails and poked a hole in the hollow of her throat. The straw he had somehow managed to keep hold of was delicately inserted and he started to relax as he heard her breathing through the tube. He ran around to the driver's side, half-man, half-wolf, wholly unrecognizable, and shoved the gearshift into Drive.

He drove through traffic like a madman, his inhuman senses allowing him an edge against the other drivers. He screamed and cursed in his guttural, indecipherable speech at the limits of the foreign import at his command.

In his mind, he cursed himself again and again. It had been such a simple set-up and he let it all get away from him, just like before. Melinda was dying, like Calle Ann, like his son, like the other members of his pack.

A bloody hand reached out from the backseat. Donovan was so startled that he nearly lost control of the car. He swerved into a lane of oncoming traffic then back again instants before he could be hit. Melinda was shuddering, spasming, trying to speak.

Lie still! he commanded in his Mindspeak. *You're not going to die! You're not!*

In the rearview mirror, he saw her blood-red eyes. She seemed desperate to tell him something. A message screamed out from her stare, but he refused to listen. He took a sharp turn and Melinda fell back. Cutting a glance over his shoulder, he saw the bloody straw on the seat beside her and heard her gasping for breath.

Ahead, the lights of a hospital winked into view.

Take the straw, he commanded in the confines of her thoughts. *Put it back in! Do it!*

He leaped the car across two lanes of oncoming traffic and kept advancing until the tires squealed to a stop a few feet before the hospital's emergency entrance. Donovan turned back, saw Melinda holding the straw to her throat, gasping for breath. Relief surged through him as he jumped out of the car, opened the back seat, and pulled her out.

The seat was soaked through with blood. The wound on the right side of her neck had torn wider, allowing a steady flow of blood to drip upon the seat. Was this what she had been trying to tell him?

He hauled her into his arms, and ran into the emergency room. The doctor on call shuddered as he saw Donovan's inhuman form.

Help her! he screamed in his Mindspeak.

No one moved near him. He considered changing back to human form, but there would be too many questions and his presence would be too great a distraction. The delirium was already striking the emergency room personnel. Setting Melinda down on a table, he turned and ran, praying that the effects of the delirium would fade once he was out of view.

An hour later, after he had stolen some human clothing, Donovan returned to the emergency room and asked about Melinda. The news made his heart slow and almost stop. She had died a few minutes after being admitted. The blood loss, the shock—it had all been too much for her.

The nurse asked if he was a relative, if he would be the one claiming the body.

"A distant relative," he said softly, tears welling up in his emerald eyes. He knew that by dawn there would *be* no body. Others of her kind would come and collect her. They always did. The Garou's was not the only Veil that must never be pierced.

On the way out, he heard an orderly and a nurse talking. They stood just outside the doors of the emergency room, staring up at the stars.

"Look at that," the nurse said. "I haven't seen a moon shine that bright in a long time."

"You know what my grandpa used to say about nights like this?" the orderly asked. "He said, 'The moon only shines this bright on nights when God pulls the wings off an angel and sends them home.' That's what he said."

Donovan shuddered and walked away.

The next morning, Donovan returned to the club. Desmond was waiting.

"The way you rabbited after your second set last night, I thought I'd seen the last of you." The old man looked into Donovan's face and frowned. "So what do you have to say for yourself?"

Donovan's lips trembled for a moment, then fell still. Instead, he walked up onto the stage, took out his guitar, plugged it into his amp, and powered up. His fingers stole over the frets as if they were desperate to recapture something that had been lost, an elusive, ethereal quality that might have been his again.

Peace.

He had found it in the arms of his wife, but she had been taken from him. He had found it in the chill of the wild, but that, too, had been taken from him. He had even glimpsed it in the wanton smile of an angel who had fallen, but not so far that she could not be picked up again and carried home.

For the first time in ten years, the music poured entirely out of his soul. The music of sadness and mourning, the fragile moonlit concerto of hopelessness and despair that had become his world.

The old man settled into a chair and grinned. "You got it, man. Don't know how you did it, but you got it back."

Donovan ignored him. The notes came freely now and in them he could sense some vestige of the escape he sought. Perhaps when he found it, he could move on again.

For today, the music played on.

Glimpses of Before

by John H. Steele

Justin's last thoughts were not of bitterness, surprisingly enough. "Don't go. You can't leave me here," he told Randi.

"I'm just going home for a few days," she answered as she stuffed clothes into her overnight bag, ignoring such niceties as folding. "You know these earthquakes wreck my nerves, and I'll never get any work done. I might as well get out of San Francisco. I can see these buildings going over like dominoes."

"A three-story brownstone is not going over like a domino," he pointed out. "Besides, what'll I do?"

"Come with me."

"You know your mother doesn't want me there, and what about the job? I'm still waiting to find out about that restaurant job. Can't you use that nervous energy here? Paint some fucking dominoes or something."

Randi stopped packing for a moment and pulled her dark hair back out of her face. "If you don't want to deal with my mother, don't come. I'm going."

"Go then. See if I care."

She stuffed in two more wadded-up shirts and zipped her bag. "Look, I'm not your baby-sitter, for Christ's sake." Her tone softened. "I love you, Justin, but I need to get away."

And so, despite his protests, she left. The next day Justin found out that the restaurant job had fallen through. What else was there to do but stop by the liquor store?

His last thoughts were not of bitterness or abandonment. Instead his mind turned to childhood, playing stickball in the wide alley behind his father's bar. The ball ricochetted off a trashcan, and Justin was running after it. As he dashed into the street, he could hear his mother's voice telling him always to stop and look both ways. The massive Buick was barrelling down on him. He froze as the seconds stretched into hours. The tires screeched. In that instant, Justin wanted to take those steps back, to undo them, but he could not.

That car had been able to stop.

Strange last thoughts, of deliverance, when he wanted to be angry—angry at himself, angry at everyone, angry at life. Justin did not ponder this for long; his life was being stripped away a layer at a time. The bitterness was already gone. The forgotten love was next, then his thoughts, memories, name, his entire sense of self, all stripped away, mercilessly, completely.

There was release. He was floating in warm water. The soothing massage washed over him, much more potent than a hot bath. He could feel himself flowing into the pool, merging, ceasing to be separate from it. What had been before was no longer. Heartbeats. Ebb and flow. Escape.

The floating continued for . . . how long? Time also was washed away, lost to the tide. There was only basking in the moist warmth, and peace. The calm was enveloping; so complete, so without contrast, that it lost meaning.

Eventually, slowly, there was movement. It was less satisfying than the tranquility but still not unpleasant. The gentle swaying, however, became a rocking and then a spinning. He saw brief flashes of rooms, ceilings spinning—evenings of revelry ended, but the consequences only beginning. He could see fingers clutching at the sheets of a bed, circles that would not end. The spinning became faster. The calm, all he wanted, was being sucked away like dirty water down a drain. He felt a cold breeze. It was not skin and nerves that felt; there were no goose bumps, yet he was chilled. The wind blew through him. It penetrated every hidden place, picking him apart, exposing that which should not be seen, sparing nothing.

Then he was plunging, being pulled and thrown down into the depths. Farther and deeper—speed, sound, motion, colors—always falling. The pressure of the Tempest was all around him, suffocating, crushing. He was being pulled in every direction at once; terror gripped him. The calm was so distant, timeless years, distanceless miles away. If only the storm would pull him apart. If only he would explode. Surely that would be better. That must be where the calm lay, the sweetness of Oblivion, an end to the chaos.

He realized suddenly that he was not alone. Among the roar and the swirling din were voiceless screams that were sensed but not heard, flailing souls that whisked past, always just out of reach. He tried to go to them, but they passed so quickly, and he could control nothing.

There were other voices also, familiar voices. Embrace the Void, they whispered. Peace lies this way. You have it within. This is truth. The voices dripped of honey. Reassurances swirled about, forming an eddy against the chaos. They beckoned. Follow this way. But there was a blackness. There were teeth behind the enticing lips, yet it would be so easy to succumb to the entreaties. An end to suffering. A lover's voice, caressing in the night. An end to fear. A mother's voice, and suckling at a breast.

An end to all. The crone's voice, crumbling to dust.

He was not strong enough to refuse them. The call of Oblivion was powerful. He might well have gone that way, but he was being pulled in another direction. There was something incomplete that would not let him go yet. They tried to hold him; they scratched and clawed, and he wanted to be embraced by their talons, but the eddy was sucked away into the distance. He heard the once-sweet voices screech and curse, raging against him. He mourned their passing as one mourns a grudgingly surrendered vice—pornography carried to the trash heap and set afire.

He was once again careening through the chaos, first this way then that. All around were more of the voiceless screams floundering in the sea of souls. Some wailed for lost pasts, others bemoaned horrific futures. Many simply howled madness. This, perhaps, was another escape—the safety of insanity, the abandoning of fettering, burdensome reason. But Oblivion lay along that road as well, and he was being pulled elsewhere still.

Gradually the screams and the deafening roar of the Tempest began to diminish, to recede if not to disappear. There was a darkness now, and a quiet of sorts, but it was far from the calm of before. It was a pregnant silence. He felt a tension, as if the cacophony of the storm and the screams was only held at bay, not far away at all, ready to rush in again at any moment. He began to visualize points of light, small flames. The light did not shine forth to dispel the darkness; rather, the darkness tolerated the light, allowed it to exist, not to be swallowed. The flames held no warmth. The dark and the cold permeated all.

Each flame was atop a smooth, white candle. No wax ran down their sides. He felt drawn toward these glimpses of the old world, the human world. He could not have turned away had he wanted. There were hundreds of them, or were they endless? The flames flickered, although there was no breeze here. He could still feel the tension pressing in upon him, the hovering storm trying to get at him, never far away.

His vision expanded. Next to the nearest candle was a glass full of bourbon. At this sight, a parade of images and sensations steamed through his consciousness. He saw three boys, young teenagers, scrunched behind trash cans in an alley splitting a stolen six-pack of beer, Pabst Blue Ribbon. The brick walls on either side of the alley seemed insubstantial, fading in and out. The scene was familiar, yet distant somehow. It tugged at him, but only fleetingly, then was gone.

The alley was replaced by a car. He felt he knew the car, yet details—year, make—were just beyond his reach, not quite available, not quite important. The car was rocking from the movements of the two older adolescents in the back seat. Their gyrations and contortions meant very little to him. On the floorboard was an empty flask. It held his attention more than anything; sparkling, it called to him.

Then the car too was gone. Where it had been was a woman. She was lying at the bottom of a staircase cradling her right arm against her body. He could not make out her face; her features were blurry. She stank of whiskey. Red tulips covered the wallpaper next to the stairs.

The images began to pass more quickly—a balding man; a cozy restaurant and bar; a woman with obsidian hair and stark, white skin. Each vision brought questions closer to the surface, but like the shimmering and dissipating visions, the questions were not fully formed. They were not whole; they were germs of ideas, remote nagging itches. He was connected once again, vaguely, tangentially, to what had been before.

The aroma of the bourbon brought him back to the candles, except now there was a glass by each candle, hundreds perhaps. He was aware of a thirst growing within him, a thirst so great that all those glasses might not quench it. He saw a hand (his hand?) reaching for the first glass. He had noticed no physical body up to this point, and he could discern no connection with the hand except that it was doing his will. He picked up the glass. The pungent odor poured from it, almost visible. As he held the glass, it began to crack. The whiskey dripped out. Then, as the fissures widened, it streamed over his hand, more liquid than the glass could possibly hold. As the last of the bourbon drained out, the cracks became jagged and sliced into his hand. He still was not sure that it was his hand. He had not felt the smoothness of the glass, the hard comfort that he almost remembered, but he could feel the sharp pain. There was no reflex to drop the glass as it became increasingly fractured and more shards bit into the flesh. The alcohol burned as it entered the wounds, but it was a sensation, an indication of being. Soon blood also dripped from the hand. The fragments of the glass were grinding each other smaller and smaller, constantly peeling away skin, embedding themselves down to the bone, until they all sifted through the red fingers. The smell of blood mingled with that of the whiskey.

He reached for the next glass which slipped in his grasp as it became smeared with blood. Once again cracks appeared and the bourbon began to flow out. It poured into the lacerations on his hand and bubbled and spit. More blood welled up from the cuts. This glass also broke apart and cut deeply into him. One sharp edge entering the palm extruded from the back of the hand. Other shards again were grinding their way down to the bone. The second glass crumbled away and was gone, leaving only the sticky, dripping, tattered hand.

He did not want to drink, but he reached for another glass. The results were the same. Again and again and again he picked up glasses only to have them crumble and cut him. The pain was intense, but it was so vital. The slice of the glass, the searing burn of the whiskey pulled memories closer to the surface. They made him more real.

How many glasses? It seemed to go on for days, one after another after another. There were always more. They did not diminish in number, nor did the pain lessen; it stayed sharp and clear. The hand disintegrated. One finger dangled below the rest, connected only by a thin muscle or tendon, a last bit of gristle. Most of the skin was peeled away. Soon the hand that reached for the glasses would be skeletal, picked clean of flesh as much as if vultures or rats had gnawed it down. He was giddy with the pain. As the last bits of flesh were sliced away, his vision began to fog. The glasses were gone. The candles began to sputter and then to blur. They were vague forms of light again, not discernible shapes. The glowing areas shrank until, one by one, they disappeared completely.

There was darkness.

The violence of the Tempest was not far away. He could hear it; he could imagine it flooding in to engulf him once more. The thought evoked fear, but fear, like pain, was familiar and comforting in a way. It gave him a point of reference.

He was in a room. It had not appeared suddenly; he simply was in it. His vision was cloudy. He wanted to rub his eyes—did he have eyes now? he was not sure—and wipe away whatever obscured his sight. The room seemed to be a basement. It had that damp, underground feel. The walls were a dingy cream color, the floor drab grey cement. On one wall thick wooden steps led upward to a closed door. The room was empty.

It had been empty, but no longer.

A man stood in the room. There was a strange familiarity about the human form. The man's face was blurred, his features indistinguishable. He knew this man, this man who radiated anger, contempt, disappointment, disapproval. All these things he could feel, he could almost remember, yet he still longed to fall into the man's arms and weep, to be held, to be safe and lose himself, to be wanted.

"Your mother was an idiot, a whore, and you're little better." Words. Human speech. The man spoke.

He wanted to respond. He wanted to speak. Hold me. What is happening? Make me safe. I want to be warm. I want to be whole. But the words would not form.

"You always were a whiner. You could have been a little girl, always running to Mommy. We were happy before you. I wanted a son I could be proud of."

A son. A father. *Father*. Hold me. If only he could reach out.

"I should have tied you in a sack and thrown you in the bay like a dog. Everything would have been okay then."

Hold me.

"You were all she cared about. She couldn't love both of us. You needed this, and you needed that. Always you."

The scene of the woman at the bottom of the stairs came back to him—the red tulips, her shattered arm, her pain. His mother's pain.

His father pushed her. She smelled of whiskey. He threw his drink at her and then pushed her down the stairs.

Rage welled up inside.

"Why don't you use it? You always were a gutless little bastard."

Use it? He realized there were two hands (disembodied? his?) holding a shotgun pointed at his father. This time he could feel the cold steel. He wanted to put it down. How could his father have hit her?

"Go ahead, shoot!"

The shotgun roared to life. No! Sparks rained from the barrel. He felt the kick, but he had not pulled the trigger. He had not fired. For only a moment he saw his father's eyes clearly, unobscured, wide with surprise, then the image was blurry again. The shot ripped apart his father's chest and stomach. Shredded flesh and blood splattered all around. But he had not fired.

"So this is the thanks I get for trying to support a family, a wife and kid. Fucking ingrate. Always wanted to blow away the old man, huh? About time you had some guts, chickenshit son of a bitch."

He could not look away from his father's churned innards. He had not pulled the trigger. He just wanted to be held. This was not how it had happened, or was it? Something was not right. Blood still gushed from his father's body, the gaping hole in his front. A pool of scarlet was spreading, covering the entire floor. His father's shredded heart kept pumping out more and more, as if it wanted to fill the entire room, floor to ceiling, with its venomous blood.

He moved toward the stairs. He was not sure how he moved or what he moved; he still could perceive no body of his own. He just knew that he was moving away from his father.

"Go on, run! That's all you ever did! Might as well keep running!" his father screamed. The walls of the room were becoming insubstantial, blurring and melting away. Only the steps were solid, and the door. From behind the walls the Tempest poured in. Waves of voiceless screams crashed in about his father, drowning his curses. The torn body was out of sight, buried by the storm. Swirling chaos filled the room. The door opened before him. He was through and it was closed, the sea of souls lapping at the other side.

He was in a restaurant, a small bar. He knew this place, a human place. His vision was still clouded. Large patches of blurriness floated slowly through his view. There was a large sign on the wall. Why was the sign not outside? The familiar setting was slightly askew. "Parker's" was the sign, with a flourish from the tail of the "s" that underlined the other letters. Parker. A name. H*is name*. His name was Parker. His father's name was Parker. He felt pieces coming together, more complete but far from whole.

Through the dimness he could see the narrow room. The brass rail along the edge of the bar shone.

The mirror behind the bar, bordered by various bottles of liquor, reflected the sparse light. The room smelled like whiskey. Across from the bar, a man sat in one of the booths along the wall. Below a severely receding hairline the man's forehead glistened with sweat. He motioned for Parker to sit. Parker was at the table, across from Uncle Vinny. From where did that knowledge come, that name? But he knew it was true. Occasionally Parker caught clear glimpses of Uncle Vinny—the whiskers on his neck and chin, the paunch, the hair sprouting from his ears.

Uncle Vinny chuckled as he spoke. He always chuckled for the benefit of others. "Well, Sonny, looks like the fat lady's singing this time. Hell, she ain't just singing, she sat right damn on top of us!" His rumbling laugh was mixed with the thick coughing of cigarettes not given up soon enough.

Sonny was not Parker's name. It was just what Uncle Vinny called him. He was sure of this.

"It's tough, I know, Sonny," Uncle Vinny's voice was softer now with concern but still deep baritone, "but it'll be better for the family, for your mother, bless her heart."

Parker wanted to respond to this soft, kind man who was . . . who was dead, who had died while Parker was in college. Parker's. It was his restaurant. There was no one else. Words eluded him still.

"I've got the papers. All you have to do is sign them, Sonny. Think about your mother. You'll both be taken care of."

There were papers on the table, and a pen. Had they appeared? Had he not seen them before? Taken care of. Someone would take care of him, and his mother. Hold me, Uncle Vinny? But why was the sign inside? Why were the barstools upholstered in blood-red? They should be green.

"Just sign them, Sonny. Trust me."

Trust. Be taken care of. Sign.

"No!" There was another voice, another person in the room, but Parker could not see him.

"Begone!" hissed Uncle Vinny in a whispery voice. "He is mine, m-i-i-ine."

"No," answered the voice. It was calm, powerful.

The papers burst into flame. The pen melted away. Uncle Vinny scurried from behind the table. He had six spindly arms ending in claws protruding from his corpulent body. "Mine, m-i-i-ine," he hissed. A thin, forked tongue snaked out from between his sharp teeth. "Mine!"

"Go!"

Uncle Vinny dropped to the floor and scampered away, a fat cockroach fleeing the light, muttering and whining as he went.

Footsteps coming closer. Shadowy form standing above him. The restaurant was fading away—bar, mirror, bottles, scent, tables. All that remained were Parker and the hazy figure before him. It reach toward him with two hands.

Suddenly the haze, the perpetual fog, lifted. In front of Parker stood his father, not the spiteful vision of earlier, but a more accurate, realistic embodiment. His father held in his hands the caul, the death mask that Parker had unknowingly worn, that had distorted his vision and his understanding. Or perhaps it had protected him. Parker had a body himself, hands that were not sliced and peeled to the bone. He threw his arms around his father, but his father did not respond, and he was cold.

Parker took a step back. He could see his father now. He had a tight smile, and those dark, piercing brown eyes. "I truly reap what I have sown," said his father. "Justin."

Justin. Justin Parker. His father, Leonard Parker. With the names came words that had to be spoken, that would not be denied. They burst out as if they had been held back, dammed, for eons. "I didn't pull the trigger. I didn't. I just wanted you to hold me; and Uncle Vinny, when he died I had to take over the bar. There was no one else, and I tried. I did everything I could, but I couldn't do it. I wouldn't sell, and I wouldn't sell, but I couldn't hold on, and we went under, and it's a fucking parking lot anyway, and we got nothing." The words would not stop. Tears were streaming down his cheeks. "And there wasn't money for the nursing home. Her mind was gone, and I couldn't help her, and I couldn't afford to put her anywhere. Part of me died with her, and I loved her, and I loved you, Daddy, and I didn't pull the trigger." His body was wracked with sobbing. He felt spent. No more words were choking his throat. He buried his head in his father's shoulder. He wanted him to rub his back or stroke his hair softly, but there was no comforting response from his father. Lacking in life, even more lacking in death.

"I know you didn't pull the trigger," said his father. "The spectres invade your dreams, your memories here. Whatever you saw before wasn't me, and that wasn't Vinny. It just wanted you to sign. It wanted your soul."

Justin stepped back. His father may have saved him from the Uncle Vinny creature, but there was no warmth, no life, no completeness to be found here. There was something else still tugging at Justin. He could feel it more distinctly now that he knew a bit more about what had been before.

His father spoke again, "There is power here, Justin. It won't be like before. You can help me. Let me teach you. I can be powerful, important. You can be important here."

Justin took another step back, away from his father. This was not what was calling him. Something was wrong. He saw the death, the hunger in those deep brown eyes.

"Come with me, Justin." A thin facade of patience was wearing away from his father's face. "Don't be an idiot. You were always a loser before. It can be different now. Come with me." Sympathetic hands reached out to Justin. He could see the white fingers with bulbous knuckles, the pale face, ichor dripping from the chin. "Come with me, Justin. Trust me."

Trust me.

Justin stepped farther back. The previous vision of his father had been false, but some truth had lurked within it, making it more believable. "You pushed her," said Justin. "You pushed her down the stairs."

"Forget the past, Justin," slavered his father. "We can make a difference here. You can finally be worth something."

"You pushed her down the stairs," continued Justin, "and I didn't pull the trigger. *You did*. You did it to yourself. You made me feel like it was my fault, you bastard."

"I removed your caul, Justin. I awakened you. I brought you into this world too. You owe me. You owe me!" His father's eyes were bulging, blood vessels about to burst. He stank of bourbon.

"No!" Justin turned and ran.

He could here his father screaming after him, "You'll regret this, boy! I'll make you regret it! You'll pay!"

Justin was running from a wave. A giant crest of the Tempest was behind him, a tidal wave of chaos and loss, and he could not escape it. It crashed down upon him, carrying him with it. The despair, the regret, overwhelmed him; they tore at his soul, trying to gain entry . . . his father's death, the muzzle in his mouth, the shotgun blast, the note accusing him; Uncle Vinny's final heart attack, bankruptcy, the parking lot; his mother's deterioration and death; his father's drinking; his drinking; so much failure, so much pain. But there was something more, something important that was missing. It pulled him, something at which he had not even guessed. That was how he avoided the pull of Oblivion. He knew he was not done yet. The storm tossed him mercilessly, still reaching for his heart. He withdrew into himself and shut out the hopelessness.

Eventually he noticed the silence. He was not sure when it had begun and when the din had faded away. The Tempest was not so close now. Its absence, or at least its remoteness, was soothing. Justin was in a room in the real world, or as close as he could come to the real world—the real world cloaked in the shadows of death. He was in an apartment that he knew in a brownstone in the Mission District. The Mission Dolores was a mile or two away. The parking lot on South Van Ness that used to be his bar was only several blocks farther.

The large living room had been turned into a studio. Brushes, tubes of paint, canvases, easels, and other painting paraphernalia were scattered about. Several of the canvases Justin knew were finished or partially completed pictures, but to him they all appeared blank white. They were not alive to him. The carpet had been pulled up to make spilled paint easier to clean. Littering the floor were a surprising number of empty forty-ounce beer bottles and several empty Jack Daniels bottles. The room reeked of stale beer and liquor.

The kitchen was much as he remembered it, as was the hallway to the bedroom. The bathroom door, on the right side of the hall, was closed. As he watched, the door bulged and then receded, pulsating slowly as if it were a beating heart. Justin turned away.

He heard the footsteps coming up the two flights of stairs. Randi was home. She was the painter; she was the one with a vision of life. He had moved in after the restaurant had closed two years ago. She had cared for him as he had slid into self-pity. He could see now, only now, how much he had hurt her in the past.

Up the steps—forty-five, forty-six, forty-seven, forty-eight—keys fumbling at the lock.

She had left late Friday night, after the earthquake. Said she had had enough of the ground moving, enough of San Francisco. She had driven to Rio Dell to be with her family on ground that was stable. He had known she would come back, but he had felt abandoned at the time. Two days of heavy drinking and everything had tumbled down upon him, all that the Tempest had found and more.

The door opened and Randi stepped in with her bulging overnight bag. She never would get a real suitcase. She set the bag down and turned on the light. Justin had not noticed that it was off. She pushed her jet-black hair out of her face. Her fair skin was touched with blush on the cheeks. The loose sweater hung from her shoulders, her small breasts barely noticeable; her skirt brushed the floor. She saw the bottles, the mess. Her mouth crinkled with concern like it did when she stared at one of her paintings in progress. Justin wanted to reach out to her, to touch her. She shivered and crossed her arms against her body. He wanted to take back everything he had ever said, everything he had done. How could he have hurt her in so many ways over the years? How could he have been so blind?

She began to walk across the room. She seemed to move so quickly. Justin allowed himself a wry smile—the quick and the dead. Randi walked toward the hallway, toward the rhythmically pulsating door which Justin could not face. He saw her pass, but he saw more: he saw within her. Inside her belly there was movement, the first stirrings of a child. *His child*. She could not even know yet. Dear God, what had he done? He had not known. He wanted to scream. How could he have failed her more? Give him another chance! Everything would be different this time.

She walked past the bathroom into the bedroom looking for him. The light was on in there now. In a moment she would come back and open the bulging door. He knew what she would find—the old, giant bathtub, his body bloated, veins opened to the once-hot water, globules of congealed blood floating. How could he have done this to her? It had been Halloween, and the call of the voices and of the full moon had been so powerful.

There was no scream. He merely heard her soft voice say, "No, baby. No." She came into the living room and leaned against the wall. She was changed; she was defeated. Justin could see death about her—extreme pallor; skin aging and falling away; the smell, the rotting flesh; and for just a moment her left eye seemed to glow eerily red. As he watched, her stomach began to swell. He could see the baby growing, struggling, tearing its way out into the cruel world. It did not break straight out. Instead it climbed upward, gouging its way through her chest, into her neck. Her body convulsed. Her mouth was forced open from within as she vomited blood and chunks of torn flesh. The semblance of a child climbed out, clawing apart Randi's cheeks as it did.

Then the vision was gone. Randi leaned against the wall, shades paler than she usually was, hair hanging in her face. The child, a boy, rested in her belly. Her eyes were clear except for the tears beginning to form. She slid down the wall until she was sitting with her head on her knees. She began to cry quietly. Justin sat on the floor next to her. Why this torturous limbo? Why couldn't he just burn in Hell? He would have eternity to find out. He was bound somehow to her; and to the unborn child, both of whom he had failed so miserably. He wanted to cry as well, but he could not. He was filled only with emptiness.

The Voice of the Hummingbird

by S. P. Somtow

Huitzilopotchtli.

It was the will of the god named Hummingbird that our people should cease to be a wandering people, a desert people, an impoverished and simpleminded people, that we should journey down into the rich, green valley at the world's heart and claim its lakes and forests for our own, and rule over all the nations of the earth. We were a people with a grand and glorious destiny; we had been called to a special covenant with our god; and if there were things that our god commanded us to do which, to those who did not share our special relationship with him, appeared brutal, cruel, uncompassionate, it was only that we alone could see the higher purpose; that we alone were charged with the guardianship of the knowledge of the secret workings of the universe.

It was the will of the god named Hummingbird that I should be the one to hear his voice and bear his message to my people; that I should lead them from the wasteland into the place where they would build the greatest of all cities, set in the center of the world as a turquoise in a circlet of gold. And it came to pass that I spoke, and the people obeyed, and we sealed our covenant with our own blood and the blood of the countless conquered. This was as it should be. Our people had been chosen.

Later I would come to understand that there were others, people no less proud than our people, no less confident of their moral rectitude, no less certain that the salvation of the entire universe lay in the application of secret knowledge that only their tribe possessed; there was even, across the great ocean to the east, a people whose god had called them to cross a great desert and seal a covenant and conquer and build a great temple. We Mexica were not, after all, unique; we were merely a repeating pattern in the wheel of history; and our history was not even the only wheel that was in motion at the time.

We didn't even have wheels then, anyway. After a dozen centuries I suppose one might be forgiven a few anachronistic metaphors. I learned about wheels a long time after the covenant was broken, in San Francisco.

I learned about the other chosen people from Julia Epstein.

There is a gap of about five hundred years in my existence. One moment, the fire was raging in the streets of Tenochtitlan, and I was watching the stars fall from the sky, and cursing the silver-clad man-beasts called Spaniards who had blundered into shattering the equilibrium of the universe. Then, in a blink's breadth, it seemed, I was lying in a glass case, an exhibit in the San Francisco Museum, being pointed at by a petulant youth.

That I might have slept for a time—a century or two even—would not have been surprising. I had done that before, though only of my own volition. I had slept all the way through the conquest of the people of Tlatztelhuatec; I knew it would be dull; they were little better than cattle. But there were no signs that I had been in suspended animation. No cognitive disjunction. No sensation of falling, falling, falling into the bottomless abyss.

The room was gloomy; it had been designed to simulate the rocky chamber in which I had been found. There was no daylight. Torches flickered, yet they did not burn; the fire in them was cold and artificial.

Even lying under the glass, unable as yet to move more than the twitch of an eyelash, fighting the inertia of the dreamless sleep, I was aware that the world had become far stranger than I could have imagined. The youth who stared down at me was a mongrel; he had the flat nose and dark skin of the Mexica, but there was also something about him that resembled the man-beasts from across the sea. He had no hair save for a crest that stood unnaturally tall and was dyed the color of quetzal feathers. His robes were of animal hide, but black and polished to an almost reflective smoothness. He was not utterly inhuman—his ears were pierced at least—but from them hung, upside-down, a pair of those silver crucifixes that symbolize the man-beasts' god, whom they call Hesuskristos, who is in reality Xipe Totec, the flayed god, as Hummingbird once revealed to me in a dream.

He called out to a companion; this one's tufted hair was the color of fresh blood, and he wore a silver thorn through his left cheek. The language, at least, I knew, though the accent was strange and there were unfamiliar words; I had taken the trouble to learn the language of the man-beasts. There are two dialects; one, spoken by the black robes, is called Español; the other is the language of their enemies, known as English. It was the second of these I heard, in a boyish voice muffled by glass.

"Dude! It says he's been dead for five hundred years."

"Pulled him out of the foundation of a fifty-story office building after that big Mexico City quake. Yeah, perfectly preserved and shit. A hollow in the rock, a natural vacuum."

"Yeah, I saw it on *20/20*."

"Did you see that? He moved, dude!"

"Yeah. Right."

Five hundred years, but that was impossible! Hummingbird himself had told me that in a few short years the world would end in an apocalypse of blood and fire. How could five hundred years have gone by? Unless, of course, the world had already ended.

That would explain the surpassing alienness of my surroundings. Even the air smelled strange. Even the blood of the two boys, which sang to me as it pumped through their arteries, exuded an unaccustomed odor, as though infused with the pulped essences of the hemp and coca plants.

The one with the crimson hair said, "No, dude, I ain't joking. Look at him, man, I swear his eyelids are like, flickering."

"You shouldn't have dropped acid at the Cure concert last night. You're still blazing, dude."

I turned my head to get a better view.

"Jesus Christ!" they screamed.

So the world had ended after all. The time of Huitzilopotchtli was over. There had been a fiery apocalypse—my memories had not deceived me—and we were now well into the World of the Fifth Sun, foretold to me by the god, and a new god was in power, the hanged god whose name those boys evoked, Hesuskristos.

I was full of despair. I did not belong here. Why had I been suffered to remain alive? Surely I should have been destroyed, along with the city of Tenochtitlan, along with the great pyramids and temples and palaces of my people. Could the gods not have been more thorough? But then that was just like them; come up with the grand concepts, leave their execution to imperfect mortals. I raged. My heart gave a little flutter, trying to bestir itself from its age-old immobility. My fury fueled me. I could feel my blood begin, sluggishly, to liquefy, to funnel upward through my veins like the magma through the twisty tunnels of Popocatapetl.

Soon I would erupt.

I lashed out. I heard shattering glass. The smells of the strange new world burst upon my senses. Then came the Hunger, swooping down on me as an owl on a mouse in the dead of night. No longer muffled, the rushing of young blood roared in my ears. The odor was sour and pungent. I seized the first creature by the arm, the one with the quetzal-feathered hair; the second, screaming, ran; I transfixed the prey with my eyes and filled him with the certainty of his own death; then, drawing him down to me, I fed.

I do not know how long we lay together, locked in that predatory embrace. His blood was youthful; it spurted; it permeated my pores; I drank it and I breathed it into my lungs; for a fleeting moment it brought back to mind those nights of furtive, unfulfilled encounters in the chill desert night; the burning curve of a young girl's thigh, the aroma of her flowing pubes. Those were the times before the god called me, when I was mortal and barely man.

At length I realized that I had completely drained him. I let go and he thudded on the polished floor like a terra-cotta doll. It was then that I became aware of a noisome clanging sound, a whirling, flashing red light, and men in strange blue clothing who brandished muskets of a sleekly futuristic design as they surrounded the plinth on which I lay. The boy who had fled stood beneath an archway, babbling and shivering and pointing at me and at his friend's desiccated corpse.

Perhaps, I decided, it would be more prudent to play dead for a little while longer.

I awakened in another chamber. It was lined with leatherbound codices of the kind the black robes favored. The room was lit by candlelight, and I sitting on a wooden chair. I tried to move, but I had been bound with ropes—metal ropes, artfully strung, and padlocked, the way the Spaniards keep their gold. Across an immense desk, cluttered with the artifacts of my people, jeweled skulls and jade statuettes and blood-cups, sat a woman.

She was of man-beast extraction, but not unattractive. I had never seen a woman of their kind before; they had brought none with them from their country, which was perhaps why they had become so ferocious. She was sharp-nosed, and had long brown hair. When she spoke to me, it was, to my amazement, in Nahuatl, the language of the Mexica people.

"I'm Julia Epstein," she said. "I'm the curator of our Latin American collection. Would you care for a little blood?"

"I'm quite full, thank you," I said.

"In that case, you might want to start telling me what the hell is going on. It's not every day that a museum exhibit gets up and starts attacking the public. Who are you?"

"It's not proper for me to give my name to you, a man-beast."

She laughed. "Man-beast! I know you Aztecs used to think that the Spaniards and their horses were some kind of hybrid monster, but times have changed. We drive automobiles now. I think it's safe for you to tell me your name. I'm not going to acquire any mystical power over you. Besides, you're just going to have to trust me; I'm the one who talked the cops into believing that that punk's story was just some kind of acid-trip fantasy; they have him under wraps now, the poor child, deciding whether to get him on murder one."

"Very well," I said, "I am Nezahualcoyotl."

"And I'm Santa Claus," said Julia Epstein, frowning.

"So you say you're the Nezahualcoyotl, who claimed descent from the great gods of Teotihuacán, the greatest poet, musician, and prophet of the Aztecs, their first great ruler, a man who was an ancient memory when Moctezuma was king and the Conquistadores swept over Mexico?"

"You are well informed," I said.

"Well, why not? It's no harder to believe that than to believe that an exceptionally well-preserved mummy, just dug up from the newly discovered catacombs in Mexico City, and my museum's prize exhibit, would get up, walk around, attack a few punks, and drink their blood. And to think that I dug you up with my own hands."

"So it is to you that owe my continued existence."

"If you want to call it living."

"What else would you call it?"

"You're a vampire."

"I'm unfamiliar with that word."

"Oh, don't give me that bullshit, Nezzy. I know everything about you guys. I can't get anyone to believe me, but I've gathered a shitload of information. Yeah, I'm an archaeologist, sure, but vampires are kind of a hobby with me, know what I mean? And this city's crawling with them. I know. I've got tons of evidence: clippings, photographs, police files. Tried to sell this shit to the E*nquirer*, and you know what? They rejected it. Said it wasn't, ah, convincing. Convincing! From the people who did the 'Alien Endorses Clinton' story and the piece about the four-headed baby! Let me tell you what really happened. They found out about it. They're everywhere. Big cities mainly, but even the smallest town has one or two. They're running everything. Your worst nightmare about the Mafia, the CIA, the Illuminati, all rolled into one. They read my submission and they squelched it! Sounds pretty damn paranoid, doesn't it? Welcome to the crackpot world of academia."

"But what is a vampire?" I said. I was beginning to feel the Hunger again; just a prickle in my veins. Normally the blood of a whole young male would have kept me going for days, but it had been so long. I glanced down at myself, saw my papery skin, knew it would take a few more feedings to restore me to the semblance of life.

"A vampire?" said Julia. "Why, you're a vampire. You drink blood. You live for a long, long time. You are a child of the shadows, a creature of the night."

"True, but—are you saying that there are others?"

"Are you saying that there aren't others?"

"There was one other." It pained me to think of my young protégé, the one who had betrayed King Moctezuma to the man-beasts, the one whom the black robes called Hortator, which signifies, in their language, the man who beats the drum to drive the galley-slaves who row in the Spaniards' men-o'-war, because of the drum he stole from me, made from the flayed skin of the god Xipe Totec himself, the one I thought would succeed me, but who instead had destroyed my whole world. "There was the god at first. He called me to his service. I had thought to hand on the power to another, but . . ."

"That's where you're wrong, my friend," said Julia. "There's a whole network of you people. You have your tentacles in everything. You run this whole planet. You're in Congress. In the UN. In the damn White House, for all I know. And all top secret. Don't worry. I won't give you away. They have a certificate on file that says I'm a paranoid schizophrenic; so who'd believe me anyway?"

"Even among the white men, people such as I?" It was hard to grasp.

"The New World was a universe unto itself in 1453. Maybe you were the only one here. Maybe your god came over the Bering Strait, nurtured his secret alone for twenty thousand years. Perhaps he forgot, even, that there was a race of creatures like himself. Perhaps, after millennia, he became lonely; who knows? Or he needed another cowherd. He made you. You, Nezahualcoyotl, coming of age with an entire continent for your domain, completely ignorant of the customs, traditions, laws, identities of your Kindred—a law unto yourself. They're not going to like you."

"I think I'll have that drink now."

Julia Epstein rose and went to a white rectangular cabinet. She opened it. A searing cold emanated from it, as though winter had been trapped within its confines. She drew out a skin of chilled blood; not a natural skin, surely, for it was clear as water. "It's my own," she said. "I have a rare blood type, so I keep some around in case something happens to me and I need a quick transfusion. Yeah, more evidence of paranoia."

She tossed the skin to me. I sank my teeth into the artificial skin. The blood was sweet, a little cloying, and freezing cold; then I remembered, from my childhood, how much I had enjoyed the snow cones flavored with berry juice that the vendors used to bring down from the mountains; I savored the nostalgia. Twice today I'd had a remembrance of the distant past, before my changing. It is strange how one's childhood haunts one.

Julia herself drank coffee, which she poured from a metal pot and blended with bleached sugar. She shook back her hair. I was taken aback at the immodest way she stared at me; truly my god had no more power in this world, or she would have been trembling with awe. There was a faint odor of attraction about her; this woman desired me. And that was strange, for no Aztec woman would have dared think sexual thoughts about one who spoke directly to the gods.

"You need me," she said. "You'll be flung into a cutthroat society of dozens of your kind, with bizarre hierarchies, internecine politics, games of control and domination. You've been asleep for five hundred years, and since then there's been a mass emigration. They like it better in the New World; fewer preconceptions, the American dream and all that, and the prey are a lot less careful than back in old Wallachia. Where everyone believes in vampires, it's hard for one to catch a decent meal."

"What? They do not give their blood willingly?" For that was the hardest new concept to grasp. Was it not the duty of humans to give freely of their flesh and blood that their gods might live? Was blood not the life-force that kept the sun and the stars in their courses?

"Willingly!" said Julia. "You do have a lot to learn."

"You'll help me."

She smiled. "Of course. But only if you help me."

"How?"

"By telling me all about yourself."

She unchained me, and I told her about the coming of the white men, and about Hortator's betrayal. And she in turn told me of her own people, who had once been nomads, who had crossed a tremendous desert to find a land flowing with milk and honey; who had made a covenant with a great and terrible deity who spoke in the voices of wind and fire; and I came to know of the vastness of the earth, and of how my people had been but one of many; how nations had risen and fallen, how even mankind itself had not always been the pinnacle of creation; how the great globe had formed out of the cold dust of the cosmos, and would one day return to dust.

In time, I came to love her; and that in itself was a strange thing, for our kind do not feel love as mortals feel it.

The man who came to be called Hortator belonged to me. I had captured him in the Flower Wars, which we hold each year when there are not enough captives from normal wars to feed the altars of the gods.

This year the war was held in a plain not far from the city. Moctezuma himself had come to watch; on a knoll overlooking the battlefield, he and the enemy king, Cozcatl, picnicked on tortillas stuffed with ground iguana, braised in a sauce of pulped cocoa beans, which the man-beasts call chocolate. I, as the mouthpiece of the god, sat above Moctezuma on a ledge lined with jaguar skin and feathers. It was a pleasant afternoon; the courtiers were wolfing down their packed lunch while I sipped, from a sacred onyx cup, the blood of a young Mayan girl who had been sacrificed only that morning; yes, the blood had been cooled with snow from the slopes of the volcano.

"It's not going well," said the king. "Look—the jaguar team has only snared about a hundred, and the quetzal team less than half that."

Once touched by the sacred flower-wand which was the only weapon used in these artificial wars, a soldier was sent to the sacrificial pen. It was a great honor, of course, to be sacrificed, and a thing of beauty to behold those hordes of young men, oiled and gleaming, rushing across the grass to embrace their several destinies. "They seem more reluctant than usual, Your Majesty," I said.

"Yes," said the king darkly. "I wonder why."

"I think," I said, trying to put it to him delicately, "it has something to do with the man-beasts from the sea."

"You'd think they'd be all the more anxious to get sacrificed, what with the present danger to the empire."

"Yes, but they've been spreading sedition, Your Majesty. I've just come from the prison; they've been interrogating that black robe they captured—a high priest of sorts. He says that our sacrifices are ignorant superstition; that the sun will rise each morning with or without them; and he's been babbling about Hesuskristos, their god, who seems to be a garbled version of Xipe Totec."

"You shouldn't say bad things about the man-beasts. Last night I dreamed that the Plumed Serpent was returning to claim his kingdom." He was speaking of Quetzalcoatl, the god-king who left our shores five hundred years before, vowing to come back.

"Quetzalcoatl will not come back, Your Majesty."

"How do you know? Am I not the king? Don't my dreams have the force of prophecy?"

"You may have dreamt of him, Your Majesty; I, on the other hand, was his friend." It was because he lost the land in a wager that he had been forced to cross the ocean to look for a new kingdom, though that part of the story never made it into our mythology.

"So you say, Nezahualcoyotl. You say that you're a thousand years old, and that you personally led our people out of the wilderness. That sort of thing is all very well for the peasants, Nezahualcoyotl. But I'm a modern king, and I know that you often use the language of metaphor in order to enhance the grandeur of the gods. No, no, I'm not blaming you; I'm a mean hand at propaganda myself. It's just that, well, you shouldn't believe your own—"

It would not do to argue. I finished my blood in silence.

"Anyhow, I think we should have a bit of propaganda right now, Nezahualcoyotl. Why don't you go down there and lead the jaguar team personally? Give them a bit of that old-time religion. Stir up their juices."

"Sire, at my age—"

"Nonsense. Guard, give him one of those flower-wands."

I sighed, took the wand, and went down the hill.

The war was being conducted in an orderly fashion.

Seeing me, members of the jaguar team made a space for me. I gave a brief and cliché-ridden harangue about the cycles of the cosmos; then it was time to charge. Boys banged on humanskin drums; musicians began a noisy caterwauling of flutes, cymbals, and shrilling voices that sang of the coming of Huitzilopochtli to the Mexica. The armies ran toward each other, chanting their war-songs, each soldier seeking out a good quarry. I too ran; not with supernatural swiftness, but like a man, my bare feet pounding the ground. Above us, the whistle of the atl-atl and the whine of flower-tipped arrows. The armies met. I searched for a suitable captive that would honor the god. I saw a man in the farthest rank of the enemy, more child than man, his limbs perfectly formed, his eyes darting fearfully from side to side. There was someone who saw no honor in dying for the god! I elbowed aside three pains of combatants and came upon him suddenly, looming above him as he ducked behind a tree.

"I am your death," I said. "Give yourself up; give honor to the gods."

I touched him with the flower-wand. He glanced at it, took it, stared me defiantly in the eye.

"I won't do it," he said.

I knew then that he had been polluted by the preachings of the man-beasts. A fury erupted in me. I said, "Why have you been listening to them? Don't you know that they're only human beings? That they bleed and die like ordinary men?"

But he began to run. I was surprised by his speed. He leaped over a bush, sprinted away from the mass of warriors toward a field of maize that bordered the battleground. My first impulse was to let him go—for there was no honor in sacrificing so abject a creature to Hummingbird—but my anger grew and grew as I watched him shrinking into the distance. I could stand it no longer. I called upon the strength of the jaguar and the swiftness of the rabbit; I funneled into the very wind; soon I was upon him again. He turned, saw me running beside him, matching him pace for pace. I could smell his terror; terror was only natural; what I could not smell was the joy, equally natural, that a man should feel when he is about to embrace the source of all joy, to die that the sun might live. He was less than a man. Only an animal could feel this terror of dying without also feeling the exhilaration. I decided to kill him as he ran. I reached out. He struggled, but I drew on my inner strength; I pinned him to the ground. The corn encircled us. Only the gods heard what we said to one another.

"I won't go," he said again. "Kill me now, but I won't die to feed a god that doesn't even exist."

"Doesn't exist!" My anger rose up, naked and terrible. I started to throttle him. The odor of his fear filled my nostrils. It was intoxicating. I wanted to feed on him right then and there. I could feel his jugular throbbing against my fingers. I knew that his blood was clean and unpolluted with alcohol or coca leaf. His blood was pure as the waters of the mountain; but I could not kill him. "How long were you among the man-beasts?"

"Three years."

I had to let him live. He knew about the foreigners, their languages, their savage ways. I could not kill him until he had divulged all he knew. With a fingernail I scratched his arm, sucked out a few droplets to assuage my Hunger. I had to bind him to me. He could become a secret weapon; perhaps I could stave off the end of the world after all.

If only I had listened to the voice of Hummingbird! But I wanted to halt the wheel of time, and though I was a thousand years old I was still too young to understand that there is no stopping time.

"Who are you?" I said.

"I don't know. I don't have a name anymore; I've forgotten it. The Spanish called me Hortator. It pleased them to let me beat the drum on one of their galley ships. I've even been to Spain—that part of Spain that they call Cuba."

"Why aren't you still with them?"

"Pirates, Lord High Priest. I escaped; the others are dead, every one of them."

"And the man-beast who is called Cortez, who the king thinks is the god Quetzalcoatl, returned to reclaim his inheritance?"

"I don't know of him. The man-beasts are many—dozens of nations and languages. And all of them are coming here. They want gold."

I laughed; what was so valuable about gold, that would make these creatures come across the ocean in their islands made of wood? Was gold then their god?

"No, my Lord. They worship Xipe Totec; their name for him is Hesuskristos."

When I escorted my prisoner back to the pen, it was getting late. Moctezuma was bored and listless; Cozcatl was annoyed at having lost the war, though it would hardly have been good manners for him to be victorious over his sovereign lord. The two kings applauded as I approached them, and bade me eat with them; they had a fresh haunch roasting. "Excellent meat," said the king. "She was good in bed, too."

"You did her great honor, Sire, to inseminate her, sacrifice her, and eat her, all with your own hands."

"It was the Queen's idea, actually; she had been getting uppity. But what have we here?" He eyed my captive with interest. "A powerful-looking fellow; I didn't know you had it in you to bring in so fine a specimen."

He cast his eye about for his obsidian knife; when

the king particularly favored someone, he was apt to sacrifice him on the spot. I had to think quickly to protect my source of information. "Your Majesty," I said, "the god has told me that this man is to be the next Unblemished Youth."

"Oh," said the king, disappointed, "we'll have to wait until the big ceremony, then." To Hortator he said, "You're a very lucky young man; you'll have the best in food, drink, and women, including four holy brides; until you're sacrificed, a year from now, you'll be worshipped as a god. Even I will have to bow to you, though you mustn't get any grand ideas."

"Yes, Sire," said Hortator. I could tell he was grateful for his reprieve. Perhaps, in time, I would be able to wash away the silly notions the man-beasts had planted in his mind. A year was time enough, surely, to persuade him to look forward to being sacrificed properly.

"You were planning to deprogram him!" Julia said, having by then become somewhat drunk. I myself was on my second skin of blood; my appearance was far less corpselike than it had been in the exhibit hall.

"I'd better take you home with me," she went on. "At least until you figure out what you're going to do with yourself. I mean—no credit cards, no social security number, no car—you could be in for some culture shock."

I was not sure what she was talking about, but a few hours later I was numb from confusion. I had ridden in a thing called BART, which is a cylindrical metal wagon that runs through tubes under the earth; I had been driven in a horseless chariot across a bridge that seemed to hang on wires above the ocean; I had seen buildings shaped like phalluses, strutting up into the sky; and the people! Tenochtitlan at its most crowded had not been like this. San Francisco—named, so Julia told me, after a nature god of the Spaniards—was a hundred times as crowded. There were people of many colors, and their costumes beggared description. In my feathers, leggings, and pendulous jade earrings, I must have looked a little odd; yet no one stared at me. This was a people accustomed to strangeness.

At length we reached Julia's home, an apartment within one of those tall buildings, reached by means of a little chamber on pulleys which seemed much more efficient than stairs; I could see that I was going to enjoy the many conveniences of this alien world.

Her home was an odd little place; she lived alone, without parents or children, without even any servants; and the apartment, though crammed with laborsaving devices, was little bigger than a peasant's hovel, and considerably more claustrophobic.

We had been there for only moments when she thrust herself at me. Her blood was racing, and scented with erotic secretions. She kissed me. I tasted blood on her chapped lips. I pulled away. "Be careful," I said. "I don't have the same desires as you. I don't feel lust. Not like that."

"Then teach me the other kind of lust."

"I'm afraid you would not like it."

"Yes, yes, I know the desolation, the loneliness of eternity. I don't care! Don't you understand? I've always wanted to be a vampire. I've never been able to get this close to one before. Not for certain. I'm a historian. I want to get the long view. I want to see man's destiny unfold, bit by bit. I hate being a human being."

"It's not what you think it is." How could I tell her about those flashes from my childhood, those faded images that still haunted me with their unattainable vividness? My world is a gray world; only the infusion of blood brings to it a fleeting color, and that only a simulacrum of color, awakened by long-lost memories; now, five hundred years beyond the end of the world, I had become even more of a tragicomic figure. How could this woman ever know, unless I made her know? And then, poor thing, there would be no turning back.

I did not want to make her like me. I had tried that once. It had not eased my loneliness. And my creation had betrayed me. But the woman could be useful. For now I would pretend to hold out the possibility that she might one day become immortal.

"Make love to me," she said.

She smiled a half-smile and beckoned me into an inner room. There were mirrors everywhere. With great deliberation, she began to remove her clothing. There was a pleasing firmness to her, though she was not young. An Aztec woman of her years would have been worn out, her fists hardened from pounding laundry or tortillas. It would be necessary for me to go through the motions of lovemaking. In the end I did not mind. She had been menstruating.

Afterwards, I lay on the bed and watched her sitting at the mirror, painting her face. She opened a drawer and took out a gold pendant in the shape of a crucified man. Suddenly I understood why I had not perished along with the rest of the world. I had unfinished business.

"Where did you get that amulet from?"

"You recognize it, don't you?" She stood up, clad only in the pendant and her long dark hair. "I'm afraid you're not the first vampire I've dated. Actually I wasn't entirely sure he was one, until now. They don't make a habit of telling. But you've just confirmed it."

"I have to find the person who gave it to you."

"I'll take you to him," she said.

* * *

Once more we crossed the bay in the steel chariot; once more my memories came flooding back.

They had seemed insane to me, those man-beasts; there were only a handful of them, yet they scoured the land as though they were an army of thousands. In only a short while they had conquered a city but a day's journey from Tenochtitlan. But in the palace of Moctezuma there was a strange calm. I did not know why. Each day, I sacrificed the requisite numbers of victims at the appropriate hours; I did nothing that dishonored the gods.

Except, of course, for the little lie I had told my king; it had not been Huitzilopochtli who had commanded that the man Hortator be consecrated as the Unblemished Youth. I had said so to ensure that the man would survive and remain useful to me. It was not the first time I had invoked the voice of the Hummingbird to bring about some personal decision. When one has been the mouthpiece of the god for centuries at a time, there are times when one's identity becomes blurred. Besides, what harm could it do? Hortator was the perfect choice, even if the god had not made it himself.

I visited him each evening in the compound sacred to Xipe Totec, where the four sacred handmaidens dressed him, bathed him, and tended to his sexual needs, for he was no longer free to walk about the city at will. He was, indeed, unblemished, a prime specimen of Aztec manhood, lean, tall, well proportioned, and fine featured. The god would be pleased when the day came for him to be flayed alive so that his skin could be worn by the priest of Xipe Totec in the annual ceremony that heals and renews the wounded earth and brings forth the rains of spring. There was only one thing wrong with it all; the Unblemished Youth did not seem particularly honored by the attention. It was all most unusual, a sign of the decadence of those times.

"I don't want to do it," he told me, "because I don't believe in it." For a nonbeliever he was certainly reaping its benefits—being massaged by one handmaiden, being fed by another, and the gods alone knew what was going on under the gold-edged table behind which he sat. "I mean that it's no use; the blood of human sacrifices isn't what makes the sun rise each morning; the god of the man-beasts is clearly more powerful than Huitzilopochtli even as Hummingbird was mightier than the gods who came before. I don't mind the pain so much as the fact that I'd be dying for no reason."

"You've been poisoning the king's mind, too, haven't you?" I said. For Moctezuma seemed to have lost all interest in the future of his empire.

"I am the Unblemished Youth," he pointed out. "It was your idea. And as you know, that means that my advice comes from the gods."

"You hear no voices from the sky!" I said. "It's all pretense with you."

"And what voice from the gods told you that I was to be kept alive to teach you the ways of the white men?"

He knew I had lied. Only one whose mind had already been tainted by the man-beasts' ideas would even have imagined such a thing. "But I do hear voices," I said.

"Then let me hear one too."

"All right."

I told him to follow me. We took a subterranean passageway—for he could not be seen to wander the streets of the city—that angled downward, deep under the great pyramid of Huitzilopochtli. The walls were damp and had a natural coolness from the waters that seeped underground from the great lake of Tenochtitlan. Hortator stopped to admire the bas-reliefs which depicted the history of the Mexica people in their long migration toward the promised land; there were sculptures in niches in the stone, some decorated with fresh human skulls or decaying flowers, some so weathered that they could no longer be identified, being the gods of unremembered peoples who had long since been conquered and assimilated by the Mexica; many parts of the tunnel were ill-kept; our torches burned but dimly here, far from the outside air.

At length we reached a chamber so sacred that even King Moctezuma had never set foot within it. It was guarded by the god of a civilization far older than ours—Um-Tzec, the Mayan god of death, whose skull-face was etched into the stone that blocked the entrance.

I whispered a word in the long-forgotten Olmec language, and the stone slid aside to reveal the chamber. Hortator gasped as he read in the flickering torchlight the calendar symbols and the glyphs that lined the walls.

"But—" he said, "this is the lost tomb of Nezahualcoyotl, your namesake, the first great king of the Aztecs!"

I smiled. I held up my torch so he could see all that the room contained—treasures of gold from ancient cities—magical objects and amulets—and a great sarcophagus, carved from solid obsidian.

"The tomb is empty!" he gasped.

"Yes," I said, "it is, and always will be, by the sacred grace and will of Huitzilopochtli, Hummingbird of the Left."

"The black robes told me of creatures like you. I've never seen you eat; you seem to subsist on blood. You're one of the undead, a creature of the devil. You sleep by day in your own coffin, and by night you prey on human blood."

I laughed. "What strange notions these man-beasts have! Though I admit that I have sometimes taken a nap inside the sarcophagus. It's roomy, and very conducive to meditation."

I showed him the treasures. Every one of them had

an ancient tale attached to it, or some mystic power. The ring of concealment and the jewel for scrying the past. The great drum fashioned from Xipe Totec's skin, which, when beaten, confers the power of celerity. "Feel it, touch its tautness. That is your skin too, for you are Xipe Totec."

"There is only one Xipe Totec, who gave his life for the redemption of the world, who was killed and rose again on the third day."

"I'm glad the Spaniards haven't robbed you of that truth!"

"On the contrary," he said, "they taught it to me. And they say that theirs is the real Xipe Totec, and yours is an illusion, the work of the powers of darkness." He pulled out an amulet from a fold of his feather robe, and showed me the image of Hesuskristos; a suffering god indeed, nailed to a tree, his torso cruelly pierced, his scalp ripped by thorns. "It is an admirable god," I said, "but I see no reason why, accepting one, you must heap scorn on the other."

"Oh, they are not so different, the new gods and the old. The black robes have sacrifices too; they burn the victims alive in a public ceremony called auto-da-fé, after first subjecting them to fiendish tortures—"

"Wonderful," I said, "at least they have some of the rudiments of civilization."

"I did not say their god was better, Nezahualcoyotl; only that he is stronger. Now show me how your god speaks."

"I will need blood."

"Take mine," he said.

I took my favorite blood-cup carved from a single, flawless piece of jade, and murmured a prayer over it. I did not want to scar the Unblemished Youth; I knelt before him and pricked him lightly in the groin with the fingernail of my left pinky, which I keep sharpened for that purpose; I drained an ounce or so into the blood-cup, then seared the wound shut with a dab of my saliva. The drawing of blood caused the man to close his eyes. He whimpered; I knew not if it was from pain or ecstasy. I called on Huitzilopochtli, drained the blood-cup, tossed it aside. The warmth shot through my ancient veins, pierced my unbeating heart; it was a bitter blood, a blood of destiny. I emptied out my soul. I waited for the god to speak.

And presently it came, a faint whisper in my left ear, like the fluttering of tiny wings. I could not see Huitzilopochtli—no one has ever seen him—but his still small voice lanced my very bones like the thunderous erupting of Popocatapetl itself. The world has turned in on itself, said the god, and the fire of the sun has turned to ashes.

"But—what have we done wrong? Didn't we slaughter hecatombs of warriors to your glory? Didn't we mortify our own flesh, build pyramids whose points grazed the very dwelling places of your Kindred?"

The god laughed. The cosmos dances, he said. We are at peace.

In my trance state I saw Hortator standing before me, no longer in the consecrated raiment of Xipe Totec, but naked, nailed to a tree, the skin scourged from his back, the blood streaming from his side and down his face, and I cried out, "You abomination! You travesty of the true faith!" and I rushed toward him. When I was with the god I was more powerful than any human. I could rip him in pieces with my bare hands. I had him by the throat, was throttling the life from him—

You will not kill him, said the god. All at once, the strength left my hands. Instead, you will make him immortal.

"He doesn't deserve—"

Obey me! He, too, is a prophet, of a sort. Do you not understand that he who rises to godhead, who creates a world, a people, a destiny, plants inevitably within his creation the seeds of his own destruction? All life is so—and the gods, who are the pinnacle of life, are as subject to its laws as any other creatures.

It seemed to me that I no longer understood the god as clearly as I had once, when I came down from the high mountain to bring his message to a tribe of wanderers. His words were confused now, tainted. But he was the god, and I obeyed him without thought. I knelt once more before Hortator, and I began to feed, mindless now of damaging his flesh, for I knew that he would never have to suffer the rites of Xipe Totec. I fed and fed until there was no more blood at all, and then, slashing my lip with my razor fingernail, I moistened his lips with a few drops of my own millennial blood, blood that ran cold as the waters under the earth.

I cried out: "Do you see now the power of Huitzilopochtli? I have killed you and brought you back from the dead; I have awakened you to the world of eternal cold . . ."

But Hortator only laughed, and he said to me, "I heard nothing. No hummingbird whispered in my left ear. The black robes were right; your gods do not exist."

"My gods have made you immortal!"

"I am already immortal; for the black robes have sprinkled me with their water of life."

I could not understand what had happened. Why had the god commanded me to make him my Kindred, then allowed him to mock me? Why could Hortator not hear the voice of the deity when it reverberated in my very bones? The very fabric of the world was unraveling. For the first time in a thousand years, I was afraid. At first I could not even recognize the emotion, it was so alien; it was almost thrilling. I reached back farther and farther through the cobwebs of memory. I saw myself as a child, scurrying beneath my mother's blanket, fleeing the music of the night. With fear came a kind of melancholy, for I knew that I would never again truly feel what it was like to be alive.

Once, it seemed, I walked with my god; daily, hourly I heard his voice echo and reecho in my heart. Then came a time when he spoke to me but rarely, and usually only in the context of the blood-ritual. And now and then, I began to speak for him, inventing his words, for the people did not hear him unless I first heard him; it was I who was his prophet. Was it those little lies that had made my god abandon me now?

I cried out, "Oh, Huitzilopochtli, Huitzilopochtli, why hast thou forsaken me?" But the god did not see fit to respond.

We stopped at a bazaar to buy clothes more suitable to my surroundings. Julia picked out some black leggings which could be pulled over my loincloth, shoes made from animal skins, and an overshirt of some soft white material; she paid for the items with a rectangular plaque, which the vendor slid through a metal device, after which she made some mysterious marks on a square of parchment.

Then we drove on to another part of the city, one where the buildings were more ornate, not the monolithic towers of stone and glass I had seen before. We stopped in front of a low, unpretentious-looking building; Julia bade me follow her.

Inside, the surroundings were considerably more ostentatious. There were paintings, a floor covered with some kind of red-tinted fur, the pieces joined together so invisibly that one could not tell what animal it had come from. The place was full of all manner of people, jabbering away in many accents, though I did not hear anyone speak Nahuatl; perhaps my native tongue had gone the way of the language of the Olmecs.

We stood, a little uncomfortably—for though no

one questioned our being there, no one made us welcome—and I began to notice a pervasive sickliness in the air—the sweetness of putrefying flesh that has been doused in cloying perfume—I knew that it was the odor of the dead—I knew that I was in the presence of others of my kind—not one or two but dozens of them. What had happened in the past five hundred years? Had I been reborn into a world of vampires? Again fear flecked my feelings, the same fear I had felt when I doubted my gods for the first time.

"Your friend is sometimes to be found there," Julia said. She pointed to a door, half-hidden by shadows. "Go along. I'll stay here and have a glass of wine."

"You're not coming with me?"

"I can't," she said. "No human being has ever come out of that room alive. But if you're really what I say you are, you won't have any trouble. That room," she went on, her voice dropping to a whisper, "is the Vampire Club."

"Why are you whispering?"

"I'm not supposed to know." Her eyes sparkled. I could see that she loved to flirt with danger; that was why she was so obsessed with my kind.

I put aside my fear. I had to confront Hortator. Already I knew that he was close by. From the dozens of clamoring voices in the building, my attenuated senses were able to isolate him. I could even hear his blood as it oozed through his veins; for every creature's lifeforce pulsates to a personal rhythm, unique as a fingerprint, if one has only the skill to pick it out.

I was becoming angry. I stalked to the door and flung it open. There came a blast of foul and icy wind. I stepped inside and slammed the door shut. There was no mistaking the odor now. I descended steep steps into a tomblike chamber where several outlandishly attired men and women sat deep in conversation, sipping delicately from snifters of blood.

"Rh negative," said one of them disgustedly, "not exactly my favorite."

"Let me have a sniff—*pe-ugh!* Touch of the AIDS virus in that one; oh, do send it back, my dear Travis."

"Whatever for? I think it lends it a certain *je ne sais quoi*," said Travis, "that ever-tantalizing bouquet *de la mort* . . ."

Two other creatures looked up from a game of cards; their faces had the pallid phosphorescence of the dead; their eyes glittered like cut glass, scintillant and emotionless.

A slightly corpulent man, sumptuously clothed in velvet and satin, waved languidly at me. "Heavens," he said, "what a surprise! We don't get many Red Indians here."

"Get him out of here," one of the cardsharps hissed. He was attired like one of the Spanish black robes.

"Yeah, dude," said a young man, of the type Julia had described to me as punk. "Or card him at least." He cackled at some incomprehensible joke.

"Whatever for? He's obviously one of us. Either that, or he's in desperate need of the services of an orthodontist," said the man in the velvet.

"We don't know him," said the other cardplayer, a woman, whose hair stood on end and fanned out like the tail of a peacock, and who wore a full-length cloak of some thick, black material.

"Perhaps we should ask him who he is. See here, old thing—very, very old, I'm afraid—I'm Sebastian Melmoth, your humble host. And you are?"

"I am Nezahualcoyotl," I said, "the Voice of the Hummingbird. I'm looking for a certain person. He calls himself Hortator."

"Oh, I see. Well, you really mustn't get to the point quite so fast; it's not very dignified, you know. Let a century or two go by first."

"I have let five centuries go by."

"Perhaps you'd care for one of our sanguinary cocktails?"

"I've already supped tonight, thank you."

"And might I ask you what Clan you belong to?"

"I know nothing of Clans. If you won't tell me the whereabouts of Hortator, please direct me to someone who can."

"Are you an anarch?" asked the woman with the peacock hair. I could only look at her in confusion.

The other cardplayer rose and sniffed at me. "Unusual bloodline," he said. "Not a pedigree I'm familiar with."

"Now look here," said Sebastian Melmoth, "he's obviously a vampire. But he doesn't seem to have the foggiest notion about how to behave like one. Tell me, Nezzy old chap, if you were in fact to find Hortator, what would you do?"

"I shall kill him."

The others began to laugh at me. I felt like some peasant on his first trip to Tenochtitlan. "Why do you mock me?" I said.

"Well!" said Sebastian Melmoth. "That's simply not done anymore. Not without the consent of the Prince. Who doesn't even know who you are, so I don't see why he would grant your request."

It was then that I heard his voice. "Kill me?" The voice had deepened with the centuries, but I still recognized it. There he stood, towering over Melmoth, in the full regalia of a Mexica warrior, the jaguar-skin cloak, the helmet fashioned from a jaguar's head, the quetzal plumes, the earrings of gold and jade. Behind him there hung a life-sized painting of the white men's Xipe Totec, the god nailed to a tree; a soldier was hammering a stake through his heart; a beautiful woman watched with tears in her eyes.

"Kill me?" he repeated. "Why, Nezahualcoyotl?"

"Because you tried to kill me!"

"That was a foolish thing. I admit it. I placed too much credence in the Spaniard's superstitions. I know now that you're not that simple to kill. In fact, you look very well for someone who hasn't had a drop of blood in half a millennium."

"You are part of the old things, the things that should have died when the world ended. I understand now why I have been preserved by the gods. It is so that I can take you with me, you impious creature who twice refused the honor of a sacrificial death. I have been sent to put an end to your anomalous existence so that no part of the Old World will taint the New."

"Did your god tell you this, old man?"

Suddenly I realized that I had heard no voices from the gods since awakening inside the glass box in the San Francisco Museum. There was no more certainty in me, there was only ambiguity and confusion. My grand revelations no longer had divine authority. Perhaps it was true that they were the hallucinations of a madman. Perhaps if I had my votive objects I could summon back the voice of the hummingbird—the sacred blood-cup, the drum, the gold-tipped thorns for piercing my own flesh.

"Huitzilopochtli!" I cried out, despairing.

"You fool," said Hortator. "No god brought you to this place. There is no divine plan. It was I who told Julia Epstein where to dig. It was I who chose the moment to bring you back out of the earth. It was I, not Huitzilopochtli, who summoned you hither!"

"Why?" I said.

"Oh, don't imagine that I want to renew some monstrous cosmic struggle between you and me. It's much simpler than that. Buried with you, in the chamber at the heart of the pyramid, there were certain artifacts, were there not? Magical artifacts that will enhance my power. Your coming back to life along with the items I need is something of an inconvenience, but I'm sure you won't last long, because you simply don't understand how things work in this new world, this age of vampires."

Then it was that the memory of the apocalypse returned to me, bursting all at once through the wall I had erected to shield myself from its pain. I could not bear these creatures or their future, with their petty rules and their ignorance of the great cycles of the cosmos. I turned and strode away, taking the steps two at a time until I reached the Alexandrian Club, where Julia was sitting nervously at a corner table.

"Where did I come from?" I screamed at her. "How did you come to possess my body? And where are the artifacts I was buried with?" I had to have them. I had to try to summon Huitzilopochtli. Surely I would hear his voice again if I went through the ritual of the sacred blood-cup.

"Quiet now," she said, "you're making a scene."

"I have to know!"

"Yes. Yes. But not here. It's dangerous for me."

We drove into the darkness. San Francisco sparkled with man-made stars. A thousand strange new odors lanced the air: frenzied copulations; murderers and thieves skulking through the back streets; and the blood music, singing to me from every mortal inhabitant of the city, from within the topless towers of stone came the pounding of a million hearts, the roar of a million bloodstreams. Oh, one could be a glutton in this city, if one were a creature such as I. No wonder they had congregated here.

"I told you," said Julia. "Things are different now."

"What did Hortator mean when he said that he had summoned me back from the dead—by telling you where to dig?"

"Oh, he was being melodramatic. But he did drop a few hints."

"Before or after he made love to you?"

"You're not jealous, are you?"

"Of course not." I was silent for a while. The woman had a way of baldly confronting me with the truth. I didn't like it. I loathed the very idea of a city crammed with vampires, living by complex rules, observing silly hierarchies. But what could I do? The car raced over the bridge once more; Tenochtitlan, too, was a city of many bridges, a floating city. San Francisco was like a bloated, savage parody of my vanished kingdom.

Julia said, "I'll tell you, if you like. We have a series of weekly lectures at the museum. Hispanic studies, you know. Hortator came to a few of them. He would ask penetrating questions. Then he started telling me things. There was a big earthquake in Mexico City, you know. The Velasquez Building was leveled to the ground. He told me—convinced me—that there was a major find hidden beneath it, a secret room, he told me, next to a secret passageway. He told me he'd seen it in a dream. I laughed when he drew me a map. Well, that was the thing, you see. We had been using sonar to excavate those tunnels, and the computer scan matched his drawing to the centimeter."

"And you found me there."

"You were lying in a massive obsidian sarcophagus. You had a stake through your heart. I assumed—foolish me—that because of that, you were quite, quite dead—too many Dracula films, I suppose—so that it would be safe to put you on exhibit."

Memories of the apocalypse . . .

The king in all his splendor. This time not on the crest of a grassy hill, watching a pretended battle, but atop a pyramid of stone, looking down on the conquistadores as they swept through the city in a river of blood and fire. Man and beast conjoined now, the man-things glittering in their silvery skins, the beasts whinnying and pawing the pathways paved with the dead, arms and legs flying in the air as the cannonballs smashed through stone and adobe and human flesh.

And I beside him, I the mouthpiece of the god of the Mexica, aghast and powerless, raging. "You didn't have to play dead for them. They're just mortals. You've treated them like gods."

"They are gods," said Moctezuma. "There was nothing I could do."

Hortator had poisoned his mind. He had fed Moctezuma a diet of his own bad dreams, told him that the Spaniard was indeed Quetzalcoatl.

I looked into the eyes of my king; and I saw such sadness, such desolation that I could not bear it. It must be a terrible destiny to be the one chosen to preside over the end of the universe. Was there no way to turn back the sun? No. Beside us as we sat, each one wrapped in his private melancholia, my deputy priests were grimly carrying on the day's duties, plucking out the hearts of victims who waited in an endless queue that stretched all the way down the thousand steps and into the conflagration in the market square.

"Don't tell me that you accepted the word of this man-beast as the word of a god!" I cried.

"Wasn't it?" the king said. "In truth, I felt a certain wrongness about it all."

"Then let me call on Hummingbird to turn back the tide of time!"

"What difference does it make now?"

"Majesty," I said, "when the king himself no longer believes in the old truths, how can the earth sustain itself?"

"Perhaps I've been a little distracted," said the king. He was wavering.

I knew that I could not stand idle. I left the king's side, I entered the sacred chamber behind the altar, whose walls were caked with the blood of ten thousand human sacrifices. I paused only to suck the juices from a fresh, still palpitating heart that one of the priests handed me. The soldiers were hacking off the limbs of the still convulsing victims, casting down the arms and legs, as has always been the custom, for the poor to dine on. The sight of the city's daily routine being carried out even now, on the brink of utter annihilation, would have moved me to tears, except that I had shed none in a thousand years. The priests worked quickly and efficiently, up to their elbows in coagulating gore. I hardly looked at them; I chucked the drained heart onto a golden platter before an image of Hummingbird, then entered the secret passageway behind the altar that led downward, downward to the hidden chamber where lay my sarcophagus and the tools of my art.

In the tunnel, the sounds of death were muffled. Cannon like the distant whisper of thunder in the rain forest. The screams of the dying faint, like the cries of jungle birds. The clash of metal on stone like the patter of rain on foliage. I took the steep steps two at a time. Soon I was in the heart of the pyramid.

When I reached the chamber, I found that the seal was broken. Not with the magic words, but shattered with gunpowder. Several of the man-beasts were already there, ransacking the place, gathering up the treasures into sacks. "How dare you?" I screamed. The man-beasts rushed at me. I summoned up my inner strength. I struck out blindly with both fists, and two of the Spaniards slammed against the stone walls. One of them died on the spot; the second more slowly, a little string of brain oozing down from his helmet. The third man-beast gaped, turned tail, started to run. Then his greed got the better of him and he returned to gather up one of the sacks of gold. He glanced at me; I was draining his dead friend's blood into the sacred blood-cup so that I could call on Hummingbird.

I closed my eyes. I called on the name of my god.

Huitzilopotchtli . . .

I felt myself sinking into the well of unconsciousness that was the presence of my god. I heard the familiar buzzing in my left ear that presaged the coming of Huitzilopotchtli. I smiled.

My child . . .

Came the whisper of the Hummingbird's wings, the tiny voice from the heart of the flames. I thrilled to its dark music. I allowed it to wash over me like the currents of the sea. I relinquished my being. The presence of the divine was more fulfilling even than the taste of blood, than the memory of women.

My child . . .

Abruptly, the trance was broken. I was jolted into consciousness. Even now, telling the story to Julia five hundred years later, the memory will not come back as a woven fabric; it is in tatters.

Hortator stands before me, no longer in the attire of the Unblemished Youth, but wrapped in a metal skin from head to toe, like one of the conquistadores. With him are a dozen of the white-skinned creatures. He has delivered to his masters an entire world, an entire civilization.

"I know what you are now," he cries, "creature of Satan. They've told me everything." Several more of the Spaniards come in behind him, brandishing their swords and their flaming torches and their muskets. Seeing their dead comrades they cry out, back away; but Hortator laughs. "I know what you are now, and the Jesuits have told me what I must do to kill you."

Confused, uncomprehending, I lash out—

He dodges my blow, leaps across the sarcophagus, seizes the drum of Xipe Totec and begins to pound on it, a slow relentless rhythm. I scream. He pounds. I lunge. He leaps, each leap drawing more celerity from the power of the drum. He flies along the walls, he twists, he turns, he is a whirlwind, a tempest—

Huitzilopotchtli! I cry out.

No answer. I reached into the profoundest darkness of the well within. Where was my god? I see Hortator bearing down on me, brandishing a sharpened wooden stake.

As though from infinitely far away I seem to see the stake rive my stony flesh, rip apart my rib cage, pierce my heart . . .

Huitzilopotchtli!

Huitzilopotchtli!

Then, and only then, the god responds. The pyramids above us start to tremble. Cracks appear in the ceiling. Rocks start to rain down.

"Flee!" cries Hortator. I hear, through the fog of pain, their footsteps, metal clanking on stone. I hear some of them cry out as the cave-in crushes them.

I clutch at the wooden stake. But it is too late. I feel its leaden weight within me, feel it still the sluggish pump that is my heart, I feel the blood slow from a spurt to an ooze. I feel my heart muscle tighten around the unyielding wood like a vagina. I feel violated. I feel powerless for the first time since my changing. Then, all at once, I am spiraling downward toward the long sleep of ultimate forgetting.

And now, another underground passageway, another secret chamber. Five hundred years in the future, in a world I did not belong in, I stood with Julia Epstein among the shelves and shelves of artifacts of my people, all labeled, boxed, marked in white paint in the strange curlicuish script of the man-beasts.

Crate after crate I ripped open. "What is it you're looking for?" said Julia. "This is valuable stuff—you can't just throw it around like it belonged to you."

"It does belong to me."

"Half a millennium ago. But they're priceless antiquities now. And they haven't been appraised by the insurance company yet, so—"

I saw a tattered quetzal-feather robe that had once belonged to King Moctezuma's grandfather. I saw my sacred blood-cup, chipped now. I lifted it from its box . . .

"Careful with that thing! It dates back to Olmec times."

"I know. I made it."

She was silent for a moment. "The drum!" I said. "There was a drum fashioned from human skin."

"I've seen that," she said, "in Hortator's apartment."

So that was how he had made it out of the collapsing tunnels—with the power of celerity conferred by the drum of Xipe Totec! I was furious now. He had no right to my ritual objects. I was more determined than ever to exact revenge. Perhaps he thought I would be a useless anachronism, but I would teach him not to usurp my magical tools. They had told me at the Vampire Club about new laws that forbade the killing of vampires without permission from some prince, but what did I know of princes? What did I care? I was more ancient than any prince.

But even as I spoke, we heard the sound of shattering glass, and the high-pitched wail that I now knew to be an alarm that would eventually summon the museum's security. Then came a distant thumping sound, uneven, like a fibrillating heart. I knew that sound well. The hollow pounding contained in it the scream of a dying man.

"Hortator!"

"Why do you have to go on fighting him?" Julia said. "Don't you realize that the war between you two has no meaning anymore?"

"Julia, I must have a little of your blood."

She closed her eyes, craned her neck, bared it to me as a warrior bares his heart for the sacrifice. "I need the blood," I said, "so I can summon forth the voice of the Hummingbird."

"There's no voice," she whispered. "It's in your mind, the right brain speaking to the left, a hallucination of godhead. Don't you understand that people don't see visions and hear voices anymore? You come from the age of gods; we live in the age of consciousness; it's not the god who commands us anymore, it's we ourselves, our ego, our individual being. People like you, people who still hear the voices of gods, they put them in insane asylums now."

What was she telling me? It made no sense. How could humans exist without prophets to transmit the commands of the gods? How lonely it must be for them in this future; to be like little islands of consciousness, not to be linked to the great cycle of the cosmos; to be not part of one great self but merely little selves, with little, meaningless lives. I could not, would not live that way. I took her in my arms; I made a tiny incision in her neck with my little fingernail; I drew a thimbleful of blood into the sacred cup; deeply I drank, and as I drank I prayed: Huitzilopotchtli, Huitzilopotchtli, do not forsake me now.

Hortator burst into the chamber. The alarms were screeching. "The rest of the treasures of the room have now been brought to San Francisco," he said. "That's why I told Julia where you could be found. I need the other ritual objects. I need the powers they can bestow on me. As for you, you're just a historical oddity."

But I could feel the strength of Huitzilopotchtli course through my flesh.

As Julia, faint from her bleeding, sat, dazed, on my old sarcophagus, still in its wooden crate, Hortator and I battled. He threw me against the wall; I lacerated his face with my fingernails; he whirled about me, pounding his drum, my drum. Each of us drew on his dark powers. A mortal would not have seen us battling at all. He would have felt now a tremor, now a flash of light, now a ripple of darkness. I leaped onto the ceiling, I sped along the walls, defying the earth's pull with my speed; but Hortator was equally swift. His fangs glistened in the man-made light. We fought hand to hand on the lid of the sarcophagus where Julia still lay. We tussled on the concrete floor of the storeroom, and still the siren wailed.

"I'll really kill you this time," Hortator shouted. "The black robes told me a stake through the heart would kill you. I know better now."

And still I had not heard the voice of the Hummingbird. It was beginning to dawn on me that there was something to what Julia said; that perhaps this was no longer an age of gods. The last time the god had spoken, had he not said, Do you not understand that he who rises to godhead, who creates a world, a people, a destiny, plants inevitably within his creation the seeds of his own destruction? I did not understand then, but I understood it now. My existence showed to ordinary men that there was something beyond mortality; but beyond my own immortality there was also a kind of entropy. In being granted the ability to see the grand scheme of the universe, to live for centuries and know the higher purposes of mankind, I had also learned that all, even the most sublime, is vanity. I was full of despair. How could I belong to this future? How could I live amongst dozens of creatures like myself, arcane hierarchies all selfishly struggling for domination over one another? I knew that Hortator would hound me to my death. I could not live in a world where I could not hear the voice of my god.

We had battled for what seemed like days, but I knew that only seconds had passed; so quick were our movements that time itself had seemed to stand still. He had me pinned to the ground. I felt not only his weight but the weight of this whole bizarre new universe. And with a free hand he continued to drum, frenzied now, his eyes maddened, his lips frothing. I waited for him to drain me of all my blood, to desiccate me, to consign me to the well of oblivion forever.

Then, at that moment, the siren ceased. Hortator relaxed his hold on me. A shadow had fallen over us. I smelled the presence of another Kindred. I could feel the concentrated power, a puissance that nearly matched my own.

"Prince," Hortator whispered. He stepped back from me, then fell to the floor in supplication. I could not see this Prince, so thoroughly had he cloaked himself in magical darkness. But I knew him in the shadow that suffused the air.

"Oh, Nezahualcoyotl," said the prince, whose voice was as reverberant as a god's, "what am I to do with you? You have arrived in this city, yet you do not even come to pay homage to me as is our custom; and already you've created all sorts of controversy. The Vampire Club talks of nothing else but you. You're an anomaly; you challenge our most basic assumptions about our people's history."

I said, "I did not mean to offend you. My quarrel with Hortator is an ancient one, and not your affair; and I see now that the things we quarrel about have become irrelevant. I have no real desire to live. Let Hortator take my ritual objects and grow in power; and let me return to the earth."

"It is true," said the prince, "that I have the authority to grant you death. But how can I? You are older than I;

you are so old that even the concept of the Masquerade is foreign to you; it is I who should bow to you, but I cannot. There can only be one prince. Nezahualcoyotl, you must find your own destiny in some other place. Or else there will always be some who will look to you for leadership, anarchs who will revere your disregard of our rules of civilization and who will claim that your greater age gives you greater authority. Nezahualcoyotl, you must leave. I cannot command you. I, a prince, must ask it of you as a favor."

And now the security guards were entering the room. It was just as it was in Tenochtitlan, the enemy storming the secret chamber just as my world was disintegrating all around me. The prince did something—used his powers of hypnosis perhaps—for the guards did not seem to see me, Hortator, or the rippling darkness that was the prince of San Francisco.

"Are you all right, Ms. Epstein?" said one of them.

Julia was struggling to get up. "I—must have passed out," she said. "Something—someone—perhaps a prowler—"

"No one here now, ma'am. But they've made quite a mess."

"Are you sure you don't want me to get a doctor?" said another guard.

"I'm fine, thanks."

"Let's see if we can find him lurking around somewhere," said the first guard, and they trooped away. Astonished, I looked up. I thought I glimpsed something—a swirl of shadow—vortices within vortices—the eyes of an ancient creature, world-weary, ruthless, yet somehow also tinged with compassion. I knew that he was right. I could not stay in San Francisco. I knew nothing of the feuding factions of the vampire world, the warring Clans, the Masquerade; I belonged to a simpler time.

"I will go," I said softly.

Then Julia said, "And I will go with you."

I said, "You don't know what you're saying. You think it's some romantic thing, that there's glamour in being undead. Look at us; look at how we have relived, again and again, ancient quarrels that the world has forgotten; the vampires that rule the world are but shadows, and I am less than a shadow of their shadow."

Julia said, "Only because you have not loved."

She came toward me. In her eyes there shone the crystalline coldness of eternity. I had not wanted to transform her into one of my kind. I had sought only to use enough blood to sustain me, to let me see my visions. She had not yet become a vampire; what I saw in her eyes was the yearning. "It's a historian's dream," she said, "to pass through the ages of man like the pages of a book, to perceive the great big arc of history. It's not just that I love you. Even if I didn't, I could learn, in eternity, to love."

Hortator hissed, "Only the prince can grant the right to sire new Kindred!"

But the prince said only, "Peace, peace, Hortator; will your anger never be slaked?" And then—and I could feel him fading from our presence as he spoke—he said, "Do what you wish, Nezahualcoyotl. Be glad. We will not meet again."

I have returned to Tenochtitlan. It is a gargantuan madhouse of twenty million souls, but it is still called by the name of my vanished tribe, the Mexica. My official title is Meso-American Studies Advisor to the San Francisco Museum Field Research Unit, Mexico City. Julia and I have a charming apartment; one side overlooks one of the few areas of greenery in the city, the other one of the worst slums.

Julia tells me that a philosopher named Jaynes has written a book called *The Origin of Consciousness in the*

Breakdown of the Bicameral Mind. It is a book that explains how, in the ancient world, men did not possess consciousness of self at all, but acted blindly, in response to voices and images projected by the right side of the brain, which they perceived to be the direct commands of gods, kings, and priests.

It is a strange world indeed, where people see no visions, and where a book has to be written explaining away the gods in terms of ganglia and synapses. I do not like it. I do not like the fact that I have been cut off forever from the divine; that I am no longer a prophet, but merely one vampire among many.

Yet the city does have its charms. Its nightlife is thriving and decadent; its music colorful; its alleyways quaint and full of titillating danger. And then there are the people, the descendants of my own people and the Spaniards who overcame them. Julia and I often make time to enjoy the inhabitants of our new home.

There are many poor people here. They pour in from the country, seeking out a better life; often they end up working as virtual slaves in huge factories that pump out cheap goods for their richer neighbors to the north. Sometimes they become gangsters or beggars. Sometimes they find a charitable person to take them in, as domestics, perhaps, or live-in prostitutes.

But sometimes, ah, sometimes, they vanish without a trace.

The Bye-Bye Club

by Ray Winninger

"Your mom is in the ground, isn't she?" whispered a thin boy with ash eyes. "And your papa's dead too!"

The new boy was too young or too unsophisticated to realize that Ash-eye's own parents must be dead or missing. No one is admitted to the Child Services Northrock Facility for any other reason.

"Did they choke each other to death 'cause they couldn't stand your shitty reek?"

The new boy couldn't respond. He stared at Ash-eye's face and nervously examined the boy's features, hoping they concealed a clue to the mystery that had tortured him all nine years of his life. As Ash-eye turned to face him, the new boy instinctively locked his fingers around the plastic kaleidoscope resting on the desk in front of him. He was determined to protect the kaleidoscope. It was the only thing he had left.

"What's that?" Ash-eye grabbed for the kaleidoscope himself and raised his voice, obviously signaling for reinforcements. "You tryin' to hide that from *us*, you shit-smelling pussy? Maybe we oughta break you off!" On cue, a full half the students in the classroom swarmed around Ash-eye and added their own voices to his taunts. One, a pasty boy in a GI Joe sweatshirt, grabbed the new boy's hand and began methodically prying each of his fingers off the kaleidoscope. When only two fingers remained, a sharp elbow to the stomach allowed Ash-eye to snatch away the kaleidoscope and disappear into the crowd.

The instant his grip slipped away, the new boy

started drooling and thrashing wildly. He grasped GI Joe's upper lip between his index finger and thumb and tugged the boy's sweaty face down toward the desktop. GI Joe reacted by bringing both hands up in an attempt to break away—a mistake that freed the new boy's other hand and sent it hurtling into the pasty boy's neck. The sudden, violent blow sent GI Joe gasping and startled the gang of tormentors. Ash-eye made his way to the corner of the classroom and steeled his fists. He recognized that he would face the enraged boy alone. No one else, save the incapacitated GI Joe, had invested reputation in the encounter.

As the students rushed back to their seats, an empty corridor opened between the new boy and Ash-eye, allowing the new boy to charge with outstretched arms. As he approached, he spread his fingers and angled his thumbs, hoping to thrust them into his tormentor's eyes and gouge into the skull. Horrified by this savagery, Ash-eye lifted his knee in a panic and drove it into the new boy's diaphragm, sending the berserker sprawling. In another beat, he pounced upon his floored prey, cocked back his fist, and grit his teeth. The new boy closed his eyes tight and brought both hands in front of his face.

Before Ash-eye could strike, something yanked him to the floor. "GOD DAMN YOU! YOU LEAVE HIM ALONE RIGHT NOW OR I'LL TEAR THIS HAIR RIGHT OUT OF YOUR HEAD! Christ! I'm five minutes late and you're already causing problems!" Ash-eye let out a yelp and started mumbling. Another shout—"Now give me that thing and go see the administrator!"—was followed by the panicked squeak of sneakers and the sound of a small plastic object rebounding on the cold floor.

The new boy opened his eyes to the sight of a chubby woman on her hands and knees, retrieving the kaleidoscope. He supposed that she reminded him of his mother, though he hadn't been able to imagine anything about his mother for weeks. "Here you go, honey. Don't be afraid; I'll make sure those little bastards leave you alone. I'm Mrs. Tremond. I'm your teacher. If you have any problems, come see me." The new boy struggled to his feet, scooped the kaleidoscope from her hand and returned to his seat. Mrs. Tremond gave him what she hoped was a comforting pat on the top of his head and went to gather her papers.

The teacher's departure cued a whisper that filled the new boy's ears with a tickling wind. "Hey, Friend." The new boy recognized the lisp. It came from one of his tormentors, a gap-toothed boy in black overalls who was seated directly behind him. "Hey, I think I like you. Umm, we have this club here at Northrock. We call it the Bye-Bye Club. If you . . . if you wanted to join, I'm sure it would be okay."

The new boy turned and greeted the invitation with a vacant stare.

"Oh. Don't worry about that other stuff—we were just teasin' ya. I'm sure we'll get along from now on." Gap-tooth paused to read the new boy's expression, which hadn't changed much since the scuffle ended. "If you decide you want to join the club, we meet in the toolshed every fifth Wednesday after lights out. We're meeting tonight. Just sneak out through the fire door and head for the shed. You'll find us there. And don't worry about the door—the alarm doesn't work."

The new boy turned and pretended to focus his attention as Mrs. Tremond began the day's lesson. He still felt Gap-tooth's breath on his neck.

"Um. One last thing." Gap-tooth waited for Mrs. Tremond to face the chalkboard before finishing his thought.

"My mom's dead too."

* * *

That evening, the new boy awoke to the sound of his bunkmate, Rust-top, sliding down to the floor and opening a drawer. Feigning sleep, he watched through squinted eyes as Rust-top pulled on a pair of trousers and slipped out into the corridor. It wasn't until the new boy noticed that Rust-top's exit failed to attract the attention of any other resident that he realized he was completely alone.

Then he remembered the toolshed and Gap-tooth's invitation. He thought about his mom in the ground and his kaleidoscope and then slipped out of bed to find his trousers.

Ten minutes later, he was gliding through the darkness. As he neared the shed, he noticed that its door was slightly ajar. A red light emanated from within and stretched along the walkway leading back to the dormitory, cutting the courtyard in half. Something about the light sent strange signals to the new boy. It soothed him, though he couldn't understand why. It reminded him of that distant evening and the traffic light he noticed and his father missed.

As he approached the shed, he heard a low whisper that abruptly dissolved into total silence. Those inside were alerted to his presence. He should have been startled, but he wasn't.

"It's okay. It's the new kid," he heard Gap-tooth whisper. "I told him to come." More whispers and a brief pause before the shed door finally creaked open.

Inside, the new boy saw his classmates seated in a semi-circle that faced the shadows blanketing the back of the shed. The red light came from a stained bare bulb that projected from a broken Mickey Mouse lamp. The glow it cast upon the faces of the assembled children lent them an unexpected familiarity. The new boy was certain that Gap-tooth was right—from now on, they'd all get along just fine.

As he entered the shed, the new boy sensed an unfamiliar presence. Disoriented, he looked around for a few moments before he noticed the two adults seated deep in the shadows. One was a fat, greasy man wearing a Marlboro hat and a dirty, black T-shirt. The other was dark, lithe, and dressed in black leather. Something about the dark man fascinated the new boy. Perhaps it was the dull red glow that may have been another reflection of the Mickey Mouse lamp, but instead seemed to emanate from deep within the man's eyes.

The dark man was the first to speak. "And who are you?"

The new boy didn't answer.

"Well, Little Cobra, welcome to our club. Do you know who this man is?" The dark man looked at fat-and-greasy.

The new boy paused for as long as it was comfortable before shaking his head "no."

"I see. Do you dream of electricity?"

The new boy never remembered his dreams, but he knew the answer was "yes"—another nod, quicker this time.

The dark man smiled and a hint of recognition crossed his face and quickly submerged beneath his icy features. "I am your friend."

"Who is the other man?" The new boy surprised himself with the words, his first in a very long time.

"Let's ask one of your classmates. Chatterjack, tell Little Cobra about George."

Across the shed, Ash-eye stood and stared at the new boy with contempt. "His name is George Feeney. People call him the Seaside Strangler. No one knows his real name but us." Ash-eye gave an abrupt nod to signal that he was finished and sat back down.

"Chatterjack, you're not finished." The dark man shot Ash-eye a cold leer, spooking the boy and urging him to stand and continue.

"George likes to cut sluts. So far, he's killed twelve of them."

The dark man was obviously appeased. "Eleven actually, but very good, Chatterjack; I see you've read those books I left you the last time George and I were here." Ash-eye sat down with a wide grin poking out from under his deep brow. "You see, Little Cobra, George has a mission—he and many others like him, scattered all across the globe. George is part of a grand plan."

"What plan?" More words—the new boy was becoming intrigued.

"I'm afraid you wouldn't understand if I told you. But no need to worry; if you're like George, you'll figure it out for yourself one day."

Fat-and-greasy giggled out loud, pleased with the compliment.

"George was once one of you. He wasn't a member of this particular club—there are many such clubs scattered across the United States—but he was a club member. Where was your club located, George? Kayenta, Arizona, wasn't it?"

Fat-and-greasy nodded vigorously and a stupid grin cut across his bloated face.

"Yes, Arizona. That's where George and I met. I remember that particular club *very* well."

"Who are you?" The new boy spoke for only the third time in almost two weeks.

"My kind are friend to George and friend to you all. George and his associates travel across the country visiting secret clubs like this one, always accompanied by a special friend like me. Tonight, George and I are here in Northrock. In five weeks, we will be in Tom's River, New Jersey, and Paul Todd Earley will be here in our place."

"Who's Paul Todd Earley?" asked Ash-eye, trying to take the dark man's eye off the new boy.

"You know him as the Red River Ripper, Chatterjack." Despite Ash-eye's best efforts, the dark man's attention soon returned to the new boy. "So far, George and I have visited Pennsylvania, New Jersey, and Connecticut."

"And Delaware," added Ash-eye. "The books say Delaware, too."

"Yes, but I'm afraid the books are wrong. George had nothing to do with that woman in Delaware. Sometimes journalists get a bit carried away."

"How do you know where to go next?" asked a petite blond girl seated near the shed door.

"Again, I'm afraid you wouldn't understand if I told you."

Gradually, the new boy came to notice something. His classmates were completely silent and attentive, almost reverent. He could feel them clinging to the dark man and his words, reaching out for attention, guidance . . . something.

"There's something else you should know, Little Cobra. George and his associates are not the only men and women with a mission. You and the other members of this club have a mission as well. It is George's job to make people go away." The red light that inhabited the dark man's eyes grew so bright that the new boy was now sure it was not a reflection of the Mickey Mouse lamp. "It is your job to decide *who* goes away."

The new boy's classmates were obviously growing anxious. Each was coiling as if to spring upon some unseen prey.

"So." The dark man produced a thick Culver Country phone book from under his seat. "Who wants to choose?"

The moment the invitation was extended, the

assembled children lashed out like sprinters starting a race. Each was trying to attract the dark man's attention by waving, grunting or shouting. Just before the noise level grew loud enough to attract the staff members stationed at the nearby dormitory, the dark man cut it off with a cold stare that quieted all the children save for the small blond girl who spoke earlier.

"I don't want to use the book," she mumbled. "I want George to make Peter Pan go away."

A few of the other children giggled, but the dark man remained patient. "We needn't use the book, but I'm afraid George can't make Peter Pan go away, dear. Peter Pan is only a story."

The little girl hung her head and slumped to the back of the crowd. The new boy noticed a pair of tears start to slip down her face.

"I have an idea, my young friends. Since this is Little Cobra's first meeting, why don't we allow him to choose?"

The children obviously didn't like the idea, but they were afraid to question the dark man's wisdom. All eyes were drawn to the new kid. "So Little Cobra . . . who should go away?"

The new kid paused and stared into the Mickey Mouse lamp. He had questions. As long as he could remember, he had questions. But something in the dark man's eyes told him that answers were finally within his grasp. He realized the dark man was right. One day, he would figure it all out for himself. Like George. He sank into the dark man's shadow and reached out for the phone book.

At the last moment, the dark man snatched the book away and tilted his head upward, obviously deep in thought. When he finally looked down to face the children again, there was a hint of a smile on his lips. Something was wrong. The dark man's voice grew tentative, almost inquisitive. "I think your classmate is right, Little Cobra. Let's not use the book this time. Who should go bye-bye?"

Suddenly, the new kid felt like an outsider again. What did the dark man want from him? Why did he take away the book? More questions. Why no answers? He needed answers more than anything in the world. He struggled to remember a name, but the only name he knew was his father's, and his father was already gone. His eyes darted around the shed in a nervous panic, looking from child to child, silently asking for help. When he noticed Ash-eye and the touch of amusement in the boy's expression, it came to him. He knew exactly one name.

Little Cobra cleared his throat. "Um. Mrs. Tremond . . . she's our teacher." The blond girl resumed her sobbing. The other children were quiet and interested, almost fascinated.

The dark man seemed to relax again. A broad smile cut across his face. "Mrs. Tremond it is," he said, shooting a glance toward George. "Our business is concluded then. Goodnight, children. You must return in exactly five weeks . . ." For a moment, his expression grew sour. ". . . and I'm sure I needn't remind you of what happens to boys and girls who talk to anyone about our club meetings."

The other children slowly filed out of the shed and started sneaking back down the path to the dormitory, but Little Cobra couldn't leave—not yet. There were still so many questions. The dark man gave George a nod of assurance, prompting the greasy whelp to make his own exit. On the way out, George grabbed the Mickey Mouse lamp.

Little Cobra and the dark man sat alone in the shadows, staring at each other. Little Cobra was afraid to speak. After a full fifteen minutes, Little Cobra finally mustered his courage. "What . . ."

The dark man cut him off in mid sentence. "No." A

knowing smile took root in his dark lips. "One day, little one." The dark man gave Little Cobra a comforting pat on the head before standing and exiting the shed.

A moment later, Little Cobra came to his senses and followed. As he stepped out of the shed, he tried to catch a glimpse of the dark man walking off into the night, but there was no man in sight. He saw only what appeared to be a large, black dog bounding across the courtyard toward the highway.

"I said give it to me right now, you cunt!" Little Cobra tore the seashell from the new kid's hand while Ash-eye watched the hallway. Feeling his grip slip away, the new kid burst into tears and started flailing his limbs. A wild left fist caught Little Cobra in the lip, but served only to enrage him.

"Quick! Someone's coming!" Ash-eye heard the click of high heels against the polished floor of the corridor. At first, he presumed that Ms. Suarez, the boys' teacher, had finished her daily chat with the social worker a bit early, though it was actually the hefty, graying administrator who rounded the corner, heading toward the classroom.

Ash-eye leapt toward his seat, but Little Cobra was too interested in the beating he was dishing out to the new kid. He was still pounding his fists into the boy's chest when the administrator entered the room.

As she crossed the threshold, the administrator froze for an instant, then bolted for Little Cobra. "GET OFF OF HIM, YOU DEVIL!" She remained surprisingly strong for her age—one swipe of her long arm easily separated the two boys. She grabbed Little Cobra's shoulders and brought her face within inches of his eyes, as if she was trying to peer into his soul to uncover a clue explaining his behavior. "You'd think you of all people would have some sympathy for a new face. You've only been here a couple of months yourself." Little Cobra just stared back. Sensing she'd get few answers from the boy, she turned to face the new kid. "Now, what's this all about?"

"He . . . he . . . he stole my favorite shell."

The administrator rolled her eyes, grabbed Little Cobra's ear, and gave it a tug. "Did you take the shell?"

Grabbing the administrator's wrist to ease the pain, Little Cobra gently shook his head "no."

"Empty your pockets!"

Little Cobra stood motionless, staring at her with clearly defiant eyes. Already tired of the whole incident, the administrator reached into the boy's hip pocket herself and tugged outward, spilling the pocket's contents on the ground. Maintaining her grip on the pocket, she stooped to pick up three items: the seashell, a plastic kaleidoscope, and a curious flat stone emblazoned with an unsettling painted rune in the form of a tight black spiral. Something about the stone sent a chill down her back. When she first touched it, its purpose and nature seemed to lie on the fringe of her conscience, just out of reach. Then, an instant later, the feeling was gone. "Where did you get this thing?" she asked, rolling the stone through her fingers.

"A friend gave it to me."

Once she decided she couldn't unravel the mystery of the stone, she placed it and the kaleidoscope back in Little Cobra's pocket and held the seashell in front of his face.

"Didn't steal it, eh? What do you have to say for yourself?"

Little Cobra stood quiet and defiant.

"Nothing at all?"

Unexpectedly, the boy's defiant expression melted

away, replaced by an unsettling grin. "Nothing to say, ma'am, but may I ask a question?"

The administrator felt a sudden chill and took an unconscious step backward. "You may."

Little Cobra's grin melted away. "What's your name?"

The Way It Goes

by Thomas Kane

Suddenly, I found myself outside Walter's Restaurant once more. It was morning again in San Francisco, just like the first time, and the colorless full moon still hung behind thin clouds. My target was sitting with Von Roon and three of his men in a corner booth, and the five of them were eating Number Two Breakfast Specials. The target had her back to me, so all I saw of her were soft golden curls and the pale-blue vinyl of the restaurant furniture. I felt the weight of the pistol in my back pocket.

It's no big deal, killing people. It happens every day.

Besides, nobody asked me to think about what I was doing. DNA Incorporated doesn't pay people to think, and neither does Mr. Praeger. I was nothing but Praeger's property—indentured servitude is a way of life in the modern corporation. If you don't accept that, you flip burgers all your life.

It's not as if I was going to make some kind of stand for high principle. *Thou shalt not kill*—what kind of garbage is that? I was living in the real world. If you fight reality, you end up like the target in there.

And so, I brushed the damp from my wiry mustache, and wiped the lenses of my glasses, which had fogged in the morning air. My hands were pale and the tendons stood out. When I looked at my skinny arms protruding from the dark gray sleeves of my imported trench coat, I knew that I was a killer, but I would get myself smeared in any kind of a real fight.

Every now and then I wondered whether I'd made the wrong decisions—whether I really had to end up as a guy who made a living by shooting people from behind. But when I looked at my arms, I knew I had the body of a coward. I remember exactly why I ended up the way I did. I never had a choice. Or, if I did have a choice, I didn't know it at the time.

I positioned myself for the shot. The waitress kept messing up my line of sight, but my position gave me the best view I could get of the target's head.

The target's name was Julie Rochon.

It didn't matter that I knew Julie's name. It was her own fault that this was happening. Julie worked in Strategic Planning, and she'd seen all kinds of the company's most secret garbage. She should have known Praeger wouldn't let her quit. Nevertheless, there she was, trying to skip out on her job at DNA and pick up a new job with another firm. She was meeting with *Von Roon*, of all people. Von Roon recruits executives for the Ries-Dillon Consortium. And as far as Praeger is concerned, Ries-Dillon isn't just the competition, it's the Antichrist.

Julie had been bitching for months. I wasn't surprised that she actually tried to quit—she was the kind of woman who seemed to think she had some kind of right to make herself happy. Julie was an idiot, and she deserved exactly what she was getting.

I reached into my jacket and gripped the pistol. The gun Mr. Praeger had given me was a hodgepodge weapon, cobbled together from the parts of half a dozen automatic pistols. It was the size of a toy. A mass of sticky cloth tape gave bulk to the handle. Even if I had owned a silencer, the gun's barrel wouldn't have held one. This was the kind of weapon that nobody could ever trace back to DNA Inc.

I cut my eyes in each direction, pulled out the pistol, gripped it in both of my gloved hands, pivoted back a step and fired. Even as I squeezed the trigger, I knew I'd botched the shot. Maybe the jury-rigged gun had a crooked barrel. Or maybe it was some kind of subconscious thing . . . because I knew Julie's name. Either way, the gunshot sang in my ears.

The bullet punched through plate glass. My shot missed Julie. The round hit the skinny, middle-aged waitress, who stood all the way on the other side of the restaurant from where I aimed. The waitress collapsed in a heap, knocking dishes off a table, spurting blood all over her white apron.

The waitress fell, and time seemed to stop. I stared at her as she flung back her head, her face all squeezed into a rictus of agony. People live a million different ways, but everybody dies the same. Cheap psychologists talk about "accepting death" but I've never really seen why it matters. When you die, it doesn't matter if you're brave and noble. You're still going to die like everyone all over the world, whimpering, helpless, and alone, with your own urine streaming down your legs. And then there's nothing.

Before I could even level my gun again, Von Roon shoved Julie down behind the booth. Chaos broke out in the restaurant. Some people headed for the waitress' body and others ran away from it. A table toppled over, and three or four plates full of breakfast dashed across the floor. I didn't have even a remote chance of getting another shot off. Von Roon's three men were fanning out, and one of them was on his knees, poking buttons on his slim cellular telephone.

I didn't notice anyone with a weapon, but I could see this vivid image of Von Roon's men returning fire, and I could practically feel gunshots rip through my body. I didn't want to die. I'd seen people die, and I knew that there was no such thing as a good death. There was no such thing as honor and no such thing as redemption. Once you die, nothing you have or did or thought matters anymore. Death just grinds you down to nothingness. So I didn't wait to see what would happen next. I ran.

I took off pell-mell up the street, stuffing the gun in my pants-pocket, my lungs screaming for air, expecting to hear sirens at any moment, if not to feel a bullet. There were a couple of shade trees just up the street. I dove into them, looking for cover. As I crashed through the moist leaves, a blue-gray pigeon burst out and flew away, squealing, into the morning stink.

I leaned up against the moist earthy bark of the tree, panting. *Why did I ever get into the business of killing people for a living*? That's just a stupid question. I knew the reasons why. For three years, I had worked my tail off at DNA and got nowhere. Then Mr. Praeger invited me to his office, the one on the thirtieth floor. Praeger looked down from his big leather throne, smiled like a frog, and asked me if I was serious about working for DNA. Then he told me about an executive manager who was a problem for him, and asked me if I could help him "deal with the man." What was I supposed to do, say no to Praeger?

The real question is why I even bothered to run away after missing Julie. I had just failed a mission. When you fail Praeger, you don't get a second chance. The moment I shot the waitress, I had killed myself.

That thought hit me like a thunderbolt. Then my memory stream got foggy.

Everything that had happened since I went to Walter's seemed familiar to me. I had lived through the scene at Walter's Restaurant a million times, as if my life was a movie playing over and over again. I wandered back onto the pavement. My foot came down over a little blister in the sidewalk. Cracks radiated out from the blister in all directions. Every time I relived this scene, I always looked down to see the rifts below my feet, like a Grand Canyon in the bumpy, black pavement.

My stream of memory ends with me gazing at the crack. As I stare into its recesses, I lapse into nightmares. I sink through the ground into a nauseous, whirling world of madness. If the shooting scene was a movie, the part where I hide in the trees would be where the film starts melting in the projector.

I can't describe the nightmares. There's nothing to talk about—just long strings of fevered dementia. I don't know how long this lasted. At last, I forced the madness from my mind. I saw the city again. The streets of San Francisco still did not seem quite real, but at least I managed to keep them from dissolving into dreams. I wandered the streets as I wandered my memories, looking for a way to get around fate.

The next thing I heard was a ringing telephone.

The phone drew me like a magnet. It was the telephone in my own apartment. Suddenly, I realized what happened after the shooting. After I had gotten away from Walter's Restaurant, I had gone back to my own place. I collapsed onto my sofa in the damp trench coat, and lay there feeling like I was going to be sick. When I think about it, it seems really stupid to screw up a murder and then just go home. On the other hand, I don't suppose that I had any better ideas.

I picked up the phone. "Yeah."

"Hello. I wish to speak with Mr. Stephen Myers, if you please." The voice on the other end was cultured and mellifluous. I recognized the tone at once. It was Mr. Donald Mozyr, who was supposed to be my boss, although everybody knew that Praeger ran the show.

"Hello Mr. Mozyr." I squeezed up my face, trying to soften my voice and steady it, while I wondered what was about to happen to me. "It's me, speaking. What can I do for you, sir?"

"Ah, Mr. Myers. You aren't busy, are you?"

I swallowed. "No, sir, not at all. I had today off . . ."

"Oh, splendid. If it wouldn't be a terrible inconvenience, I was hoping you'd come down to the office for a few hours. It seems there is something Mr. Praeger wants to speak with you about." Mozyr's voice sounded like a cheerful, beckoning songbird.

"Sure." My hand shook a little, and I accidentally rapped my mouth with the phone. "Is something, you know, wrong?"

"Oh, no, nothing like that." Mozyr laughed in a lovely, reassuring bass tone. "Mr. Praeger simply wishes to go over some matters with you—nothing very serious I'm sure. But I do wish you'd hurry. Mr. Praeger does seem eager to get started."

"Be right there." I fumbled for my cigarettes—I needed a smoke badly. There was an irony. I needed to smoke because I needed to do something meaningless and get my death.

I had no idea how to escape. I paced back and forth in my apartment. I knew this call to the office was a set-up, but Mozyr said it was OK, and besides, what choice did I have? If I didn't go, they'd come for me. My fingers trembled like jackhammers as I reached for the cigarettes. I couldn't get the pack out of my pocket. I couldn't have handled a match anyway.

Death awaited me at the office. I knew that. I also knew that, whether going to the office was a good idea or not, I wouldn't be able to force myself to do it.

I shoved some things into my pockets, emptied my bank account at the nearest ATM, and bought a ticket for the Greyhound bus to San Diego. I thought maybe I'd cross the border into Mexico on foot, at night, and disappear forever. The bus was late, and I paced around the terminal. I glanced from the battered soda machine to the tired-looking passengers to the gang of men in sweat-stained blue coveralls, scrambling to load and unload busses.

The bus finally came. I took a seat in the back corner, by a dusty window. A clan of half a dozen Mexicans trickled in after me, filling all the seats in my area. The driver climbed on board in a few minutes, but he promptly returned to the station, and spent an interminable amount of time in there. I fidgeted in torment. However, as the bus finally trundled onto the interstate, I relaxed enough to watch the people in the nearby seats.

The Mexicans had a full-fledged family. A thin man in denim seemed to be the father. He had the responsibility of standing up and unzipping the luggage in the overhead baggage compartment whenever the baby whimpered for a toy. A golden-skinned woman in a flower-print dress sat next to him, apparently the mother. An elderly man, his tanned skin all wrinkles, sat in the seat in front of them and occasionally turned to offer a sage word.

After perhaps half an hour, the mother put the plump baby into the aisle, patted him on the back, and sent him toddling toward the remaining two members of the family. These were two young women, apparently young aunts or elder daughters. The one by the aisle scooped the infant up and set him on her lap, cooing at him.

The young women chatted as the bus drove on. They had lively faces and their dark eyes flashed as they spoke. The flow of their conversation rose and fell in incomprehensible Spanish. Occasionally, one of them chuckled, and then they both broke into gales of hilarity. Nothing seemed phony or malicious about their laughter.

The more I watched these people, the more I realized that I had nothing whatsoever in common with them. This went far beyond the fact that I didn't know a word of Spanish. The father looked vigorous; the girls seemed warm and cheerful, and they all were wholesome and content. It was easy to envy them. However, whether their lives were good or bad, they seemed utterly alien to me. I could no more have fit into that family than Mr. Praeger could go in his suit and tie to a playground, and join in the games like one of the children.

I felt an emptiness that I had never felt before. An emptiness that had always existed on the fringes of my being. I had never allowed myself to let it affect me and I hated this perfect family for delivering me my pain. Praeger hadn't had me shot yet, but inside I knew that I had already died a long and pathetic death.

By the time we get to Los Angeles, I knew that Mexico would give me no redemption. I was an empty man—a killer. I would have nothing to live for no matter where I went. And so, I bought a new ticket. I waited for five hours in the urine-smelling concrete warrens of the Los Angeles bus terminal, and then I took the bus back to San Francisco. We pulled across the Golden Gate bridge early the next morning. Up the arching bridge we went, with the suspension cables soaring to the sky on either side. Steam rose from the Bay, slowly diffusing into the air.

I returned to my apartment almost twenty-four hours after the moment I shot the waitress. Once I locked the door, I scooped the pistol out of my pocket with both hands, trying to keep it from clattering to the floor. Then I stared at the dull-gray thing. Possibilities ran through my mind. I could have bought a real gun, pushed the sofa up against the door and defended myself. I'd shot people before, and I could have shot whomever Praeger sent to waste me.

But that was not going to save me. It would not save me from the welling emptiness in the pit of my stomach. And what if had killed one of Praeger's men? He'd have sent somebody else to do the job, someone who knew what he was doing. Either that, or he'd wait. Eventually, I'd have come out, and then he'd have wasted me. Or, he might have just tipped off the police, and I'd have gone to the gas chamber. You can kill all the people you want, but nobody has invented a way to keep someone else from killing you.

I jiggled the clip out of the gun's handle. Little brass bullets rattled in their track. I pushed the clip back in and massaged it until it clicked into place. Then I put the pistol up to my eye, looking down the barrel to the shadow inside. I even caressed the seam that ran down the middle of the trigger. A tear rolled down my cheek and my head reeled. Time ticked away in a rhythmic, pulsing staccato of thumps. The thumping was the beat of my cold and heart.

It all came down to this. Everything in my life had really just led up to this point. I was going to die in my own hole, and that was going to be the end of everything for me. I never had much and now I was going to have nothing.

Still, those thoughts didn't explain the terror I felt inside. When I looked into my gun, my insides felt sour, from the base of my throat to the hollows of my bowels. There was something primal about this fear. It was the fear that every living thing feels in the face of death, and it was more potent than anything I had ever felt before.

Whenever I've made a decision, I've always tried to do the smartest thing. I've been rational. However, even though I knew it would be best to shoot myself, I realized that there was more to it than that. Hard realities were not the only things that shaped me. I didn't know if love existed, or hope, or honor or morality, but I was face-to-face with pure, animal horror. If I'd known that sooner, I might have been a different man, but it was too late.

When you die, it's too late for anything.

I hurled the pistol across the room. Then I waited. Sooner or later, Praeger's men would come and kill me for me. If my shot had missed entirely, maybe Mr. Praeger would have let me live, punished me, but let me live. However, I'd killed a bystander. That meant police and a real investigation. Mr. Praeger was going to arrange for me to commit suicide and then let the cops pin it all on a dead man.

Sure enough, I heared a single, reverberating knock on the door.

I had no idea what came after the knock. That

memory always trails off into a typhoon of horror. I do recall pain tearing through my chest, bubbling up into my head, choking out everything. I do not think anyone survives such pain. There isn't really much doubt in my mind about what happened. Praeger's men came in and drilled a bullet through my body.

Even before the bullet came, I plunged into delirium. I sank through the floor into the dream-world, screaming at the top of my lungs. My body faded before my eyes, and my whole consciousness dissolved into a crimson nightmare.

This wasn't supposed to happen to me, it was supposed to happen to Julie. I thought of her and the world faded around me. As I plunged into dreams again, memories of her rose around me. This was from before she went to Von Roon. It was from before Praeger sent me to kill her. This was the moment when I first met Julie.

I tasted liquor in my throat. Muffled strains of music rumbled from the walls, confused by the babble of conversations. The lights were dim, and the springs of a hotel bed creaked beneath the weight of two people. Julie sat on the bed next to me, her red dress a little rumpled, her face flushed with alcohol.

I was on my back, a little dizzy, and she was sitting up. I eased my arm around her hips, far less smoothly than I might have hoped. Then I propped myself up a little on one elbow, my other arm still wrapped around Julie. "Great party."

Julie just nodded. She wasn't really smiling. She looked down at me, her blue eyes steady, and as focused as they could get at that stage of drinking. I tickled her stomach through her dress, but she moved her body and kept looking at me.

"Hey Steve, are you . . . satisfied?"

"Huh?" I tried to slide my hand a little lower, but she shifts away. "What d'you mean?"

"Satisfied." She sighed with the sincerity of the drunk. "With your job . . . with your life. I mean, I know I'm not. I keep trying to imagine my life as being different. Do you want things to be different? I mean, are you happy?"

I just grunt. What kind of dumb question was that? I slid my hand upward, brushing her bosom with my knuckles.

Julie kept looking at me.

"We all sell our souls." I pulled in closer to her, working my hand closer. "That's just how it goes."

"OK, Steve." Julie wraps her arms around herself. "But is it worth it?"

I had no answer for that. I breathed heavily in her ear, dismissing what she had said. She pulled back, as if she wanted to say something more, but I ignored her. I reached up for her breast. When I touched her, it was as if something had snapped between us. She jerked away.

Julie stood up, leaving me still lying on the bed, with my arm around nothing. She pulled open the door of the hotel room and headed back toward the rest of the party, her arm protecting her breasts. And as she left the room, she looked back at me, and wrinkled up her face, as if she was looking at a snake.

I just lay on my back, half drunk and miserable. Julie was the only woman I'd come close to having in years. That was the first thing on my mind—I had blown it. But that was not the only reason I felt so miserable. Julie's questions dug into my mind like burrowing worms.

It was only a few days after that Mr. Praeger told me he wanted Julie dead. And I accepted the job.

Now, as I live through the scene again, I think about Julie's questions. Was it worth it? I don't dare try to answer that.

Then the nightmares begin again.

When I regain consciousness, I feel more lucid than

I've felt for . . . for a long time. The things at Walter's, and the things in my apartment—those were just memories. What's happening now is new. I haven't remembered it before. I don't think I'm living old events any more. The things I see are real.

My gaze falls on the telephone again. Then it falls on the gun, which still lies in the corner, by my VCR. My apartment is almost the way I remember it. However, strips of yellow tape crisscross the window and run around the room. A circle of tape runs around the gun. A brownish stain marks the floor. Someone has drawn chalk marks all around the stain.

I had only one more question and my mind searched for an answer. What happened to Julie? She was the person who didn't cave in to Praeger. She was the person who made me wonder if I could defy him too. She was also the person I had tried to kill, and in trying to kill her, I had brought on my own doom. Julie was the only chance I ever had to make my life different. Now, I desperately wanted to know her fate.

I track Julie until I find her. Although Julie does not seem to see me, I cling to her unnoticed, like a piece of lint on her black satin blouse. Julie is in Praeger's office—the upper-story office where I used to meet with him. She sits upright before his broad mahogany desk, her hands clasped in the lap of her skirt, her exquisite lips pressed together. Praeger has his back turned, and he makes Julie wait, which is what he always does. Julie's cheeks look soft and creamy, with all the signs of weeping cleansed away, but I can see where tears have melted her mascara. Every muscle in her body looks taut.

Neither Julie nor Praeger seems aware of me. Being in the office is like being in a dream. The office is real, the people are real, but I am not. And so, I watch.

Slowly, magnificently, Praeger swivels in his seat, turning to face Julie. Praeger sits in a huge office chair, upholstered in alligator hide, with a high back that rises behind him like a dragon's folded wings. He stares down at Julie through his glasses, his face as plump as a baby's. "Ah, Ms. Rochon. I hear we had a . . . frightening experience."

Julie just smiles a polite, little smile. I can see her quiver.

"It is so fortunate that we were not harmed." Praeger speaks with a European accent that lends his voice a piquant air of arrogance. "In the future we will be more careful . . . no?"

"Oh—yes, sir." Julie nods and looks up at Praeger, batting her curled eyelashes as if looking at a lover. If there was ever a trace of defiance or independence in Julie, it is gone now, scrubbed away without a trace.

"Hmm—very good." Praeger chuckles, moving his Adam's apple but not his lips. "And so, Ms. Rochon, do we need a bit of time to be getting over the shock? A brief vacation?"

Julie shakes her head. "No, sir. I'm ready for work."

"Ah . . ." Praeger's voice boomed. "Then it's back to work, back to work. You're industrious, Ms. Rochon. I like that. What do you think about a promotion, Ms. Rochon?"

Julie gasps. Her mouth forms a little O. I guess I'd be shocked too, if Praeger sent someone to shoot me and then offered me a promotion.

"Yes, yes. For some time I consider you for this job—ideal. You step up, become Export Consultant for joint ventures in the Amazon Basin. Of course, we increase your salary, what, maybe ten, fifteen percent."

"I'll do my best, sir—I really will." Julie beams, and her voice chokes a little. Relief transfigures her face. Her ecstasy looks positively sexual.

"Of course, this is a highly sensitive project." Praeger folds his hands and stares Julie in the eyes. "If you accept, you will be placed under our Executive

Security Program. We will have people keeping an eye on you, to make sure no more scary things have to happen. Do you understand?"

"I understand." Julie takes a deep breath and lets it out. Tears sparkle in her eyes. "I really am grateful, sir. I know I've made some very, very foolish choices. But you've been so wonderful . . ."

Praeger shrugs and turns up his palms, an expression of good humor on his roly-poly face. "Ah, yes, but that is what I am here for, no?"

Julie laughs. Then she turns her head to the side and gazes at Praeger out of the corner of her eye, with a fond, admiring smile.

I see now that Praeger is a genius. He hasn't merely intimidated Julie. He's crushed her, broken her down to nothing, and then built her up again. Julie is more than a loyal DNA employee now. She's a worshiper. To Julie, Praeger has become a combination of lover, father, and god.

It is possible that when Praeger gave the order for me to waste Julie, he never meant for me to succeed. This is exactly what he had planned. Praeger got what he wanted. Julie got what she wanted as well. As for me, well, I had to play my part to make Julie believe that the threat to her life was real, to make her feel properly shocked and terrified and desperate. I gave substance to the ritual, like a goat with his guts pulled out on a heathen altar. I was a sacrifice. In fact, Praeger was probably ready to get rid of me anyway—I knew too much, and had been doing dirty work too long. I did what I was told, and I got the shaft. It's that simple.

After a few moments, Julie looks up at Praeger as if he's her best and closest friend. "The man who shot at me . . ."

"Yes. What about him?" Praeger was talking faster, and after years of working for him, I could tell he was losing interest in the conversation.

"I saw his face." Julie continued breathlessly. "I know him . . . his name's Steve Myers . . . he works in this building."

"Oh—yes." Praeger threw up his hands. "We forget about Mr. Myers now. Steve Myers is gone. We never see him again. So don't worry—get to work." Praeger laughs again, curls his mouth into a U-shaped smile, and then turns away in his chair.

My teeth grate together. I want to make Praeger—and Julie—remember who I was. I'm standing right in front of them, but they don't see me. Julie walks right through me as she heads for the door. I feel her body heat, but she doesn't even flinch, much less look at me.

I chase after Julie to the exit. I want to ask her the same question she asked me. Is she satisfied? Will she stay satisfied? Ten years from now, when she ends up the way I did, will she think working for Mr. Praeger is worth it?

I call her name. "Ju-lie . . ." My voice rings in the cavernous office but Julie does not turn and the door closes in my face. I reach out to open it, but although I can feel the cool brass knob, and the tacky spots where Julie gripped it with moist fingers, I cannot make the door open. My fingers do not even wiggle the knob.

Then I hear a hollow command. "Come through the door."

I step right into the door, and the polished wood doesn't stop me from going through. Even the metal knob seems no more substantial than shadow to me.

Outside, I see three figures, looming in the broad corridor of the thirtieth floor. Julie walks away, paying no more attention to them than she does to us. An elderly secretary with her hair up in a gray bun ignores us all as well. However, we appear quite real to each other.

As the three approach, I can see them more clearly. They all wear suits and ties. The one on the left looks young. He's a little twit, with round glasses and a shock of blond hair that stands straight up. When his eyes meet mine, he grins. "You're ours, Larva."

The guy on the right has a smug, pudgy face. He puts me in mind of a well-fed worm. Worm nods a mocking greeting. "Smile . . . you're among friends."

However, neither Twit nor Worm comes too close to me. The one in the center walks right up and places a heavy hand on my shoulder. He is older than the other two, with heavy square spectacles and a strand of hair that artfully covers his balding scalp. "We've been following your progress for some time, Mr. Myers."

"Yeah." I curl my lip and look up at him. Suddenly I recognize the man. His name was Halperin. Halperin worked for DNA Inc. about five years ago, before his heart attack . . . his *fatal* heart attack.

"You are eligible to enter the society of the dead. My friends and I have made it possible for you to exist in that society, Mr. Myers." Halperin appraises me, his lower lip extended in a glum expression. "We are doing you a favor by bringing you to full spiritual consciousness. In return for this, you entail certain obligations to us. I trust you understand the significance of such obligations."

"We own you lock, stock, and barrel." Twit breaks out in an obnoxious little chortle. "You know how it works."

I nod. I realize that this was how I had lived my life. My skull aches with that realization, and a numbness fills my brain. People like Praeger rule our lives and our deaths. I had always thought death was meaningless, but death is worse than that. Death is when people like Praeger triumph.

Then Halperin reaches toward my eyes with ashen fingers. Before I can flinch, his fingers close, and he peels a foggy membrane from my face. For the first time, I look with clear vision upon the world of dead souls. This was a world I already understood. I had lived it for years. And now, as far as I knew, I was going to live it forever.

The Scarlet Letters

by Scott H. Urban

The fog was just beginning to roll in as Corrinda found Café Prague. Thin, white wisps crept around corners like sentries for an invading army of oblivion. Emerging from the mouth of an alley, like something born of the mist, came a huge dog of uncertain breed. Surely he's too big to be someone's pet in the city? she wondered. The canine ran across the road with an easy lope, not even giving a sniff in her direction, and was swallowed back up by the enveloping shadows of a narrow side-street.

Over her head, a sputtering neon sign caused the fog to glow in a blue nimbus. She could still see where someone, many years ago, had painted the name of the coffee house on the tall front window, using varicolored daisies and asters to give shape to the letters. Only in Haight-Ashbury, thought Corrinda, where the flower is in power. A handwritten sign taped to the window's lower left corner read "Open Mike Poetry Reading—9 PM Until ???"

Corrinda brought herself close to the glass. As she did, another face approached her. She gave a start, then realized it was her own reflection. The bruise under her right eye was only now beginning to lose some of its purplish bloom. She winced and wished she had learned to use makeup somewhere along the line.

A plywood stage rose on the other side of the window. Two interior spotlights mounted on the ceiling were aimed at the stage. Someone was onstage speaking, but the glare prevented her from determining whether the person was male or female. She took another step and pushed open the door.

In all her fifteen years she had never been to San Francisco, but she immediately felt more at home here than she ever had in Homily, some five hundred miles to the north. The atmosphere was thick with smoke. It hung in spiraling coils like the thin ghosts of snakes. Her nose detected not only tobacco, but also cloves and pot. Ten circular tables, each with five or six chairs and most of them occupied, filled the center of the room. Ten additional chairs were lined up against the left-hand wall. The patrons seemed divided equally between gray-haired day-trippers who had somehow missed the word that the '60s were over, and khaki-shorted out-of-towners who wanted a safe brush with the counter-culture. The bar was to the right, and a chalkboard hanging behind it proclaimed, "The Perk of the Day." Irregularly spaced around the walls were vintage Peter Maxx posters and psychedelically lettered broadsides announcing concerts by Jefferson Airplane and The Grateful Dead.

A lanky man with hair to the small of his back was shouting onstage. In his left hand he held a sheaf of wrinkled, stained papers. His right hand fluttered as if trying to work itself free of the confining wrist. He was saying something about government atrocities in Central America, but it was somehow mixed up with what his older brother had done to him when they were young.

She followed a roundabout course to the bar. Behind it stood a woman with thick, curly red hair, fair skin, and freckles the color and size of pennies. Corrinda ordered coffee, black, and watched it poured, thick and steaming, from a waiting pot. She passed a five-dollar bill over the counter, wincing as she realized she was now down to ones. She blew across the top of the mug while waiting for her change. She turned slightly, looking back at the stage, trying to get into the flow of the poet's declamations.

"Are you going to read tonight?"

The voice, right behind her ear, was unexpected. She gave a start, nearly slopping scalding coffee on her fingers. Cursing, she set down the mug and turned. She could have sworn there was no one behind her when she walked up to the bar, but a man now stood only inches away.

He was swarthy, stocky, and of medium height. He wore a black turtleneck sweater and loose-fitting black slacks. His hair, also black, was swept straight back from his forehead. She could see little of his eyes. They were set deep amidst his other features, whereas his nose was just a touch too prominent. He frowned with concern.

"I'm sorry. I didn't mean to frighten you."

"It's all right. I just didn't see you there." She began to ask him where he had come from when she caught a warning. Her palm was resting on the smooth, oak top of the bar, and she felt the message travel up her fingers, through her arms, and into her brain. Her pupils and nostrils flared wide.

She looked up at the newcomer. "Brace yourself against something," she said breathlessly.

His brows drew together in question, but before he could ask her what she meant, a rumble—at first distant—seemed to approach at supersonic speed. The floor beneath them rippled, as if they somehow stood on the surface of a wave. Glasses and plates beneath the bar shimmied against one another, trying to see how violently they could shake without shattering, though many fell and burst. A couple of the cafe patrons screamed, but by the time their cries faded so had the tremor, the faultline agitation flowing back into the mantle to be absorbed. Most of the audience was laughing now, releasing nervous tension. The bartender was standing up toppled bottles.

"It wasn't the Big One, folks," the lanky poet

onstage announced, "so God must be telling me it's all right to finish my poem."

The man in black focused his attention on Corrinda. "You knew that was coming. You knew it before it happened."

She nodded, using a wad of napkins to mop up coffee that had spilled from her mug. "Sometimes I . . . catch things. I think of it as catching because I know there are messages flying around us all the time, out here"—she used her finger to point in ten different directions—"and sometimes I just happen to be in a position to pick them up. It's like catching a baseball blindfolded. Most of the time you'll miss. But if you hold your mitt just right, you might catch one pitch out of a thousand. Sometimes I learn things about the past. Sometimes I learn about the future. Sometimes I know what another person is thinking right at that moment."

"What a gift to possess." The stranger smiled. "You have been blessed."

Suddenly she looked down and bit her lip. "You wouldn't think so. Not if you'd caught . . . some of the thoughts I have."

He nodded, accepting that without question. "So. As I was asking you before San Andreas interrupted, are you going to read tonight?"

She felt the blush rising on her cheeks. "I wanted to. Is it so obvious? It's the reason I came, I guess. But now I'm not sure. I don't know if my stuff is good enough. I don't know if it . . . sings."

"Ah." His eyebrows rose slightly. "Are you the new Belle of Amherst?"

She quickly shook her head. "No. Nothing like that. I write more about . . . the darker side of life."

"Emily understood that as well. She knew Death would stop for her and take her to the Narrow House. But that's beside the point. I would like to hear you read."

"I'm afraid I'll make a fool of myself . . ."

He nodded at the stage. "You couldn't do any worse than that one. You may get some applause. You may even feel like doing it again." He looked her up and down appraisingly, and she discovered, much to her surprise, she didn't mind. "What's your name?"

She hesitated. She had no idea who he was—for all she knew, he could have been a mugger, a psycho, a serial killer. She could lie, make up a name—but then she realized she would never see him again after tonight anyway.

"Corrinda. What's yours?"

He repeated her name in a low whisper. It had always seemed awkward before, but in his voice her name became something exotic and glamorous.

"That's different. Very beautiful." He glanced at the stage. "Go on up there. Before you can talk yourself out of it." The audience was clapping, seemingly with relief, as the lanky poet stepped from the stage.

She made her way between the tables, feeling as if she were walking toward a sacrificial altar. She had to keep swallowing. Stepping onstage, she turned toward the audience. The spotlights in her eyes jarred her, but she felt relieved she didn't have to look into any faces.

"Ummm." She brought her hands up nervously, brushed her hair back, then laced her fingers in front of her. "My name is Corrinda, and . . . I write poetry." Someone over to the right coughed. "OK." She didn't put her poetry on paper. The twenty or so pieces she had composed that she was satisfied with she had committed to memory. Now she almost wished she had then written down so that her hands would have something to do while she recited.

The words came, tremulous at first. Sweat dotted her forehead, prickled under her arms, but she gained confidence with each minute, her voice becoming increasingly stronger and firmer. She spoke of a mother's love turned into something venomous when the mother abandoned the family. She was able to take a stepfather's abusive and incestuous advances and turn them into something tragic, while they yet remained repulsive. She sang of an anger frustrated because there was nothing at which to strike. She mourned for dreams that were bittersweet to begin with because they could never come true. The lights, the audience, Café Prague itself evaporated; she spoke in a void, a place white yet without illumination, where words were the only things to console her. She was surprised when she reached her last word; it brought her back to the mundane. She blinked, now seeing patrons hunched forward in their seats, silent—waiting for her to continue.

"Ummm. That's it. Thank you."

She stepped from the stage and was taken aback at the applause that erupted around her. She was certain it was a mistake; they must have been clapping for someone who just entered. She headed for the door. Well, you did it, she told herself. You shared your poetry with the world. Now you have to figure out what to do with no money and no place to go home to.

She was just about to slip outside when an arm shot across her path—not touching her, but barring her exit.

"That was incredible!" It was the dark-haired man from the bar. "Please don't leave just yet." Flecks of purple and black swirled in his eyes, now revealed in better light.

"I . . . I really have to go."

"At least come finish your cup of coffee. I was saving it for you." He removed his arm, ushering her back to the bar.

She blinked several times, clearing her eyes, then nodded and preceded him to the back of the cafe. Now on the platform a woman sporting Marinecropped hair, tattered T-shirt, and camouflage pants avowed she was a "feminist-revolutionary-lesbian," and she began to stomp on the plywood in time with her poetry.

"I could almost believe the Muse had descended and spoken through you." He picked up her mug and handed it to her.

She shook her head. "Please. It wasn't that good." She accepted the coffee and took a long sip.

"You underestimate yourself. Your poems are emotional and touching, but not maudlin. You can trust what I say. I've been . . . condemned to follow beauty." He leaned forward, peering intently at her face. "Your poems. Some of them come from life, don't they?"

She couldn't meet his unflinching gaze. "All of them." She dabbed at the hated tears with the already-soiled cuff of her military-surplus jacket. "When no one would listen to me, hold me, I found poetry. For the first time I had a world that accepted me and made me feel safe. The Romantics, the Symbolists, the Beat poets. . . . They seemed to understand the hurt I felt. They had fought against the unfairness of the world, and although they may not have won any battles, they did leave some beauty behind."

"It never ceases to amaze me. Humans' ability to hurt each other . . ." He brought his hand up near her cheek but refrained from actually touching her. "'Monster I must be . . .'"

"'Lest monster I become,'" Corrinda finished. For the first time, the man seemed rattled. "Where did you hear that?" he demanded.

Corrinda's eyes darted left and right, as if she had done something wrong and now sought an exit. "It's a line from a poem," she said hastily. She reached into her jacket and pulled a thin book from an interior pocket. "In this book." It was smaller than a hardback, with an ash-gray cover and the title in a bold, red typeface:

The Scarlet Letters
by Virgil

At the sight of it the man's eyes narrowed, almost as if it were a poisonous snake suddenly discovered too close. "By the blood!" His voice was nearly a hiss. "Where did you find this?"

She didn't know whether to drop the book, put it back in her pocket, or give it to him. "I—I bought it in a used bookstore. They usually only carry trashy romance novels, but one time I found this. . . . It was only two bucks, and I really liked the poetry. Have—have you read it, too?"

He ignored her question, as he had all her others. "Would you consider selling this to me?" His voice, up until now calm and resonant, quivered, as if its possessor were an alcoholic suddenly denied the bottle.

"I—I don't know." She looked at the chapbook uncomprehendingly. "It's my favorite. They're poems in the form of letters from a vampire to a mortal. They talk about the horrible Embrace of darkness . . . the uncontrollable thirst for blood . . . and the eternal longing for a final release. It depicts a world of night and shadows and death—more beautiful and more terrifying than our own world. It's a world I wanted to enter . . . I felt like the poet had read what was written in my soul . . ."

The stranger was so focused on the chapbook it seemed he had forgotten her presence. "Damnation! I thought I had rounded up and destroyed all of these years ago . . ." As if the volume were a fragile find at an archaeological dig, he lightly stroked the cover. As he did so, his fingers, thin and cool, brushed against her.

And she caught another of her messages.

Her jaw dropped, causing her to appear more

frightened than when the tremor had struck. "Oh, my God." Her voice was no more than a whisper. "How can you be standing here—when you're—"

She couldn't complete her question. He gripped her wrist and cinched. She gasped, cutting off her own words. His eyes bore into hers. "You've got to come with me." He was speaking—so softly she was certain no one else could hear him. "To a place where we can talk in private. You mustn't make a sound, understand?"

He began pulling her from the bar. She looked frantically around the cafe; no one seemed to be taking notice of them. She considered making a sound—plenty of loud, shrill screaming sounds—but she had no idea what he would do to her wrist, let alone the rest of her form, if she didn't cooperate.

He led her to a door in the rear wall. The red-haired bartender, who had gone into the back to load up on silverware, came through and almost walked into them. At the last moment he pulled Corrinda back out of the way. It was like she couldn't see us! Corrinda thought, nearly crying out. He squeezed her wrist sharply: Stay quiet.

They pushed through the door and found themselves in a small kitchen. The gleaming, stainless steel surfaces of an oven, refrigerator, sink, and preparation table ran along the walls. He led her to a second door in the far right corner. He looked back over his shoulder and was apparently satisfied with what he saw, or didn't see. "You caught something about me when we touched, didn't you?" He spoke quietly and earnestly, yet she could make out each of his words. He opened the door: wooden steps with peeling paint made a right angle turn as they led to a basement below.

As they made their descent, Corrinda spoke as if in a drug-induced stupor. "I saw—everything that is the opposite of light—shadows, darkness, night, the Void . . . And I saw blood—an ocean of blood—and you—floating on its surface—not breathing—not even alive."

They stepped onto the floor of a stone-lined basement. The air was much cooler down here than it had been in the stuffy cafe upstairs. The chamber was illuminated by a single bare bulb of low wattage hanging from the middle of the ceiling. The center of the floor was taken up by tables and chairs, all in need of repair. Boxes with indeterminate contents were piled against one wall.

Only now were connections falling together in Corrinda's mind to link words, messages, and omissions. It was not that she was naive or incapable of inductive reasoning. It was simply that, even with her unfocused prescience, the image she arrived at ran counter to all she had been taught to expect from a blind, heedless universe.

He bent to the floor and found a fingerhold that had been undetectable to Corrinda. He pulled up what looked like a solid stone slab and held it while motioning her over. "Sit down and swing your feet inside. You'll feel rungs. Climb down carefully. You'll be all right. This used to be a rum-runner's storage room during Prohibition."

She thought once more about bolting for the stairs but knew the time for that was long gone. She sat on the trapdoor's lip. "You wrote those poems, didn't you?" She peered at him so intently her gaze might have seared the flesh from his skull. "You're Virgil. The one who led Dante into Hell." She looked down into the dimly lit opening. "Should I abandon all hope?"

He wouldn't turn from her stare. "Haven't you already?"

She had no answer for that, and began to climb down.

At the bottom, she hugged her arms to her chest and waited for him to lower the trapdoor and descend. The chamber in which she stood was a mixture of the contemporary and the archaic. It was slightly larger than the main room upstairs. There was soft track lighting around the perimeter of the ceiling, but the primary source of illumination came from a pair of elaborate candelabra on a heavy oaken trestle table perhaps ten feet long. Aside from the candles, the table supported teetering piles of books, scattered papers, and a bottle or two of wine. In a far corner stood a huge bed with Mediterranean-style headboard and footboard. There were four or five photographs to either side of the bed. Corrinda stepped closer and examined them, her eyes growing wide with disbelief as she did so. The photographs all depicted Virgil with other people, some of whom she thought she recognized. "God! That's Jack London! And that's you and Kerouac—outside City Lights bookshop!"

Virgil nodded. "Can I get you something to drink? I keep some wine down here for my infrequent . . . guests."

"No, thanks." She sat on the edge of the mattress and looked up at him. "London died in 1916. *The Scarlet Letters* was published in 1955. But you can't be any older than thirty-five or so. How can that be? How can you walk—when I can't feel any pulse of life inside you?"

He had turned away from her so that she was addressing his back. "Corrinda, you are not the only one who writes from personal experience." His words came haltingly, as if it pained him even to say them out loud. "You must understand that those poems describe my life—if what I wake to each evening can be called a life." He whirled on his heel toward her once more, hands outstretched as if imploring her to believe him, and she shrank back on the bed reflexively.

"There are those who live only by night. I don't just mean thieves and gang-bangers. There are things most people don't believe in . . . things they laugh at, because their laughter conceals the fear they feel in their hearts."

"So the Kindred—the vampires you wrote about in the *Letters*—they do exist." She shook her head in wonder. "Have you . . . been here . . . since the Roman Empire?"

He couldn't hold back a self-mocking chuckle. "No, I am not the Virgil of the *Aeneid*. I had another name once, but I haven't used it in decades. I was born in Sicily in . . . well, the year wasn't in this century; let's leave it at that. I traveled across the States and wound up in San Francisco. I became a correspondent, sending stories to various European newspapers."

"How did you get like this?"

He stood by one of the photographs, running his fingers over the smooth glass. "In 1914 the Old Gringo, Ambrose Bierce, decided he wanted to cover the Mexican Revolution. The cynical bastard joined Pancho Villa's band. He didn't know what he was getting into. He was Embraced by a south-of-the-border Cainite—he never knew his Sire. It seems fitting that the author of *The Devil's Dictionary* was transformed into one of the Damned.

"He made his way back to San Francisco, the only home he had ever known. We knew each other from our newspaper days in the 1890s. He found me and made me one of his Progeny." Virgil rapped his knuckles against the grainy black-and-white image of a seated man with salt-and-pepper sideburns and mustache. The man's expression indicated he didn't think much of sitting still for the camera.

"Bierce was as bitter in death as he was in life. He said, 'All of life is a rehearsal for death and I must have made a poor understudy, for I have died, and yet here I walk.' It wasn't for long, though. He just couldn't help making enemies. He enraged one of his own Brood, who slew him some sixty years ago."

"This is incredible." Corrinda had absently knotted the fingers of her free hand in the bedsheets. "You're telling me some of the most famous people in America have become vampires?"

Virgil arched one of his eyebrows. "I'm only giving you a hint of the truth. I don't know it all myself. I try to stay out of Clan maneuvering. I don't want to run afoul of Prince Vannevar and his politics. I once got myself in enough trouble, over this." He tapped the little book Corrinda still held.

"What happened?"

"I am of the Kindred Clan Toreadors. We are . . . drawn to the aesthetic arts. I have always watched over Bay Area writers and poets. During the '50s, I began keeping company with some writers who were determined to express themselves in innovative styles no one had used before. Lawrence Ferlinghetti, Jack Kerouac, Gary Snyder. They resisted what authority told them. They experimented, both with their bodies and their minds. They held readings that captivated me as nothing I had ever heard before. I spent time with them, spoke with them, read their work—never revealing my true nature, of course.

"They inspired me. I had written poems and stories before, but only for my own amusement. But I decided I wanted to capture the essence of what I had become. I wanted to portray both the wonder and the grotesqueness of the Masquerade—immortals doomed to feed off others to satisfy the cravings burning inside. I wrote them in the form of a series of letters to a mortal. I had the poems published privately and distributed in bookstores around town. I couldn't see them purchased during the day, but I understand they were quite popular at the time." He looked at Corrinda's book as if he couldn't quite believe he had produced such a thing.

"But of course, I had gone too far. I had broken the

facade of the Masquerade. The Prince was outraged, and nearly called a Lextalionis—a Blood Hunt—upon me for making public secrets of the Kindred. Crawling on my belly, I swore that no human would ever take my poems as truth. I had to promise to retrieve and destroy all copies of *The Scarlet Letters*. I've been tracking them down for three decades. . . . Yours must be one of the few remaining."

Tears glinted in the corners of Corrinda's eyes. "I'm only human . . . but I know what you feel. Your poems are too lovely to destroy. They described exactly what I felt when I wanted to . . . damn it, kill my fuckin' stepfather!" She reached out suddenly and grabbed Virgil's sweater. "Please! Make me one of you! Take me too! Embrace me—do whatever it takes . . ."

With an animalistic growl he stepped back, freeing himself. "No!" he snapped. "You don't know what you're asking! Only now is Vannevar close to forgiving me. He's even attending a party here tonight."

She slid from the bed to her knees on the floor. "I do. I understand . . ."

"Fool! If you had the slightest notion what it is like to stalk your own kind, feed off their blood, you would run screaming from me! I've only told you as much as I have because I need your book and I owe you an explanation for what I'm about to do. I'm going to . . . touch your mind. It won't hurt you. You'll forget we ever spoke, and you'll forget you ever read a book called *The Scarlet Letters*. You can go back home and—"

It was her turn to shout defiantly. "No! I don't have a home anymore! My mom left us three months ago. Last weekend my stepfather came into my room in the middle of the night. He was walking in a cloud of sweat and smoke and beer. He . . . slipped into bed with me. He said . . . it wouldn't be wrong because we weren't really related. When he touched me, I caught a warning from him. He was going to rape me until he tired of me, then he was going to kill me. I pushed him away, and he slapped me, hard."

She gestured at the bruise under her eye. "I shoved him again, and he fell back, smacking his head on my nightstand. While he was unconscious, I grabbed his money and whatever I could stuff in my pockets. I ran into town and waited until I could hop the bus."

"Surely you have some other family to turn to—"

"There's nobody! I picked San Francisco because I knew there were poetry readings here, and I wanted to share what I had written with other people. But now I don't know what I'm going to do. I can only sleep in the bus terminal and wash up in the public restroom so long. There's no way I'm gonna turn tricks for some crack-freak pimp." Her words were distorted, catching in her throat. "I could wait on tables, but where am I going to live? I mean . . . I'd be better off jumping from the goddamned Golden Gate Bridge!"

Virgil scowled. "What a typically adolescent thing to say."

"Please." She dropped the book and folded her hands. "I caught something else from you, when we touched. I know why you left home—why you traveled to America."

"Stop it!" He almost seemed frightened of the girl at his feet. "You're not to speak of—"

"You were beaten, too, weren't you?" She brought her hands to her neck. "See, we're two of a kind. We understand each other." She undid the top three buttons of her blouse. "Here. I won't cry. I won't back out. Write me into your lines. Make me part of your poem. I want you to. Put your teeth in me. Kill me." She arched her head back, waiting for the strike.

His lips were pulled back. His incisors had descended instinctively, involuntarily. His hands came toward her as if rising through tar. Then he spun away, tearing himself from the sight of her pale, exposed flesh. "I can't! It's forbidden! If I Embraced you, Prince Vannevar would have me staked for the dawn!"

"Fine." She sprang to her feet and bolted toward the table. "There's nothing left for me anymore." She grasped one of the wine bottles by the neck and smashed it against the edge of the table. The crystalline shatter shredded their eardrums. "If you won't take me, I'll do it myself."

"Stupid bitch!" Virgil cried, starting for the table, but even with his preternatural celerity she was too quick for him. She brought the jagged point of turquoise glass up underneath her jaw and jabbed—

Both of them were screaming. Their positions from just a few minutes ago were reversed: Corrinda was now wavering on her feet; Virgil was on his knees, his arms outspread, looking up at her in shock. The sight of blood gently pulsing from her neck brought the Beast close to the surface. He felt himself hovering at the edge, a fraction of an inch from lunging at the thick red wash flowing down her shoulder.

"I love you . . . for helping me read tonight," she managed to say. "I want to . . . give you part of me . . ."

Eyes blinking rapidly, she walked behind the table and slumped against the wall. She bent forward from the shoulders and cupped her left hand between her small breasts. A warm, rich flow coursed down her neck, spilled down her chest, and pooled in her palm. She brought up her right hand and dipped her forefinger in the deepening well. She then put her finger to the wall and began to write—her finger the pen, her blood the ink, a poem her message.

If I die, let it be with you.

The words were not as beautiful as she wanted them to be. Some of the letters ran, and some were difficult to make out. She had a hard time keeping on a horizontal line, and the words near the end of the line began to slope downward.

Hold me close while the world falls in on me.

"Corrinda!" Virgil's mouth drew down at the corners. "There's a way for me to stop the bleeding! You can still return to the world where you belong—"

Whisper my name as the darkness rises

She didn't know if she could keep going now. The blood was overflowing her cupped palm and dripping to the floor below with heavy wet splashes. She had to consciously focus her eyes in order to see. "Shhh. It's all right." Her words were slurred. Her tongue felt thick and unresponsive.

And I fall into the dream that never ends

Her legs wouldn't stay straight any longer; it felt as if her bones were dissolving, leaving only the cold stone to support her. Some of her hair caught in the still-damp letters and trailed downward, red, as she slid to the floor. "Damn it! Damn it!" Virgil violently brushed away crimson tears. "You're going to cost me . . ."

He scrambled to her side as her eyelids met a final time. He took her hair in his left hand and lifted her head. He brought his right wrist up to his mouth and savaged it—taking out his frustration on his own flesh rather than hers. Thin drops of deoxygenated blood welled up from the inside of his arm. He wiped them across her lips.

"Drink. Drink well and come back from death, knowing you've cursed me."

There was a flutter against his skin. Her lips, like an infant's smacked pleasurably. A small, pink tongue darted into the red stains and licked. He felt suction as she began to actively nurse his arm, and the feeling that flowed through him was the closest to sexual ecstasy he was capable of experiencing anymore.

"They will make me pay for you," he said aloud, more to himself than the small form curled embryonically at his knees. "Oh, how they will make me pay."

Descent

by Sam Chupp

"Really, Anastasia, I didn't think you'd show, especially after that earthquake." Selena smiled. It was a shark's smile, sure and predatory. She was dressed to kill, as well: a velvet dress, green, with a beautiful stone circle Sumerian pendant depicting Inanna, Queen of Heaven. Anastasia smiled back the same way, her eyes hard. It had been a long time since she had been forced to play dominance games with another vampire.

"Oh, Selena, you know, I so dearly love Luigi's. That's why I'm here, really. Ah, isn't that Inanna! Wasn't she the one who lost her life in the Underworld?" Anastasia said, smiling.

"She found great power with the Queen of the Damned, actually. And returned to rule." Selena's eyes glittered.

"Who's your blond friend?" Anastasia smiled. She brushed her thick, auburn hair back from her face and her dark eyes glittered. The maitre d' hadn't even noticed her leather jacket and jeans: perhaps he'd been expecting her.

Selena prodded the teenaged, blond surfer boy with a single, gloved hand. The boy was obviously uncomfortable in his white tuxedo, and he stumbled forward. Selena smiled wickedly back at Ana through the veil of her midnight hair. She smoothed the silk sheath dress she was wearing as she watched Anastasia's reaction. "Go on, boy. Tell Mistress Ana your name." Selena's leer, her red lips and tongue, disgusted Ana.

The surfer smiled, dully, slowly. "I'm . . . my name's Dinner, ma'am." His voice was thick and sleepy.

Anastasia flinched, almost imperceptibly. But Selena caught it. "What is it, Ana? Do you not like your wine white? I imported him from Marin County. Would you prefer a less fruity, more robust vintage?" Selena had a habit of referring to blood as wine.

Anastasia smiled slowly. "Although your hospitality is without question, Selena, I'm not thirsty at the moment. Thank you for the offer, however."

"Not thirsty? How strange. I myself am never one to turn down fresh, young things like this one. But I understand: you prefer a more feminine blush these days. What's her name? Susie?" Selena motioned for the surfer to step back to her.

"Sofie. Her name's Sofie. I thought you wanted to talk about old times?"

Selena brushed her hair aside, her green eyes narrowing. She smiled impishly, her whole demeanor changing in a second. "Oh? A sore spot for you? Don't tell me you've gone and fallen in love with her?"

Anastasia returned Selena's look with stony silence. A waiter took this opportunity to change the plates on the table: the soup went away, replaced by the salad.

Selena was first to break the silence. "Well, so. I see that's not a topic you're interested in discussing. Is there something beside the weather that we can discuss?" Selena's voice was icy.

"I would imagine you'd be full of gossip from the east. How is Jeremiah, Tabitha? I've not heard from them in some time," Anastasia said, picking at her salad. She was amazed at how old habits returned to her. She used to be a master at maintaining the Masquerade, especially in public and especially in restaurants. She noticed that Selena made no such pretense—perhaps Luigi's was Kindred-owned.

"Jeremiah is doing boring Toreador things, and Tabitha is doing boring Tremere things. They're both boring. And you would know that if you weren't hiding in your ivory tower here in San Francisco." She motioned to the surfer, who kneeled next to her and presented his wrist.

"Oh look, Ana. Poor boy's got slash scars. Probably has a rough life. Poor thing. Well, you're about to feel better, honey." Then, there, in the balcony of Luigi's, Selena sunk her fangs into the surfer's wrist and began to suck deep draughts of blood. He smiled in dull pleasure, closing his eyes and savoring the feeling.

"Don't you think you should leave him some to get home on?" Anastasia said, trying to keep her composure. Even though she was not hungry, and had not needed to feed as much lately, the smell of the rich surfer vitae was tempting.

"Oh really, Ana. You're so very droll. The last bits are the sweetest, you know," Selena said, smiling, licking her lips. The totally drained surfer was lifted onto a cart and taken out. A waiter stepped forward with a napkin, and Ana looked up at him in surprise.

Selena smiled, dabbing some vitae from her chin. "I wanted us to be completely comfortable this evening, Anastasia. So I took the liberty of arranging things. Don't worry about your precious Masquerade tonight. None will be the wiser for our celebration." Selena's skin had grown pink, her hair shinier, her whole body more shapely.

"Oh? And what are we celebrating?" Anastasia felt a wave of nausea well up inside her, and forced herself to maintain a mask of propriety.

"Our friendship, of course. And independence. You are independent of the Camarilla, the Circle of Seven's iron grip. And so am I," Selena said, smiling victoriously.

"What? How did you swing that? Your Sire get you a research grant?" Anastasia narrowed her eyes.

"Hardly. I've decided to go freelance. Totally.

Tremere for hire. And I tell you, Ana, I've met the most interesting people in Mexico."

"Mexico? Why would you want to go there? The place is crawling with the Sabbat," Anastasia said.

"Exactly," Selena said, smiling, her eyes gleaming.

Anastasia put down her fork. She looked at Selena, looked at the inhuman coldness in her eyes, for the first time seeing it. Then she looked away. "Oh, Ana. Ana. You are so naive. You and your hermitage, your cloister. You're right to turn away from the Camarilla—what have they ever offered you that was of value? They ask you to deny what is truly you. The Beast Within."

Anastasia looked up at her, eyes afire. "I . . . I may not be involved with the Camarilla. But I am still loyal to my Sire."

"Your Sire? And when was the last time you spoke with Etrius?" Selena said, smiling.

Anastasia's eyes narrowed to slits. "I speak with him at the Esbats, as you well know. Or have you forgotten the lore that the Tremere taught you?"

Selena licked her lips and brushed her raven hair aside again. "Ana, that's just it. I've learned so much more among the Sabbat. They have powers, and paths, and rituals that are much more potent than any of those taught to us in the Camarilla."

"Yes, I imagine so. It's quite easy to gain power when you sell your soul for it. So tell me, Selena: who is your infernal master?" Anastasia said, finally finding her anger. She felt it building within her, welling up.

"Those old wives' tales about the Sabbat and the Infernal are just that. And I never took you for an old wife, really Anastasia. How dramatic. The way you talk, you'd expect me to burst into flame at any moment."

Anastasia rose and smiled as sweetly as she could manage. "Don't give me any ideas, Selena. Now, if you'll excuse me, I've suddenly lost my appetite for this conversation." She whirled and stalked down the stairs.

From the balcony, Anastasia could hear her laughing. "You'll be back, my sweet. You'll be back," Selena called.

Ana took a cab across town, and made her way to the market, where she purchased a handmade wicker picnic basket from a street vendor. She began to fill the basket with wonderful things, things that she knew Sofie loved.

Ana loved tasting the sweet flavor of the warm Valpolicella wine in her blood, loved the sweet tang that garlic and basil and oregano brought to her lovers' vitae. She threw herself into shopping, trying to forget the disturbing things Selena had said.

Ana decided she would take Sofie and drive up to the beachhouse, where they'd spend the rest of the night. It would be nice to get away, away from Selena, away from San Francisco, away from other vampires.

She smiled thinking of the light Sofie's eyes would have when she saw the caviar, the *foie gras*, and the anchovies, all wrapped in green foil. She even smiled at the vendors who wished to haggle with her, and who were surprised that, be it Italian, Greek, or even Chinese, she answered all in their native tongue. Soon her basket was filled with jewel-like parcels, wrapped neatly in their individual packages, giving off a redolent scent of luxury.

All this preparation was for the midnight picnic on the beach that had become their tradition at the house. Ana shook out her hair and smiled absently as she thought of the daring race they would play with the sun as it burned over the cliffs and pierced to the ocean: about how sweet those last kisses were, before retiring for the day. Sofie would be able to sleep next to her while the jealous sun burned in the sky. It would be heaven.

Ana began to feel filled up with the combination of anticipation and longing that she felt. It consumed her. Sofie was the moon and sun in her life. Sofie was what made each step worthwhile. Sophia, bringer of wisdom, Sophia, bringer of peace. That gentle spirit, a magical woman who did not even know the simple magic that she carried in her fingers, the grace and beauty that she held in her eyes. This was why Ana loved her, why Ana had forsaken her own kind for a simple life with her, away from the intrigues of the Kindred.

Anastasia had met Sofie by pure chance, had stumbled into her life as the result of an accident, and had stayed with her because of something totally coincidental and unexplainable. Sofie painted Ana's dreams, painted the landscapes of her daytime slumbers. She did so with a clarity and accuracy that was unnerving and disturbing to Ana, who held herself quite an authority on the occult and magick. Sofie fell in love with Ana's dreams, and with the vision of Ana, and finally with the reality of Ana. When it came time to reveal her nature, Anastasia had steeled herself for the possibility that she would have to blot out her existence by commanding Sofie to forget her forever.

She needn't have worried. Sofie had smiled her sweetest smile and said, "Then, my love, let us seize the night, as we can never be together during the day."

Ana could almost feel the love that she shared with Sofie as a palpable thing: it surrounded her, kept her warm, kept her calm. Just now, relaxing, she realized how much Selena had goaded her, how close she had been to losing control. She walked the rest of the way up Russian Hill, and through a secret garden to get to the well-nigh hidden brownstone they rented.

The door to the attic apartment in the brownstone

was properly locked, so Anastasia was spared that initial shock of dread and panic when one finds one's door ajar, hanging open there like a murderer on a noose. No, she was lulled into a sense of security as she opened the door and made her way through the silent attic, intent on the meal she would soon be creating. It was not until the pungent smell of her lover's blood wafted up to her nostrils that she was hit with the wave of terror.

Ana screamed. She ran down the spiral staircase that joined the lightproof attic with Sofie's studio. She ran through the studio, following the blood trail that had been left, sickened by the panic and the fear and the intangible desire she felt spring from the warm blood. The blood trail led up to a beautiful antique dressing mirror, one that Anastasia herself had procured for Sofie, who so loved mirrors. The bloody footprints around the body led up to the mirror, and vanished.

Anastasia threw back her head, unwillingly, totally consumed in her frenzy. Skirling, whipping winds rocketed through the suite, breaking ancient porcelain and toppling an expensive antique laboratory set of glassware, shattering it. She lifted her arms up in total submission to the rage, allowing it to consume her and fill her up completely.

The winds stopped, but as if in answer to this chorus of destruction, another sound replaced blowing winds: the crashing of shattered glass. One by one, every pane, cup, plate, mirror, picture frame, and blown-glass art piece exploded in a shower of tiny glass fragments.

And, like the eye of a hurricane, there was sudden calm. Anastasia sank to her knees and then to the floor in supplication to ever dark power and every God she had ever known. She even cried out to Caine in her agony, to come and take her from this pain.

She sank into a timeless state, where her senses dulled and she was unaware of the shards of glass that peppered her skin. She held her eyes, weeping bloody tears, unable to move otherwise. She crouched there for a long time, until the first light of dawn crept over the tops of the expensive houses on the hill.

That light, as faint as it was, caused her to look up. Ana saw through blood-sheened eyes the dawn approaching, and began to feel drawn to it, as she always did. Only now she felt that she would not have the self-control to swing close the heavy shutters that would protect her from the sun.

Anastasia looked at the dawn, helpless to stop it. She knew that she would soon be struck by a sunbeam, but she could not bring herself to care. She looked about the room for something of Sofie's, something she could gaze upon in the bright sunshine before it took her unlife forever.

She saw Sofie's first painting, a beautiful seascape, with a little girl and a dog, hanging slantways in its now-glassless frame. She looked up at it, and sighed, smiling through her tears. She would soon join Sofie. She felt a warmth on the back of her neck, and felt her skin start to bubble under the heat.

And then, as if in answer, she felt a twinge, a definite pang of some kind, some sense which begged to be listened to. She focused her awareness on that twinge, on that merest sliver of a feeling, and felt it brighten. She felt her certainty grow that Sofie was indeed still alive. Her powers, latent and bound though they were, did not fail her. Sofie was still alive, no matter how ridiculous that seemed.

Pain. Pain was needed. Pain, after so much shock, after so much delirium. Pain, to awaken her senses and focus her priorities. She grabbed a shard of glass and jabbed it into her palm, watching it sink in, watching her black blood well up around it. The pain was enough.

She got to her feet and slammed closed first one, then the other heavy shutter, collapsing against it. Anastasia slumped down until she was resting on the floor, her back against the warm shutter.

Then, from exhaustion and wounds, Anastasia fell into unconsciousness.

She dreamed. She dreamed of a happier time, a night almost four years ago. She saw herself and Sofie, on the beach. The moon was bright. Sofie was naked, as she always was on beach, and wet from the water. "No, Ana, no. I want you to promise me. I want you to put away your super powers. I don't want you to use them anymore."

Anastasia shook her head, trying to focus on Sofie. "Why my love? Why? They are a part of me."

Sofie put her fingertip to Ana's lips. "No. No, Ana. They are a part of your old life. Your old ways. And now you're with me. Remember what you told me about that Goal-condra thing?"

"Golconda. Yes. I remember." Anastasia was smiling at Sofie. When she wanted to be charming, she was charming. It didn't hurt that she was teasing Ana the entire time, turning slightly in the firelight.

"Well, that proves it. No more ESP. No more spoon bending or door opening. Nothin'. Okay? You got it?" Sofie was smiling, but her voice was firm.

Anastasia looked very serious. "You're serious, aren't you? You really want me to throw everything away?"

"Not everything, Anastasia. You'll still have me. What do you want? Maybe that's what you have to ask yourself."

Anastasia watched the surf come in, watched it wash out. "I want . . . I want to be with you . . ."

"So promise me. Promise me, and I won't bitch about it anymore." Sofie dug in the sand with her toes.

"But . . . what if I need my powers to protect you?" Ana said, looking far out to sea.

"I'm not saying you should throw them away . . . just don't use them. Unless you have to. And I mean, there better be a damn good reason. Now, will you pinky swear?"

"Pinky swear? What's that?"

Sofie laughed. It sounded like the surf in her dream. "You know, a solemn promise. How would you put it? An oath. You gotta swear."

Anastasia smiled at Sofie. She shook out her hair and drew her close. "No, Sofie. I have a better idea. A much better idea."

Then she was suddenly in the beach house, bent over a leaf of parchment. The parchment contained the carefully worded terms of her promise, and she signed it in her own blood. Sofie looked solemnly at Ana, and realized that it was one of those issues that she would not bend on. Ana held her hand while she made the pin prick. Sofie signed her part of the contract in her own blood. She remembered celebrating that pact as one might celebrate a marriage; it was a honeymoon of sorts. The dream turned to the silvery nights they spent by the sea.

The telephone rang. It rang again, incessantly. Ana's eyes were nearly sealed shut from the bloody tears she'd cried, but she managed to open them and find the telephone. The digital clock on the VCR told her it was evening again.

It was Selena's voice. "I imagine by now you've discovered my little plot."

Frenzy boiled up inside her, and she choked it back down. "Where is she, you bitch!"

"Please, please Anastasia. Such language. Let's be civilized shall we? You can certainly sense that she is still alive, no? Or are your powers weak from disuse?"

Anastasia struggled to hold on to her rage. Although

she couldn't sense Sofie with her Pact-bound powers, she felt strongly that she would know if Sofie was dead—the sense she had felt earlier had not diminished.

"What do you want with me? What do you want to secure Sofie's release?"

"Ah. 'Secure.' 'Release.' You're talking like a general, Ana. Why not come down from that high horse and talk to me? Remember me, your Selena, your Moon? I have not changed. Perhaps it is you who has changed. Tell me, are you happy under the yoke of your Sire? Are you pleased that he can control what you do? Are you happy in the Camarilla?"

Anastasia nearly dropped the phone. Looking around, she noticed where she was for the first time. She had managed to crawl, bloody from the piercing glass in her skin, to Sofie's futon, which was ruined now with her black blood. She was weak, hungry, and the Beast within her was rattling its cage.

"Selena. I'll do anything. Just don't harm her. I swear, if you hurt her, I'll make sure you burn in the sun."

"Anything, Anastasia? My, my. The Ana I once knew would've never been so desperate-sounding. She would've steeled herself, and even sacrificed a petty mortal if it suited her purpose. Where is the Ana who faced the Primogen of New York?" She laughed. "Oh, and Ana—I don't have to remind you that you're in no position to make threats."

"Don't toy with me, Selena. Name your price."

"My price? My price? Why, that implies that it is something that can be paid, as a debt is paid. As a Boon is paid. No, no, Anastasia, what I want is something much more than a price. I want your oath. I want your loyalty. I want your soul. I want your blood. I want you, Ana, sweet Ana. And you can have your pretty girlfriend as a pet, if you wish. But you'll serve me. Me, and the sacred Order of the Black Hand, the Sabbat."

Hearing this began to free the Beast, the collar around its neck loosening, weakening. Anastasia's fangs slid into her mouth, and she felt their sharpness next to her tongue.

"And if I refuse?" she whispered, trying to sound cowed when she wanted to loose her hate on the Sabbat bitch.

"Your Sofie will be made glad to join us, and be our cute plaything for a time until we stake her for the sun. You remember what I do with playthings, don't you Ana? Or perhaps you have been neglecting that side of you, as well?" Selena's voice was like frozen diamonds.

Anastasia shuddered. The Beast began to howl against its collar, the leash slipping out of her hands. She watched her fingernails change into talons. "Yes. I remember."

"Very well then. I hope you won't be offended, but I have taken the liberty of preparing an initiation rite for you. Tomorrow evening, when the moon is new, we will perform it. We will welcome either you, or a newly Embraced Sofie, into our brood. If you wish to join us, you'll be there. The church on Beacon Street. But I'm sure you already know that, you being such the clever girl. And so well behaved!"

Her voice was rasping, irritating, provoking. She knew what she was doing, and Anastasia was powerless to prevent the Frenzy she was provoking.

"I will be there, Selena," Anastasia said. Her hand shook as she put the phone down on the cradle. She moved to the vase on the fireplace, picked it up, looked at it, considering. Her palsy got worse, her taloned nails scraped against the fine porcelain, and then the vase slipped from her hands. It shattered on the hearth.

Looking down, her eyes clouded with red, she saw the parchment with her blood pact written on it. Her monstrous claws caressed the paper, and she felt a twinge of pain as she saw Sofie's signature in blood there on the page. Her powers, her old life, her old self was waiting, contained in the words of the pact, waiting to be released. And it could only be released one way: through fire, pure cleansing fire. That would make the pact null and void. She thought a moment of Sofie—how she would be alone, terrified, weak, helpless to resist the powers of the vampiress who held her. Her head felt numb, dull, cloudy. She couldn't think straight. She knew that if she took this step she would be breaking a solemn oath, one that she had made in all serious dedication. But Sofie was in danger, a heartbeat away from living life as one of the Damned.

Her claws parted the stiff parchment of the pact with ease. It shredded into long, narrow strips with one pass. They fluttered to the floor. Ana felt her power returning, slowly, being freed as it was bit by bit. Without a word, she summoned fire from her blood magic, fire from her own hand to destroy the pact that she had signed.

It burst into flame, another tie gone, another step taken.

Then the Beast struggled again, and this time caught Anastasia unaware. It slipped loose its chain and ran free, blood hunger driving it onward, on to the Hunt.

Time blurred. Ana ran through the streets, her powers cloaking her, her bloodthirst driving her every step. Turning down an alley, she fell upon another kind of hunter and his prey. She fell upon the unlucky rapist, tearing the man apart and feasting on his blood as it welled out of the wounds, rending his flesh as she fed. It wasn't long before the man's heart beat its, and the world was free of one less foulness. But it had been so long since she had fed, and she was so thirsty, and the Beast demanded more. Her will was like a feeble reed in a torrent of floodwater, and the Beast set her upon the hapless victim as well.

The woman started to flee, but in her frenzy she caught her as well, and could not stop herself from draining the victim, the fear and pain in the victim's blood changing to ecstasy as she drained the last drop, desperately, unthinkingly. Then the cloud of blood-fire lifted, and she realized what she had done, and she held the empty corpse of the woman and cried blood tears over it, having taken one more step closer to her old life.

It was as if the stench and foulness of the city rose up around her to coat her in corruption, to make her its own, to Embrace her again. Standing up to leave, she looked at her blood-soaked hands and realized that she had taken another step down the path away from the light she had shared with Sofie.

"Aren't y'all gonna take care of that little messiness before you go?" A coarse female voice whispered in the dark. Anastasia whirled, her Beast still near the surface, and her night vision revealed a harlot stepping from the shadows.

The harlot looked at her, up and down. "You must be a new lick in town. I'm Princess Victoria. Pleased to meet you." The harlot smiled for a brief moment, and Anastasia's senses flared around the woman, telling her that she was Kindred—as well as a man in whore's costume.

Anastasia waved her hand and the two corpses burst into flames. "Does that satisfy my lady?" she said, her eyes narrowing. She was used to more respect from other Kindred. But that had been long ago.

The Princess immediately reacted to her power, stepping back. "Ah, ah'm terribly sorry ma'am . . . I had no idea that one of the Tray-mare would be stalkin' about my part o' town. I didn't mean no disrespect, you understand . . ."

"I see. Well, then, you can go about your business then. And say nothing to anyone about this."

"That's what I was gonna say, ma'am. That I wasn't gonna say anythin'. But, you see, the Prince, his name's Vannevar, he's a wonderful man. He asked us to tell him if any new licks come into town. And, well, ma'am, I feel kinda obliged to tell him. Unless you were just on your way to see him. You know, to present yourself . . ."

Anastasia's eyes narrowed to slits, and she reached out with her long-unused powers of domination. "Listen to me, you false strumpet, I'll do as I please, and you'll forget that you saw any of this! Do you understand me?"

The Princess's eyes blurred, her body went lax, and she nodded. "Yes ma'am. I do. Thank you, ma'am."

"Very well. Walk north until you reach the street, and awaken to yourself there. Begone!"

Anastasia watched the Princess walk out of sight, and turned and stepped out of the alleyway. The fires had already died down, leaving nothing but gray ash to swirl about in the eddies of wind that blew through the city.

She shuddered, realizing how far she had fallen in so short a time. She contemplated things: if she continued along this path, she would have to present herself before the Prince before too much longer, or else her Sire would have to defend her before the Camarilla.

As she walked home, healing the thousands of tiny cuts on her body as she walked, she failed to notice a pair of gleaming red eyes watching her from a darkened alley.

* * *

Anastasia invoked the powers of the Path of Finding, the path she had herself created, and followed the threads of possibility through the city to the church that Selena had described over the phone.

A white-haired vampire met her at the door to the ancient church, black, woolen cowl draped across his mocking grin. She had garbed herself in her ritual Tremere robes. The Eye, the Wand, and the Athame of her office hung from the sash. The vampire turned and called out to the gaping hole of a stairwell leading down: "One comes before the Gate, demanding to be allowed in to Hell! What should I tell her?"

"Tell her that all are equal in Hell, and that she seeks her own doom," came a voice, the ritual response. Ana thought it was Selena's, echoing up the stairwell.

The white-haired vampire smiled and blood oozed from the sides of his mouth. "Blood. Blood. Blood. We are all equal in the Blood." He grinned and reached out his hand; in it he held a burlap bag, open. "Your things of office, you will leave them behind. All are the same in Hell."

She heard a girlish scream, a human scream, echoing up from someplace, someplace far away. "Ana! Don't listen to them! Ana! Get away! Get away from here!" It was Sofie. She was silenced, Ana knew not how, but the quiet was brutal.

Anastasia hesitatingly placed her Wand in the bag, followed by her Athame, and finally, her hands shaking and knuckles white, her Eye, the dark, round onyx jewel glittering in the candlelight. Glad she was that he did not ask to remove her ruby earrings. The white-haired devil vampire then began to laugh, threw back his head and let his fangs grow. She saw his forked tongue dancing about his lips and she shuddered.

"The toll is paid! Lay open the gates for the Damned!" he said, his voice a shrill mockery of humanity.

Two heavy cast-iron gates, which had obviously been a decoration in the days when this place was a working sanctuary, flung open. They were covered with entrails from some unrecognizable sacrifice, and the charnel smell coming up from the steps was enough to cause nausea in even Anastasia, whose tastes had been dulled by centuries of unlife.

She carefully stepped down the stairs, bracing herself: they were slippery with blood. She would've certainly been driven close to frenzy if she hadn't been so full with blood, she realized. Everything seemed to appeal to the Beast within her, and she knew it would soon wake from its uneasy slumber.

She suddenly felt a revolting caress, felt sinuous fingers touching her body from all around, and she stood stock-still, knowing that anything that happened here would be a test of sorts. She felt softness on her arm and around her neck and smelled a mixture of woman scent, fresh blood, and earth. She felt a kiss on her shoulders, on her cheek, and on her forehead, and she endured them. She saw the blood-and-earth-streaked face of the one who blocked her way further: a Sabbat woman with streaked red hair, and a wicked smile.

The woman turned and called down the steps as the man had, before. "Hey-yah! Hey! There's one here at the stairs of Hell, coming down the stairs! She wants to pass! What shall I tell her?"

"Tell her that she is doomed, and follows her own folly! Tell her that all truths are bared in Hell, and in Hell, all are naked, so that fires may burn them." Selena's voice again, Ana thought for sure.

The Sabbat bitch smiled a greedy smile as she put her claws up to Anastasia's fine Tremere robes, and ripped it off, exposing her naked body underneath. The woman leered at her. She threw the fine velvet aside and growled at Anastasia. "Go forth with you, Damned soul! Get ye hence!"

She felt a strong hand push her down the stairs, and nearly fell the intervening distance, but caught herself as she came in sight of the floor. The room was bathed in red, the heat was thick and heavy here. Black smoke choked the ceiling, blackened the place, from the many small fires that had been lit here. A hole rose up in the center of the place, and that was the only way smoke could get out.

Selena stood, naked, the headdress of Hell on her head. Two large oiled and tattooed men stood to either side of her, and she had a black glass dagger in her hand.

"So, there comes one to the fires of Hell, to see what she can see! Why do you come, little girl?" Selena said, mockingly, laughing.

"I come to join the Black Hand," Anastasia said, hoping that the reply was sufficient, not knowing the proper response.

"You? You? Foul creature, do you think you're worthy for the strength of the mighty Black Hand? Do you think the Strength of Caine would take you into their order? How arrogant and stupid a child you are. Take her! Punish her for her insolence!"

The two guards grabbed Ana from either side, and she did not resist them. They bound her feet together, and clasped iron around her wrists. She felt totally powerless, and it was only the comforting presence of the twin ruby earrings that kept her from losing control.

She recoiled in horror, however, when the wooden stake struck her heart, and then she was mostly paralyzed—her heart was not fully penetrated, so she could still move a little. Then she felt twin spikes, twin hooks pierce her back in throbbing pain, and felt her entire weight placed on them. She was hanging on twin meathooks, her feet dangling in the air. Her feet left the ground. She felt her supply of blood leaking down the sides of the wounds, felt the terrible cold of the steel that passed through her whole body. She was totally immobile.

Ana felt the Hunger begin to well up in her as the blood flowed out of her faster and faster. Staked though she was, she began to struggle in her grisly bond, and for the first time a sound issued from her mouth, a low growl, animalistic, and full of hunger.

"Yes!! Yes, Anastasia! Now you see! Now you know! Let it come, Anastasia. Do not fight it. You will be reborn! You will be reborn as one of the rightful daughters of Caine! Let it come! Let your hate reforge you!" Selena whispered in her ear, and she retched blood in response. Selena petted her as if she were a sick child.

Anastasia knew that they were trying to make her one of their own, breaking down her humanity and forcing the Beast in her to come out. She shook with impotent rage.

Then she saw Sofie. The white smock she'd been wearing when they took her was torn and bloody, but she was still breathing, still alive. The two brutes brought her in and chained her to the wall, her hands over her head, facing it. Selena then took a scalpel and began to cut the smock from her, and Anastasia had to watch in horror.

Sofie's back was a network of lines that were bleeding once the smock was cut away, and the fresh smell of the blood wafted over to Anastasia and filled her with self-loathing, desire, and disgust.

"Do you desire her, still, Anastasia? Well, I'm afraid that there's another who does as well. The right of feeding has already been claimed." Selena waved to the white-haired devil, who laughed maniacally and leaped forward. He grabbed Sofie's arm and sunk his fangs into her, feeding on her rich vitae.

Anastasia howled. She struggled on her hooks, so much so that Selena was afraid she'd be ripped in two by the meat hooks. Frenzy was past her as she watched what that white devil did to Sofie while he fed, and she felt every ounce of her humanity straining as she was forced to endure the torture along with her love.

When it was over, they opened the manacles and Sofie slid down the wall, the blood from her wounds causing a sickly wet slap on the flagstones.

Anastasia was an angry Beast then, and it was only Selena's powers of domination that kept her in control. Fixing a look in Ana's eyes, Selena told her "Silence!" With that, Anastasia calmed, but the fire behind her eyes was still there.

Selena stepped before Anastasia, who mustered all the control she had. In her hand was a bloody piece of cotton, one of the shredded strips of Sofie's frock. "Do you find this delicious? Did you like what we did?" she asked Anastasia, holding the strip under her nose.

Anastasia swallowed back the black bile rising in her throat and nodded, trying to let the feral fire in her eyes reflect madness, trying to convince Selena that her attempts at destroying her humanity had been successful. Selena smiled as Ana licked at the blood on the cloth.

Selena stepped quietly over to Anastasia and removed the meat hooks from her back. She unlocked the chains that bound her arms and legs, and the stake which pierced her heart. "You must now stand, newest member of the Sabbat. You must now partake in our Rite of Initiation. Share blood with us, Anastasia. Prepare to become known by the One-Who-Walks."

Anastasia smiled dully, but said nothing more, trying to show feral light in her eyes. She barely retained her sense, her humanity, but as long as she had will left, she would survive.

While they prepared the cup of blood for their hated ritual, she quietly undid the earrings on her ears, and popped the ruby stones from their fastenings. Anastasia watched in horror as Selena raised her hands in silent supplication to an unseen force. "Oh, One-Who-Walks, Dread Zarastus, I implore thee, come forth and mark one of your own!" Selena lit, one by one, big black candles that were arranged on the altar where the blood cup rested.

Anastasia slipped the rubies into her mouth and closed her eyes, willing them free of their enchantments. She had to swallow quickly as potent vitae washed into her, flooded through her. Just two quarts of blood from her Sire, but it was potent blood at that, the blood of Etrius, the archmage! When next she spoke, it was not only in her own voice. Her Sire's voice mingled with her own, and she spoke with unearthly tones.

"Selena! Long have I sought another chance to battle you, now it seems my Childe will carry the fight for me!"

Selena whirled, hearing the voice of her ancient enemy, Etrius who had betrayed her and all her kind and branded them all with the Curse of Tremere.

"Etrius?" she called aloud, her voice quavering with barely controlled fear. Her hands dropped to her sides, and the flames on the black candles were snuffed immediately.

"Etrius?"

"Let us say my power is in the blood, Selena! Taste its strength!" And with that, Anastasia sent twin curling bolts of lightning shooting at the Sabbat priestess.

She had no time to delay, and took the full brunt of the powerful blast, her hair singeing off in the process. Again, twin blasts flew forth from Anastasia, and she could feel the waning power of her Sire's blood being spent in their very essence. She screamed aloud in pain, but that did not stop her from reacting to the attack. With two grand gestures, she raised her arms and made a flinging motion at Anastasia.

Almost immediately, Anastasia felt invisible shackles to replace the iron ones that had held her before. With her Sire's blood gone from within her, and with the near-shattering of her own mind, she could not think of a counter-charm to break the bonds. They were proof against her magic, as well. She struggled against them, in vain.

Selena smiled as she watched Anastasia struggle, the Sabbat priestess's face scarred with black gashes from the lightning. With a simple gesture, Selena sent the nearby stake back into Ana's heart, paralyzing her again. The white-haired Sabbat brought Selena the twin earring settings.

Selena smiled. "I see. 'Principle Focus of Vitae Infusion,' isn't it called . . . your Master's vitae? Tsk, tsk. Your sincerity was ever at suspicion, of course, but I had begun to believe that you were ready to embrace the Beast within you. I can see that I was foolish to think one of Etrius's whelps would ever see the true source of Kindred magic. I have risked much in initiating you to this, our sacred order, Anastasia! You have cost me much, and caused a sacred ritual to be ruined. And now you will pay the price for your lack of vision!"

With a gesture, Selena made the invisible chains pull her down to the floor, where she was forced into a kneeling position near the center of the room.

"Sofie doesn't seem to be feeling well. Poor dear. I'm afraid she's going to bleed to death. You're going to be forced to watch her slowly die, unable to do a thing to help her." Anastasia struggled again, but to no avail.

"I imagine that we will see your attitude change during the night, and I think that tomorrow night you may be ready to join our ranks. That is, if you are still alive. You see, the sun comes in to this place. There's a tiny hole in the ceiling, and a little beam of light filters down here on sunny days. Of course, tomorrow could be dreary. I do hope so for your benefit."

Behind her, Selena's warlocks were gathering together the items they had used in the ritual.

"Oh, and, Anastasia, in case you were wondering: this room is warded against all Disciplines and magicks, except mine. It was only the potency of your Sire's blood that broke the ward, and then only briefly. You'll not find an easy escape from this place!"

Selena left after donning her robes, sweeping her cloak behind her, her pack of Sabbat warlocks following. She heard Selena say, "No! Leave those here. They can only be used by her Sire to follow us." There was the soft clink of a bag dropped to the ground, and the group departed. Upstairs, she heard the scrape of iron against stone as the gates were slammed shut.

Anastasia passed into a numbness, locked as she was by the magical chains. Her mind raced, going back through all her magical training, trying to find something, anything that would save her. There was a gray time, and Sofie moaned and passed in and out of consciousness.

Soon, the light of the sun began to show down from the hole in the ceiling. Sofie stirred. Anastasia turned her head slightly toward her, having discovered that the magical chains allowed her a little freedom of movement.

"Sofie! Sofie! Are you awake?" Anastasia called. A wave of sleepiness washed over her as the sun was rising in the sky.

"Sofie!"

Sofie's eyes were half-open, and she looked up at Anastasia. "Ana?"

"Sofie! You have to get me that bag. Get me the bag, sugar. I can save us both."

Sofie crawled her way toward the white cotton bag, wordlessly. Ana wasn't sure if she realized what she was doing. She carried it back in her teeth, and Ana saw in horror that one of her legs had twisted around, broken and utterly useless.

Sofie upended the bag and Anastasia watched as her Eye, her Wand, and her Athame spilled out onto the floor. "The Wand, Sofie. Give me the wand. That stick there. Tuck it in my hand."

The sunbeam was burning its way across the floor. Anastasia's heavy-lidded eyes were barely able to stay open. Sofie uttered a muffled shriek of pain as she moved her body to put the Wand in Anastasia's hand.

Closing her eyes, Anastasia invoked her will, the Blood within her, and the power that streams through both. She felt the Wand react to the power, felt it growing warmer and warmer. She felt the power within her begin to form. When she had shaped it to completion, she let the power go. She felt a surge go through her chains and then . . . nothing. Nothing had happened.

"Damn it! The power wasn't enough, and now I have only a scarcity of vitae! I've failed you Sofie!"

Sofie looked at Anastasia. "Ana? Is that you? I'm gonna die, aren't I? You're really here?"

Anastasia nodded. "Yes, I'm here"

Sofie looked wide-eyed at the sunbeam, burning its way across the floor. "You need blood? I could give you mine."

Anastasia turned away from her. "No, hon, that's fine. You need all of yours. I'm just trying to figure out . . ."

Then she smelled the fresh scent of her lover's vitae. Sofie had cut her wrist with the Athame. "Don't waste it," she said, as she moved forward, forcing her wrist to Ana's mouth. Ana looked at her, and saw the commitment in Sofie's eyes.

"I love you Ana," Sofie said. "I can't live life without you."

Ana took Sofie's wrist into her mouth. Ana steeled herself but could not resist the tremendous ecstasy that flowed through her. Giving in to that feeling, Ana brushed Sofie's mind in a familiar way, and the mental bond they always shared during lovemaking was established. For a second it was as if time stood still, and their souls mingled in that connection. Sofie had made her decision, and gave of herself. Ana felt her lover's last drops of blood leaving her body, felt her essence slip across the connection.

With but single gesture of the Wand, Anastasia was free.

Anastasia put the white rose on the gravestone, and finished her ritual. A drop of blood was called for, and she took it from her tears. She drew a pentacle on the marker, calling for all spirits in the area to watch this place and keep it safe. She took some of the earth from the fresh grave and put it in a pouch.

She had called Etrius to arrange for the burial, he was happy to hear from her and even managed to show sadness at her having lost Sofie. He was more than willing to help her with the financial arrangements: provided that she present herself to the Prince of San Francisco immediately.

She walked back down the hill, closed the cemetery gate behind her, and stepped to the waiting limousine. Her driver was a ghoul of the Tremere elder, who had already telephoned her at her brownstone to pay his respects. As the limo passed through town, up Russian Hill, on the way to Sebastian's Club, she caught a glimpse of her former home, her Ivory Tower, the brownstone she and Sofie shared. She realized that it would never do as a Haven in this city, that she would have to move uptown, perhaps closer to the Chantry.

Whether Selena had known she had escaped or not, the Sabbat bitch had not come seeking her. Perhaps she wasn't as powerful as she had thought. Anastasia was still deeply concerned about the name Zarastus, One-Who-Walks . . . could that be her Sire? Or perhaps a darker creature, for the Sabbat were said to truck with forces from Hell?

She would meet the Prince garbed in her robes of office, having reclaimed and mended them from the vestibule of the church. Checking them before she changed in the limo, she found something, something which told her that Selena wasn't finished with her.

It was a pendant, a stone circle. On one side was Sumerian art, the visage of the Goddess Inanna, Queen of Heaven, and on the other, the Crescent Moon, Selena's sigil.

Wolf Trap

by Richard Lee Byers

The fence was wrought iron, sixteen feet high, and topped with sharp-edged arrowheads: a heavy-duty perimeter defense for a hospital. But I'd climbed tougher barriers, and didn't need to shift out of human form. As I swung myself over, the full moon, my birth moon, came out from behind the clouds. A thrill sang down my nerves.

I did my best to quash the feeling. That sort of exhilaration's nice (in a mindless kind of way), but I didn't want to bounce around like a puppy while I was trying to sneak into an enemy installation. I adjusted my ski mask and slunk on, creeping from one patch of cover to the next.

The well-tended grounds were extensive. It was a while before I caught a glimpse of the hospital itself, and that first look surprised me. My client had mentioned that there'd been some kind of insane asylum here since the mid-nineteenth century, but I hadn't expected to find the original building still standing. The sprawling, three-story structure was as ugly as its surroundings were pleasant. The brick walls were grimy, the few small windows, barred. The place reminded me of every nasty thing I'd ever read about Victorian England, of Bedlam, Newgate Prison, and the workhouse. It seemed out of place on the outskirts of contemporary San Francisco.

Still, aesthetics aside, I was glad it was old. Old buildings are usually easier to crack than new ones.

I looked about, didn't see anyone, and eased around the structure until I spotted a side door. As I'd expected I needed my picks. The lock was a good one; it put up a fight, and despite decades of practice, the gloves still made my fingers a bit clumsier than they would have been otherwise. I'd nearly made up my mind to peel them off when the latch finally clicked open.

I cracked the door open and peeked inside. Beyond the door was a deserted hallway. It wasn't too dark to see down, but it was gloomy; most of the ceiling fixtures were switched off. The air smelled of disinfectant. Somewhere a sound whispered, too faint to identify.

I headed down the passage. Doors with little windows lined both walls. On the other side were small, cell-like bedrooms, all vacant. Evidently, the hospital wasn't overcrowded.

I turned a corner, kept moving toward the noise. Eventually, it resolved into Jimmy Stewart's stammer. Brighter light shone ahead.

Skulking on, I discovered that the hall ended in a sort of lobby adjacent to the main entrance. Other passages ran off it, a staircase led upward, and one corner was glassed in; the nurses' station, by the looks of it. Inside, two guys in white coats sat watching a colorized movie on a portable TV. Apparently, they didn't have any work to do (one of the perks of the graveyard shift).

There was something odd about the scene, and after a second, I realized what it was. The lobby was too bare—just tables and chairs; no decorations, even though it was Halloween night; no projects that the patients had made in art therapy, or whatever on display; no Ping-Pong or pool table. Come to think of it, I hadn't noticed a baseball diamond or basketball court outside, either.

But hell, what did I care? I hadn't come to critique the facility—just to bust somebody out. And to do that, I needed to get to one of the other corridors and continue my search.

So I just walked out into the open. With luck, the attendants wouldn't look away from the TV. And if they did, well, that was why I'd brought the mask and my Beretta.

The men didn't turn. I chose another hall at random and discovered that its bedroom doors had name cards mounted on them. Bingo.

I found Jennifer Ryan's room halfway down the corridor. She was locked in, but this one only took a second to pick. I eased the door open, then stiffened in surprise.

The teenage girl was in four-point restraints. Leather cuffs bound her wrists and ankles to the bed. An IV ran into one pale, skinny arm. Someone had shaved her head, the better, I assumed, to attach the wires that ran to some sort of monitor. A visor, linked by a cable to the same console, covered her eyes and ears and hooked metal prongs into her nostrils. Dressed in a pungent, urine-stained hospital gown, her coltish body twitched and writhed. Somehow, I didn't think it was going to be a problem to convince her to leave with me.

Intent on pulling the hardware off her, I moved toward the bed. The soft scuff of a footfall sounded behind me. When I whirled, there was a figure silhouetted in the doorway. I lunged, but I was already out of time. The stubby, black gun in its hands made a funny whir. For an instant, my face and chest burned, then I couldn't feel anything. My knees buckled, and the room got even darker. As I passed out, I marveled at just how quickly and completely the job had gone south. And to think that when I'd heard about it, I'd figured it was going to be a cakewalk.

I supposed that Nikos Ripthroat and I were a study in contrasts. He was slim, handsome, his skin so smooth and his bones so fine that his face just missed effeminate. He was elegant with his sculpted hair and pearl-gray Armani suit. I was hulking, shaggy, and, I knew, somehow uncouth despite a decent suit of my own and a stylish black leather trenchcoat. Plus, he was in a wheelchair and I was on my feet.

"Erik Mikkelsen." He said my name as if he were tasting it, not sure he liked the flavor. Maybe he thought it discreditable that I no longer used my bombastic Get of Fenris handle. "They tell me you don't like to shake hands."

I fought the urge to shove my fists deeper into my pockets. The urge won. "I'd just as soon you didn't sniff my ass, either."

Nikos flushed. "They also told me you were insolent."

"I'm guessing you didn't fly me three thousand miles to talk about my quirks. Why don't you tell me what you do want."

He grimaced. "All right. Please, sit down." I dropped into the armchair in front of his huge teak desk. "You understand this has to be kept completely confidential."

"Uh huh."

"All right, then." Nikos paused, hitched the wheelchair around as if looking away from me would help him get started. Or maybe he was just checking out the view. It was worth it. His office took up most of the top floor of a skyscraper in the financial district, and the walls on two sides were made of glass. Behind him I could see the Transamerica Pyramid, the Bay Bridge, freighters and sailboats traversing the sun-dappled waters of the Bay.

"Sixteen years ago" Nikos explained, "I had a human secretary named Peggy Travis. She worked here, in the legitimate part of the operation. She was a wonderful girl, full of joy and fire, and we fell in love, or at least I loved her—enough to want to marry her.

But while I was still trying to find a way to tell her what kind of being I really am, she ended the affair and quit her job. To this day, I don't know why."

I figured I did. She'd caught a whiff of the beast inside him. It was the way ape-werewolf romances usually ended, or so I'd been told. There was no way I'd know firsthand; my sex life was limited to hookers and one-night stands.

"Anyway," Nikos continued, "I kept tabs on her to make sure she didn't run out of money before she found another position—that, in general, she was going to be all right. I knew when she married her high-school sweetheart, a boy named Scott Ryan, three months after she left me, and when she gave birth to a daughter named Jennifer, four months after that."

"Yours, unless she cheated on you," I said, showing off my arithmetic. "I assume that after that, you kept an eye on the kid."

He hesitated. Nikos reached the part of the story he was ashamed of. "At first. If she was only Kinfolk, I meant to leave her alone to live a normal human life. But if she was Garou, she'd need my help.

"Unfortunately, it hurt me to think about her, because I still loved her mother; loved her, too, in a way, even though I'd never met her. I had plenty of other matters to distract me. Jennifer turned eleven, twelve, thirteen without showing any sign of the Change. The upshot of it all was that, gradually, I just stopped checking on her."

"Until recently, I gather. When you found out things were different."

"Yes. She'd started having nightmares and temper tantrums, fighting, destroying things, and running away. The usual picture. Naturally, Peggy and Scott thought she was having some sort of breakdown and dragged her to a shrink. The shrink recommended

Jennifer be hospitalized, and when her first placement couldn't handle her she was transferred to what I'm told is a state-of-the-art experimental program for explosive teens."

Nikos paused, rubbed his forehead, and continued. "I want you to break her out, so I can guide her through the Change before she really does lose her mind."

"One question," I said. "You're a pack leader. You have plenty of flunkies you could send. Why do you need me?"

Nikos scowled. "Because of this." He rapped the arm of the wheelchair. "A Bane got me. The wound's slowly healing, but until it does—"

"You'll worry," I said, suddenly comprehending, "that one of your underlings will try to grab your throne. Your Shadow Lords are notorious for that kind of crap." Actually, as far as I was concerned, most Garou were too locked into the senseless, endless struggle for dominance, but Nikos' tribe was a particularly egregious example.

Nikos nodded. "I don't know who I can trust. And if a rival got his hands on Jennifer, he could use her against me. So, will you help me? I'll pay you $20,000 and make a place for you in the pack."

I'm sure I gaped at him, stupidly, in fact. It was the first time in a long while that I'd found myself so completely at a loss for words.

"I guarantee you'll be welcome," Nikos continued. "Everyone's heard about the victories you've won—"

"I fought for money," I said, more harshly than I'd intended. "Not for your precious Gaia, and certainly not to impress anyone. You can give my 'place' to the next ronin who wanders through here."

Nikos frowned. "Are you sure?" he asked. Modern as he looked in his high-tech, corporate surroundings, complete with the computer and conference phone on his desk and the big-screen video system in the corner, he was really an old-fashioned Garou at heart. He couldn't fathom why any werewolf would opt out of the hidebound system of tribe, sept, and pack if given a halfway reasonable alternative. No doubt he'd been certain the invitation would clinch the deal.

"Yeah," I said. "Hard to believe, isn't it? I mean, you make the Shadows sound like such a true-blue, fun-loving bunch of folks."

"All right," he said. "Then will you do the job for just the cash?"

"Sure," I said. "Why not?"

Ah, why not, indeed?

I dreamed I was lying in the bottom of a pitching rowboat with a fat fly buzzing around my head. Gradually, I realized the cold, hard surface beneath me wasn't moving. I was just dizzy and sick to my stomach. And the buzz became a droning baritone voice.

I cracked my eyes open and found that my vision was blurry. But I could see that I was sprawled naked on the linoleum in the middle of the lobby. A crowd of people surrounded me, many wearing blue coveralls and a number pointing guns at me—not tranq guns like the one that had knocked me out, but killing weapons, all loaded with silver bullets, I suspected. The voice belonged to a pudgy, pink-faced guy with a wispy, ginger mustache. He was holding one end of a three-foot rod. The other was attached to the steel collar encircling Jennifer's neck. The visor was gone and she was standing unassisted, but it was obvious from her slack jaw and glassy blue eyes that she was still only semiconscious.

"Look at him," the pudgy man said, "and you'll see that he's only flesh and blood. Nothing to be afraid of, just an odd kind of animal driven by instinct. That's why we caught him so easily. Despite the tricks he can do, he's no match for a rational human being."

"What's the deal with his hands?" an Asian woman asked.

"Ordinarily, a Garou mates with a human or a wolf. Sex between two werewolves is as unnatural as incest between a human brother and sister. The offspring of such a union is called a metis, or mule. They're always born deformed and are regarded as freaks even by their own race of monsters." He sounded as if he relished the thought of my childhood loneliness and humiliation.

"Actually," I said, "the other Garou always told me I had an endearing pixie-like quality. And everyone adored my blueberry muffins."

When I spoke, some of my captors jerked in surprise. The pudgy guy said, "I thought it was about time you were waking up. Who are you and what's your interest in this girl? Answer, or we'll hurt you."

"My name's Rolf Hendricks," I said. "Jennifer's my daughter, though she doesn't know it. I came to get her out of here and help her through the Change." A good merc always protects the client, though at moments when my own head is on the block, it's hard to feel enthusiastic about it. "Now, who are you and what were you doing to her?"

The pudgy man sneered. "Why should I tell you?"

Because it will give you a chance to gloat and strut, I thought. He seemed like the type. I just needed to provide an excuse. "Well, it sounded like you want to teach your buddies about the Garou. If we chat for awhile, maybe I'll display the inadequacies of my dimwitted animal brain." More to the point, from my perspective, if I stalled for time, maybe I could shake off the effects of the tranq before he and the goon squad started hurting me.

The pudgy man chuckled. "All right, when you put it

like that, why not? It's not as if you'll get a chance to repeat what you hear, and it might be educational for the students to observe your reaction." He glanced around at his audience. "He could fly into one of the werewolves' legendary psychotic rages, so stay ready to shoot. My name is Howard Cooper. I'm a psychiatrist, a neurophysiologist, and a Project Head for the Aesop Research Company."

"A division of Pentex," I said. No wonder he knew all about the Garou. The tribes didn't have a deadlier enemy than the Wyrm-controlled megacorporation. I was in about as deep as I could get.

Cooper frowned. He didn't like it that I knew that much about his organization. "Well, yes. Recently ARC acquired this facility and informed the psychiatric community that we were converting it into a residential treatment program for troubled adolescents. Since our goal was research, we'd be offering our services free of charge. Naturally, we were inundated with referrals. After that, it was just a matter of using genetic testing to identify the children we actually wanted to work on—"

"Mislaid Garou-to-be," I said.

"Precisely." He stood up straighter, preening. "Needed to test a hypothesis of mine—namely, that the right combination of aversive conditioning and chemotherapy can make it impossible for a young werewolf to complete the Change."

I blinked and squinted. My eyes still refused to focus. "So what? The majority of lost cubs never achieve their potential anyway. And most kids aren't forgotten. Their Garou parents take them in hand as soon as they start showing signs of their heritage. So what do you hope to accomplish?"

The pudgy guy smirked. "As I expected, you lack the abstract reasoning ability to grasp the implications. Once I invent the treatment, I can refine it into a form we can administer to the entire population. The drugs will go into the food supply. The hypnotic stimuli will air subliminally on television. Every Garou child growing up in a human community will be affected. And since there aren't many being raised by wolf packs anymore, in just a few years the supply of new werewolves will dry up without your people ever even knowing why."

The gunmen tensed just in case I did go into a frenzy. "They would have loved you at Auschwitz," I said mildly. "But it'll never work." I wished I were certain of that.

"Oh no, I assure you, it will. I'm on the brink. Too bad you won't be around to see it."

"Why not? I figured there was an IV and a tin blindfold in my future."

"Sorry. You've already accessed your powers. The treatment was never intended to work on someone like you. But we do have a use for you."

"What a relief," I said. "I'd hate to think I couldn't pull my weight."

"I wear a lot of hats at Pentex," Cooper said. "One of my responsibilities is training First Team operatives. Garou killers. They reside here, providing security, until they're ready to go into the field. You're about to become the object of a training exercise."

"Let me guess," I said. "Slow me down with dope, turn me loose, and let the posse hunt me down. Only, what if I refuse to play?"

"Then we'll regretfully blow you apart where you lie."

"In that case, I'll play."

He grinned. "I thought you might." He gestured, and the ring of people surrounding me opened, clearing a path to the door. "We'll give you a head start. By the way, the fence is now electrified."

"Well, gosh," I said, rising. "If there's no way out, I'll just have to kill every one of you monkeys, won't I?"

Unfortunately, at that point my legs went rubbery and I staggered, making my threat less intimidating than it might otherwise have been. A couple people laughed. Trying to look undaunted, I ambled to the exit.

Once outside, I started running, putting distance between me and the enemy. I wracked my brains for a plan. Hell, I ought to be able to think my way out of this, no sweat. After all, I'd been a real Einstein so far.

For instance, I could have found out who owned the hospital *before* coming out here, could have retreated when I sensed there was something strange about the setup, or at least proceeded more cautiously, maybe avoided tripping the alarm or whatever it was I'd done to give away my presence.

But no, I'd waltzed blindly up the gallows steps and stuck my head in the noose—proof positive that a Goof of Fenris could take himself out of the tribe, but that there was no way to take the infamous tribal recklessness out of the Goof.

I did my best to stop kicking myself. It couldn't help me now. Instead I'd better decide what form to take. Either of the four-legged forms, Cujo or Rin Tin Tin, would have advantages. With sharper senses, I'd have a better chance of detecting enemies before they saw me, while being built low to the ground would help me hide.

But as Cooper had pointed out, I'm a freak. No matter what shape I shift to, my oversized Larry Talbot hands stay the same regardless of form. They don't shed their talons and fur when I turn human, and they don't shrink into paws when I go lupine. That makes the four-legged forms clumsy, and I didn't think I could afford clumsy.

Be Larry Talbot, then: the wolfman, the powerhouse. Except that that would make me ten feet tall and very easy to spot. Okay, then be the troglodyte, Alley Oop. At least I'd be a little stronger. I crouched behind a purple-flowered glorybush and willed myself to transform.

When I did, I got another nasty surprise. I'd hoped Oop's high-performance metabolism would burn off the lingering effects of the drug. It didn't. Apparently the stuff was Wyrm-tainted.

Well, no use worrying about it. It wasn't as if I had much of a chance in any case. It occurred to me that if there was a tall tree growing near the fence, I could climb it and jump over the barrier without getting fried. I dashed to the edge of the property.

No dice. There'd been big trees here once, but somebody had cut them down. Somehow, I wasn't surprised.

Behind me, I heard doors opening, the hunters spreading out into the night. Afraid of being pinned against the fence, I ran back toward the hospital, hunkered down behind a fragrant eucalyptus, and strained to come up with another idea.

After a minute, I got one. I could at least screw up the enemy's night vision. Concentrating, I tried to activate one of my Gifts.

It was hard. The tranq didn't just throw off my balance and coordination; it made me feel drunk, undercut my ability to focus my will. Finally, just when I was about to give up and move on, I felt the power kick in, like a key turning inside my head.

Through the darkness sounded a quick succession of pops, like a bunch of inflated paper bags being swatted all at once. Small fires burst into existence in bushes and trees. Unfortunately, with only green growth to consume, most would gutter out quickly, but I hoped that at least a few would burn for a while.

Startled hunters cried out. Grinning, I slunk on, shoes swished through grass.

I lunged behind an oak, flattened myself against the rough bark. The footsteps continued toward me.

One man murmured and another replied. It was hard to believe they didn't hear my heart pounding.

Obviously they didn't, because they walked right past me; two of them, with assault rifles, Kevlar jackets, and helmets equipped with modular nightvision goggles and radios. I eased out of my hiding place to attack them from behind.

I clawed the first one's carotid arteries. Blood spurted, suffusing the air with its copper scent, and he dropped. As I pivoted, the other guy, a burly Chicano with two tattooed tears, did the same, bringing his weapon to bear. Feeling horribly slow and clumsy, I barely managed to slap the rifle out of line, then punched him in the jaw. His neck snapped and he fell, too.

For the first time, I though I might have an outside chance of surviving. Now that I'd taken down the gunmen, I could seize a weapon for myself. Not only would it narrow the long odds against me, but I could use it to blast open the gate in the fence.

I wrenched the Chicano's rifle out of his deathgrip. With its box magazine and folding steel butt, it looked a lot like an AKMS with some extra bells and whistles; probably the latest design from one of Pentex's munitions companies. Wishing that the one of the helmet and jacket sets would fit Oop's beetle-browed, anthropoid body, I crept back toward the edge of the grounds.

I knelt behind a bush, held my breath until four goons went by, moved on, swinging left to avoid the halo of light cast by one of my fires. I sensed motion at my back.

I pivoted. Nothing there. I did my best to blink the haze out of my eyes and still couldn't see anything.

Maybe my nerves were playing tricks on me. After all, I wasn't even sure I'd heard anything. I just had a feeling. Backing up, I took a last look around, then turned and stalked on.

For four paces, it was all right. Then the hairs on the back of my neck stood on end. I spun around.

For a second, I still didn't see him. Then he was right in front of me, a piece of the night molded into human form. A more prosaic description: he was a guy in black pajamas, hood, gloves, and shoes, wearing black pigment on his upraised samurai sword.

Damn my cloudy vision! Still, it was all right. I'd spotted him in time, and now he was going to wish he'd brought a gun instead of relying on this ninja crap. I pulled my rifle's trigger. Nothing happened. Maybe the gun was Wyrm-tainted, too. At any rate, it was gimmicked somehow so a Garou couldn't fire it—one more way this game was rigged against me.

For one precious instant, I froze in shock. By the time I recovered, the sword was whizzing at my head. Frantically I jerked up the gun to block. The blade swooped around my guard and slashed my shoulder. The ninja whirled past me.

No pain yet. Ordinarily, that would come in a moment, but I invoked another Gift and shut it out. At the same time, I wheeled to keep the swordsman in front of me.

He lunged, cutting, feinting, bellowing kais. He was a better swordsman than I was, or might have been even if I hadn't had the tranq slowing me down. Over the next few seconds, my superior strength and reach barely sufficed to hold him off. Meanwhile, blood streamed down my arm; the gash wasn't closing. Evidently, the blade was silver-coated.

Finally I got lucky. Swinging with all my might, I managed to bash the sword out of his grip. Spinning end over end, it vanished into the shadows. I rushed in, trying to brain him, but he sidestepped and tripped me. By the time I scrambled to my feet, he had a dagger in each hand.

I suspected he was as proficient with those as he

was with a sword. Still, he'd have to get in close to score with them, and that might give me the chance I needed.

I dropped the rifle, brandished my hands in a your-knives-against-my-claws gesture, then swayed, trying to make it appear that my wound was draining what was left of my strength. Since it wasn't that far from the truth, I figured I'd look reasonably convincing.

He pounced at me. I jabbed my talons at his face, a feeble thrust, and he brushed the attack aside with his forearm.

I guessed Cooper hadn't taught the class about the Gift that lets certain Garou drop an opponent with the slightest touch. Or maybe Sho Kosugi here had been absent that day. At any rate, his feet flew out from under him. I threw myself on top of him, ripped through cloth, flesh, and cracking ribs to shred his heart and lungs.

Afterwards, I needed to lie still, gasping in chestsful of air. But I could already hear running footsteps pounding toward me. The ninja's shouts and the clangor of sword and rifle had drawn the other hunters.

My shoulder throbbed. My gaze fell on the useless gun, and a black, despairing rage welled up inside me. Suddenly, I didn't care about eking out another few fearful, painful minutes of life. I wanted to turn and charge my tormentors, kill and kill until they brought me down. My spine and limbs lengthened. My teeth grew points and my jaws began to stretch into a muzzle.

Shuddering, I clamped down on my fury. I refused to go berserk, not when it would mean losing, not with so much at stake. After several moments, my head cleared, and the shift to wolfman form reversed itself. Clutching my wound, hoping I wasn't leaving a trail of blood, I jumped up and ran.

A gun barked. I threw myself flat, then realized that the bullet hadn't come anywhere near me. Someone had fired at a shadow, or maybe at one of his fellow goons. For the time being, I was in the clear.

Which meant it was time to hatch Plan C. Much to my surprise, I finally did dredge up one last idea. It was a long shot; it meant trying something I hadn't done in years, and hadn't been good at even when in practice, but it also looked to be the only shot left.

Unfortunately, I couldn't take it out here in the dark. I got up and headed for the hospital.

After a minute, the black pile of the building loomed out of the night. I crept toward the door I'd entered through before. Guns banged and chattered. Bullets split the air around my head.

I sprinted, zigzagging, certain every instant that the next shot would take me out. But the gunmen kept missing. Chalk it up to the dark and the fact that the clowns were still trainees.

Knowing the door had relocked itself when it closed, I hurled my weight against it. It crashed inward and I fell on top of the wreckage, jarring a burst of pain through my injured shoulder. I scrambled up and ran on.

I was afraid the lobby would be full of hunters, but it wasn't. The only people there were the two attendants I'd first seen, still manning the nurses' station. Since I didn't want them telling my pursuers which way I'd gone, I charged the enclosure.

One guy frantically locked the door, so I leaped at a window instead. As the glass exploded, I noticed the other man had a red left eye. I wondered fleetingly what that was all about, but by the time I touched down, I'd forgotten about it. I had more pressing things to think about.

I tore red eye's face off, then pivoted to kill his partner. No need. A flying shard of glass had opened his throat for me. I smashed a console that looked like it monitored an alarm system, then grabbed a piece of window. Then, I dashed up two flights of stairs, around a corner, and stopped, panting, under a light.

Below me, radios crackled and voices called back and forth. Knowing I'd reentered the hospital, the hunters would seal and sweep it. I was treed.

So I'd better get to work, I thought.

I held the shard up, tilted it to reflect the maximum amount of light, stared into the sheen, tried to push fear, anger, and pain aside so I could slip into the proper meditative frame of mind.

I felt the power stir inside me, but nothing tangible happened. Ordinarily, that wouldn't have been any reason to panic. On my best day, I'd never done this trick in less than fifteen minutes. But now I didn't have fifteen minutes to spare.

I concentrated harder. Drops of blood plopped from my elbow onto the linoleum. Footsteps clumped from the first floor to the second.

I kept straining, heard the hunters ascend again, and felt the world shift.

The ceiling fixtures went dark and turned to spider webs, deepening the gloom. Now, the only light was a sourceless gray phosphorescence. The linoleum changed into wood, while the antiseptic tang in the air gave way to a faint stink of excrement and rot.

I laughed. I'd done it, stepped sideways into the spirit world. The enemy couldn't get at me anymore.

Or so I thought. Then two riflemen stalked around the corner.

One Garou can lead a band of comrades through the Gauntlet. Though it was supposed to be impossible, somehow I'd drawn my pursuers after me. Which meant my last ploy had crapped out, and I guessed I was going to die. Still laughing, I charged the riflemen as they drew beads on me. I saw that I wouldn't close with them in time.

But before they could shoot, a ring of giggling shadows materialized around them, clutched at them with gray translucent fingers. The humans squawked, punched, and thrashed, but feebly, as if the phantoms touch had sucked away their strength. In seconds the shadows disarmed them, then hustled each into a different cell.

I dropped into a fighting stance, but the spooks didn't attack me. After a few seconds, shrieks and gunfire began echoing through the building.

It sounded as if the hunters suddenly had bigger problems than bagging me. Emboldened, I sneaked toward the stairs to check out the situation.

Down the hall, another band of wraiths was stomping a fallen goon. On the second floor, they were wrapping the hunters in straitjackets. A few yards away, cell doors swung open by themselves. Startled gunmen pivoted toward them, then found themselves unable to look away. Sobbing and shuddering, resisting with all their might, they shuffled through. The doors slammed behind them.

Meanwhile, still unmolested, I tried to figure out what was going on.

Nikos said the hospital had been an asylum since the 1800s. Maybe it had been a snake pit, and the old-time inmates who'd suffered here were getting their revenge. Not that the shadows were their souls, trapped in this place for generations (or at least I hoped not). But Umbral sites remember their histories, and sometimes create emanations to reenact them. Or to settle somebody's old score.

Evidently, my step sideways had somehow enabled the spooks to pull my enemies into their reach. Not that I was complaining, but I wondered why they weren't messing with me as well. Maybe it was because I wasn't human and had never held anyone prisoner here. Unlike the Pentex guys, I didn't have much in common with the people the inmates once hated.

So I guessed I was home free. Then someone yelled, "Hendricks!" It took me a second to remember that that was the alias I'd given, but I didn't have any trouble recognizing the voice—now shrill with fear—of Howard Cooper. Perhaps, hoping to witness the kill, he'd been following some of the goons around, and so had been yanked into the Umbra along with them.

"Come out!" the scientist shouted. "I've still got the girl! Tell him!"

A shaky female voice cried, "Yes! I'm here, too!"

At last I understood why Cooper had taken Jennifer out of her cell: to use her as a hostage, just in case, against all probability, I somehow managed to turn the tables on him and his men. He was either remarkably farsighted or astonishingly gutless. "Where?" I called.

"In the lobby!" she replied.

"Don't be afraid," I said. "I'm coming down to help you."

They were standing by the front door. Cooper had a snub-nosed .38 revolver pressed to Jennifer's temple. He had choked up on the rod-leash to hold her in front of him human-shield fashion. Maybe that was why none of the shadows had taken him out.

The girl's eyes widened when she saw me.

"I thought you'd be interested in learning about another difference between us inferior Garou and you godlike humans," I said, advancing. "We can open the way into a place called the Umbra—"

"I know where we are!" Cooper yapped. "Stay back!"

"Or else what?" I kept walking forward. "If you understand what I did, then you know you need me to take you back to the physical world."

"It doesn't matter. I'll shoot her anyway!"

"All right," I growled, "I guess you win." Then charged.

Cooper shoved the hostage at me. I tumbled her out of the way. The revolver pointed at my chest. I dove trying to get under the shot. The gun banged once as it plowed into him, taking him down with a flying tackle.

As soon I got my claws in him, it was over, but I'd grown to hate him so much that I felt an urge to keep mangling his corpse.

Instead, I got up and turned to Jennifer. She was cowering with her back against the wall—scared, but not terrified, which made sense when I thought about it. On the one hand, I was a naked, blood-spattered ogre who'd just torn a guy into cold cuts, but on the other, my victim was the doc who'd been torturing her. To some extent, it ought to balance out.

Hoping it would reassure her, I shifted back to human form. Jennifer gasped and recoiled, but once the change was done, her trembling abated. "I'm a friend," I said. "Really. I came to take you out of here."

"But you," she swallowed, "you didn't stop when he said he'd shoot me."

"Yeah, well, even doped up like I am, I'm pretty fast. Cooper couldn't count on having enough time to kill you and turn the gun on me. I hoped he'd realize that and be more interested in protecting his ass than carrying out his threat.

"I admit it was a gamble, but what was the alternative? I could have stood a safe distance away from him and tried to shift us all back across the Gauntlet, but since Cooper wasn't a Garou, ordinarily it wouldn't even work. Then again, I got the two of you here, so who knows? Say it worked. Next thing, he shoots me and locks you back in the brainwashing gizmo. I couldn't see much percentage in that."

Jennifer's lips quirked into a fleeting smile. "Easy

for you to say. I'd still have been alive. Maybe the next rescuer would have gotten me out."

"Maybe," I said, "but there was another side to it, too. Cooper claimed he could destroy my people, who are your people, too, even if you don't know it yet. That made killing him more important than saving your life or mine. I couldn't even risk simply marooning him here because his organization has agents who could cross over and bring him out. Can you understand that?"

"Kind of," she said. "Could you be a little more vague?"

I grinned. "I still have work to do. I'll explain things as we go. That is, if you feel up to helping me."

"You mean, help you free the other kids?" I nodded. "Sure," she said.

The mop-up took some time, but it was easy. Despite the fact that my companion had yet to come into her powers, I had no trouble carrying her back to mundane reality. Maybe the shadows helped me, I don't know. Afterwards, I killed the noncombatant Pentex staffer I found hiding in the building. Jennifer bandaged my shoulder. Together we found clothing. Then we trashed Cooper's files, drugs, and equipment.

Finally, we walked mumbling, stumbling teenagers around until they came to, then parked them in the lobby. Some couldn't stop crying; others wouldn't speak; many flinched at any noise or sudden movement. Though they weren't emaciated, their demeanor reminded me of photos I'd seen of death-camp survivors.

"You wimps make me sick!" I bellowed in my best drill-sergeant snarl. The teenagers jumped. "Don't you know why Cooper picked you to hurt? Because you're special! You have magic powers and a heroic destiny. Fate has chosen you to defend the world. So act like it, damn it! Stop sniveling. Stand up straight, and don't huddle together."

It worked to a degree. I jolted some of them out of their funk. A chunky black girl said, "What are you talking about? What's going to happen to us?"

And I realized it was a good question.

I didn't doubt that Nikos's pack would take them in. Like most troops, Nikos's pack was almost certainly eager for new blood. In fact, a mass recruitment might shore up the crippled leader's shaky position considerably. The problem was what would happen after that.

Garou aren't known for coddling their young. Certainly, the grim, cold Shadow Lords didn't. The kids would face a grueling series of tests, and for all I knew, they weren't up to it. There was no way to guess how much damage Cooper's experiment had done.

It was a disgusting thought, but I was afraid they were going to need a friend.

"Soon," I said, "you can go home if you want to. But first you have to spend some time with a secret society of people like yourselves. They'll teach you how to harness your hidden talents. It's what you need, and they're a good group—so good that I'm joining them myself. It's part of my reward for shutting this dungeon down."

Which only goes to show that there's more than one kind of wolf trap, and it's hard for any one Garou to dodge them all.

Shards

by Phil Brucato

"We've got to talk." Gerald's words had an ominous chill. Sara glanced up at him as they walked, and his eyes were as cold and distant as the San Francisco mist. *Here it comes*, she thought. She'd seen it coming, but felt no better for the knowledge. Tanglewood had meant what he had said. The loremaster's rites were more powerful than she would have guessed.

Gerald quietly refused to meet her gaze, but looked off into the fog. The cool sheen on his face reflected the orange glow of streetlights. Finally, he spoke. "I think that it may . . . we might . . . maybe we shouldn't see each other like this anymore."

A blow prepared for hurts just the same. Sara swallowed, and for a long time she said nothing, feeling the chilly, damp sand beneath her feet. They walked in silence for a time before she answered. "Just like that?" The words grated in her throat like glass. Gerald nodded. He had no answer. Sara hadn't expected him to. "Well, this certainly comes out of nowhere," she said, but she was lying. She had an idea of exactly where it had come from.

"Stand by the fire," Tanglewood had said. The loremaster's eyes reflected dancing flames as the bonfire bled its warmth into the August night. Sara padded carefully through the rock-studded clearing and took up a place by the fire, feeling the gaze of the pack upon her.

"You disappoint me," said Tanglewood. His voice

was heavy with sadness and anger. "You are Garou, but you are not pack to us. You dwell in your own life and wall out those who are your family. You shirk responsibility and set yourself apart, and yet you still have no wholeness, no sense of Gaia in your heart. The wolf and the woman are not one within you. Your soul is selfish and alone."

"That's not true!" Sara shot back. "And it's not fair! I'm new to all this! I'm just trying to get my bearings! This stuff takes time—"

"You have had time," Tanglewood thundered, "and you have wasted it. You see our tribe as some great new game, but you do not aspire what you must become! You are separate now, as you were two years ago, still woman and wolf, and not a whole Garou!"

"But—"

"We try to help you," he continued, "and you do not care. Your old life is still too important to you, and you cling to it like a child! Until you let it go, we can waste no more time with you." Sara shivered, and she crossed her arms against the hostile glare of her tribe. "If you wish to stand alone," said Tanglewood, "You shall."

Tanglewood's words rang hollow in her mind. Primal Rage stirred in her gut, black, frightening, all too familiar. Gerald, oblivious, walked beside her, searching the night mist for answers. "So, how long have you been thinking about this?" she asked.

"A few weeks."

"How long?"

"Over a month," he admitted. Sara glanced up sharply. The Rite had been three weeks earlier. "Any particular reason?" she demanded.

He shook his head. "A lot of reasons. I can't put them all into words."

"How about trying?" She looked at her feet, sticky with sand, as they walked. Doubt, fear, anger swirled up the back of her throat like bile. She bit her lip, feeding Rage with her own blood.

"I haven't felt too good about us lately," he admitted. "It's a lot of little things. Look," he said, stopping, "we're pretty young, okay?" This was true; Sara was just shy of eighteen, Gerald a little older. "Things never last at this age. I'm thinking about college after all, and I don't want to go to Berkeley. I just wanna go somewhere else."

"And leave me here."

"You never needed me to take care of you or anything," he said. Was there an accusation in his voice? "You'll find someone else."

"And so will you." She started walking again. She felt scabs pulled off deep inside, and the cuts were still raw underneath. The blood from her lip tasted good. "Bastard," she muttered. Gerald didn't answer, and they both walked in silence for a while. "Well," she demanded at length, "don't you have anything else to say?"

He shook his head and extended his hand, but she refused to take it. "Sara," he implored, "don't be this way."

"What way?" Her tone was bitter. "I saw it coming, you know. I did. I just want a reason. I want an explanation. After almost two years, I think I deserve one. Why are you doing this?" The question was a plea for some normal, rational, human reason beyond Tanglewood's curses. She said it knowing that Gerald had no answer, but wanting one all the same.

She met him soon after the First Change, when her life was in fragments. The taste of bad wine had been strong in her mouth that night, and her eyes were swollen from crying. Gerald had touched her shoulder and asked if she were all right. Sara had always been a bad liar, but she had refined it to an artform since that night.

He'd been a sweet guy, then, not quite eighteen and a bit awkward, too polite for his own good. It was always easy to keep her temper around him, and he accepted everything she told him with quiet deference. Sara had built a house of deceit to shield him from her new life, and had kept him as a barrier against the wolf. Gerald was soft, in a good way, a comfortable anchor, and she felt freer with him than she did with the pack. These walks on the beach became a ritual, a cleansing of her spirit. He had stood at the gateway to her humanity, the woman that the wolf could not command.

Now his voice was cold as the ocean and his eyes were hard as glass.

He stopped and turned away, looking out into the endless dark. Waves rumbled and hissed just out of sight, scattering the sands. "I'm not sure where we're going, Sara." he said after awhile. "We've been together for a long time, but I don't see where we're going."

"That's a lot of crap." Her tone was quiet and sharp. She restrained a sudden urge to shove him down into the sand and scream out the fury just beneath her words. Deep inside, below her human mask, Sara felt another, darker urge to hurt. Something inside her twisted and uncoiled. "Don't give me that shit, Gerald," she snarled. "I know you too well. Be straight with me, dammit! Is there someone else, or are you just bored?"

The words stung him. "Fuck you!" he snapped. "This isn't easy for me, dammit!"

"It's a real treat for me!" she shot back.

"Listen to me!" he shouted. Their eyes locked.

"You're asking for something I don't have," he said. "There is nobody else, Sara, no. I just . . . feelings don't always make sense. We can't . . . I have to go. I'm sorry."

You will be, said the wolf.

Sara had blinked back tears that night. The campfire stung her eyes, and she could not meet Tanglewood's gaze. Beside her, Bessa, in natural lupine form, snarled at the loremaster. Tanglewood glared in return as Bessa trotted up to her friend and brushed against Sara's legs, interposing herself in between the human cub and the angry loremaster. "Don't defend your charge, Bessa," Tanglewood growled. "She stands between two roads and will not choose. Until she does, she is of no use to us or to herself."

They performed the Outcast Rite and sent her away.

The wolf inside her reared its head. Sara felt its heat behind her eyes and fought to drive it down again. Gerald took her silence for speechlessness and reached for her. "Don't!" she snapped, and he flinched. Around him, the mist seemed to brighten. Sara's vision sharpened, and her heart jumped. The taste of Change, like a mouthful of summer grass, rose unbidden in her mouth. *Not now!* A voice inside her screamed. A sudden strong gust blew in from the sea, biting through her damp jeans and leather jacket, raising goosebumps on her bare skin. She shivered, but the chill went deeper, far deeper, than a cold misty breeze. She snarled. Gerald met her gaze, and she pinned him in place without raising a hand.

She had wandered the park for hours after the rite, daring some mugger to hassle her. None had. When she reached home, her Rage had built to a fever pitch, barely clenched by sheer will, and she paced the hardwood floor, muttering to herself until the dam broke inside and she hurled the first thing that came to hand—an incense burner shaped like a Chinese foo dog—and hurled it hard against the mirror. The bitter smash sent her into a frenzy of destruction, ripping furniture, trashing knick-knacks, baying in rabid fury.

The wolf had her in its jaws. Its Rage had shredded her apartment.

When her fury was spent, she sagged to the floor, weeping as she reverted to her human shape. Her clothes hung in tatters, and the mirrored glass bit into her knees. Blood welled up with the tears. She cried until she couldn't breathe, then reached for the phone.

When he came, he asked no questions. He only held her until she finished shaking, then helped her clean up the mess, his brown eyes clouded with concern.

"Sara?" Gerald's eyes were wide, his voice uncertain. The wolf in her wanted to rip those eyes from his head. It would be so easy, here, alone, to share her pain with him in ways he'd never forget. Words, torrents of fire, bloodlust, and worse boiled just out of reach. "Go home, Gerald," she said suddenly, breaking eye contact and turning away.

Was he to blame? Would things have ended this way if not for Tanglewood's rite? Did things run deeper than the rite, down below the surface of things they never talked about? Sara had built a wall of lies, to her pack, her lover, her self. What lies had Gerald built? He knew so little about her, really. How little did she know in return? She hurt too badly, now, to think about it. Better to puzzle through this later, when the wounds weren't raw.

"Hey, wait," Gerald called as Sara walked away. "We can talk about this!" Now he was beside her, reaching for her arm. She pulled away. "There's nothing to talk about," she replied. "You've said enough. Just go."

"I'm sorry."

"So am I, Gerald. Leave me alone. For your own good." Hurt lodged in her heart like a sliver of glass. Rage buzzed just beneath the surface. She had to get away.

"Is this it?"

"That was your decision." The wolf gnawed at her self-control; pain and loneliness, Rage, confusion and sadness washed through her like cold waves. Had she loved him, ever? Did she now? "Please just go." Too many questions, too many doubts.

Sara had sensed the difference in Gerald after that, the half-hidden glances when he thought she wasn't looking. No questions, ever. He hadn't thought to ask her what was wrong, not that she could've told him. He simply withdrew, like the pack, but without anger or recrimination. Less than three weeks after that night, Tanglewood's rite was complete. Or was it? Was this the loremaster's doing, or Gerald's, or her own?

"I'll take you home." He reached for her again.

"*Go!*" The word was a lash, and there was blood behind it. She dropped her human mask, and Gerald cowered, finally seeing the wolf in her eyes. Change bristled just beneath her skin. *Let me have him!* cried the wolf, and Sara stepped forward. Her prey stumbled backwards, sprawling in the sand. The fear in his eyes dimmed as she blocked the light, throwing her shadow across the sand. She could smell his sudden fear above the salty air. Her fingers curled into hooks, claws inching to extend from beneath the nails. Her teeth ached, sharpening into fangs. Only slivers of humanity kept her claws from his throat. Only shards of will kept the wolf inside.

"Get out of here," she rasped. Gerald scrambled to his feet, eyes rabbit-wide. Sara trembled, wanting to hug him, wanting to kill him, and turned away instead, striding ankle-deep into the freezing surf. She waited there, hugging her sides, until the Rage subsided. When she turned around, he was gone.

She howled until her throat was raw. The sound was lost in the roaring surf.

Hours later, Sara stood alone on the beach, awash with memories and cleansed by the Pacific wind. Her eyes stung, but she refused herself the luxury of crying. The sliver moon was hidden, wrapped in shimmering mist that enveloped her like a mother's womb. This womb, though, was damp and cold, like the icy part inside of her. Sara's breath was mist before her face, and waves washed her bare feet. There was a chill, pristine beauty in the night, and both wolf and woman welcomed it together. The cool wind soothed Sara. Her sadness lingered, but the bitterness had faded. It was about time, she thought, to be reborn.

"The wolf and the woman are not one within you," Tanglewood had said. After the last few hours, though, Sara felt that they had come to some sort of understanding. With no one else to run interference, neither had a choice.

In the distance along the beach, the flicker of beach bonfires warmed the dancing mist. From one came the sound of drums, laughter, and off-key singing, all mingling with the roar of endless waves. Sara paused, recalling similar nights with Gerald, with Rick and Ray, Shelly and the mousy blonde with a name no one could pronounce. Cool wet nights in the fog with a fire and a beer and a pack of old friends. Gone now, only memories. It was a good night for sorrow, but sorrow was a waste of time. Her life was smashed to splinters, now. Better to bury the pieces and move on.

Down the beach a ways, firelight glittered on a rash of broken glass, bottles jutting from a blackened mound of sand. Sara swore as she approached the mess. The campfire embers guttered, smoke rose into fog, and the tracks of the bastards who'd left this disaster led up to the pavement and away. By the look of the fire, they were long gone. Pity.

She knelt beside the fire and carefully scooped up the largest pieces, tossing them into a paper bag. As she worked, Sara remembered Gerald, cleaning up bits of broken mirror. Maybe I'm not the only one, she thought, who got stuck cleaning up someone else's mess. The larger pieces were easy to find, Sara thought. The hard part was finding the splinters, the stubborn shards of glass half-hidden in the sand. No matter how carefully you picked them away, she reflected, some always waited below the surface, any one of them large enough to draw blood or to lodge painfully in bare skin. You could sift the sand all night and never catch all the shards.

But a few tiny shards in the sand evaded her grasp, leaving large, sharp fragments laying around. Given time, the sea would wear away the splinters until the shards and sand were one. Until then, she guessed, you just took your chances and hoped that you never stepped on the broken glass.

Her legs were cramped by the time she finished. She stretched and grunted, then carefully took the bag. The glass inside rustled thinly as she searched the sand a final time. You can never get them all, she thought. Sara brushed damp hair from her eyes with a sandy hand. It would have to do. She dumped the bag of shards in a nearby trashcan and headed back across the sand to the ocean's edge.

One less bag of glass. A few less shards to litter the beach. Not a clean sweep, but it would have to do.

Rootbound

by R. S. Martin

I wake up with the ground grinding against itself like teeth. Earthquake. All around, my house is shivering loose from itself. Has this happened before? I don't remember.

It's dark in here and it's dark outside, so it's night. What time is it? This is one of those times when a clock would come in handy, but they always stop. Call it three in the morning for want of working clocks. A good time for teeth to grind. A cityful of broken bones screeching like yellow chalk when they touch, making sure they hit each other's sore spots. The ground's not supposed to do that. It's supposed to lie there, buried underfoot, and carry its burdens in peace.

While the firm ground gnashes its teeth and snarls on all sides, I start to panic, hoping that the world didn't change while I slept. So I pull on my eyes and look out the cracks in the window glass. My hair falls in my eyes almost at once, force of habit, and I brush it back again. I don't know what color it is or what I look like, so I don't ask. I forget.

Outside my window there's Richmond, same as it ever was. Rows of close-trimmed yards, unassuming houses reflecting each other across long, undistinguished streets. Richmond. My neighborhood of square houses embroidered with personal touches that distract us in the suburbs from the numbness of the days. Land of garden furniture and quaint wicker arches, where lawns are taken seriously. If ever a neighborhood were to put off grinding the teeth in its foundations until three in the morning, to keep the neighbors from hearing, it would be Richmond. I can respect that philosophy.

Always a relief when your neighborhood doesn't die in your sleep. It's happened. You lay your body down to rest a little piece, and when you wake up, they've bulldozed your house and you're in a parking lot. Every time I fall asleep, I'm always a little afraid it'll happen to me. I'll wake up, and it'll be the year 2525 or something. Everything and all the people will be gone, and that will be that.

The ground keeps straining against the foundations of the house. One by one the splinters of the broken windows fall from their frames, making sounds like sighing. Upstairs, something heavy falls to the floor, and the roots of the house creak in sympathy. A crash like that is about as close to coffee as I get these days. I am awake.

There's a fog up tonight, but between the streetlamps' haze and the thick moonlight, the trees along the street look like autumn. Hard to tell, though. With a few of them bare of leaves and the rest of them gold and black, it's hard to tell. Could be the tail end of winter, just before budding starts. Could be October. Call it October.

Out of the broken corner of the window, the beacon at Saint Ignatius's shimmies at me through the fog. Such a tease. I already have a girl.

Girl. Angel. I'm in love with a statue, you know, a wooden statue of an angel. I know full well what "statue" means. Inanimate person-shaped object. Mute, immobile, insensate for all I know. Doll. Around here, though, you take love where you find it.

I keep her upstairs. Where I just heard something heavy fall. I drop my eyes to the floor and I'm up the stairs and in the Angel's room now and she's in bad shape.

The earthquake must have knocked her off her pedestal. Instead of smiling down at me, she grimaces up from the floor, almost snapped in half, with dry leaves and dust pouring out from all these new cracks in her. In her willowy figure. She always was slim. There's a branching fracture in her left side, just under . . . just under her heart.

I really don't want to see any more, but I've seen worse. It may be my job to see worse, but I still feel sick to see you like this, Angel. What's this, a dull spot on the wall behind you, like a bruise made of sawdust? Did you hit yourself against the wall? Why are your wings just hanging there, all crumpled? They've shaken loose. Why are you holding your arm like that? It looks like it's broken. Is there something wrong with your face? Don't tell me. It can wait.

My poor wooden angel. The earthquake's shaken her all loose from herself. I know all about that.

I'm not going to let her suffer any longer than she has to.

It hurts to see her like this, unanchored. I try to lever her back to her place on her pedestal, make her comfortable, but she's heavy. I'd forgotten how heavy she is. Every few minutes her head and shoulders bounce a bit against the wall when the ground reminds us to take it seriously. I remember, I remember how that feels.

Push. Pull. Sick. Shove. Swear. Plead. Pull, don't cry. There are splinters where her hair was.

This isn't working. I've got to get focused here. I'm in San Francisco. California. My name is Andrew. Andrew Patrick Malone. I go to the University of San Francisco. Dick Nixon is president. There's a war on. Focus.

Hold her hands. My hands hold her. She lurches, half-doll, half-dancer, and I pull her upright again. As I pull, her wedged, twisted, bent parts scrape against the wall, spilling the dust of her insides everywhere. But she's upright.

I made her myself, a long time ago. There's birch

bark in her, and brown, papery leaves for her wingfeathers. I found a smashed chair in the garage and made the pieces into a skeleton for her. Slats for her ribcage, chair legs for her delicate forearm bones, and the seat for her hips. Then I worked outward, tying everything together with roots twined and knotted together. Roots are what bind her together, binding everything to make a single Angel.

I feel a little lightheaded. Something's changed. Roots. Roots are beautiful things. The tragedy's that they're almost always buried, down in the earth where no one can see them. The smallest, palest flowers, blooming upside down in the dark, whispering to each other with no one else to hear. In my Angel, like everything else here in the shadows, everything works upside down, and for once the roots walk around out in the open, above ground. That's the secret. Here, it's the flowers that work to bind the roots in place.

The aftershocks are finally winding down. The ground loses interest in saying whatever it had to say and trails off, mumbling to itself more and more quietly until the night is silent again.

I hate earthquakes. Either they wake you up at three in the morning or they kill you before your eyes are open. I'm always afraid I won't be able to tell which is which before it's too late: whether I'm awake or dead, whether it's the first day of the world or the last.

Outside my windows, morning's breaking and the sky cuts itself on the pieces. Dawn turns the sky red in streaks like gashes and they bleed for awhile, but then the white sun finally rises through the fog and the clouds go white again. Gradually, the room goes gray. It settles into the routine of morning like the colorless dust on floors and walls. Dust trying to settle in an empty, wooden room.

Someone used to like to say I always "took the

weather too personally." I wonder if I should remember who it was. Whether I take the morning too personally or not, the light helps me evaluate the damage, which is the important thing. The house really doesn't matter, but there doesn't seem to be anything wrong that wasn't wrong before. The plaster's still cracked, the pipes are still rusting, the window's still broken. If anything, the earthquake only managed to shake the dust off things. It's a tough old house.

The important thing is always the Angel. Her wings need new weaving before I lace them back into her shoulders, but first I need to mend that hole in her side. Experimentally, I trace the jagged, splintery edges of the crack and gently kiss her dust off my fingers. My poor, shaken Angel. It won't hurt long.

What if I can't fix this? For courage, I look down into the perfect curves of her face, to draw balance from her, but instead, I draw only dust. I can hardly recognize her. The fall shifted something in her cheek. Now when she smiles at me, her roots unwoven and exposed, I feel weaker. Weaker and so very tired. Please don't look at me like that.

There's also something wrong with her eyes. I made them out of heartwood, the palest, tenderest treasure of the vegetable kingdom. This morning, they're infected with something red, accusing, and feverish. Instead of looking softly at me, they glare. It's not my fault. Does her left look darker? Bloodshot as dawn. I wonder what it means for an angel's eyes to go all red in earthquake weather. Something in the air? The delicate fibers in the heartwood chips seem dried out, like fruits left out in the air for too long. Red in heartwood. A bad sign, whatever it is, and it needs to be fixed.

It reminds me of how Ceille looked, how red and tired-looking her eyes got when we had the argument and didn't look back. They looked like golden islands in a watery red sea. The first continents must have looked like that, when everything was earthquakes and Atlantis swam on the magma ocean and rain fell for a hundred thousand years. I remember thinking, "This must be what real life is like: red and bottomless, brimming over, dilating, afraid to blink."

Ceille. Celatia. That was her name. She always used to tease me about taking the weather too personally, getting too nervous when it was just the world.

Now it's my Angel who's crying. It's not my fault. I'd do the crying for her if I could take the time, but there's too much to do and it's not my fault. I didn't mean to say the wrong thing, Ceille. It just got to where I couldn't keep quiet any more.

I wish I'd told you sooner.

This Angel of mine. She may be made of wood, but even broken like this, she's the only angel I have. That means something.

Whatever happened to Ceille, I wonder. I don't think I ever saw her again, after the gold continents of her eyes got red. I went off to school and woke up every day and made my face and voice work. She wrote me for a few months, but I could never bring myself to open the letters. Finally, I had the accident, and the mail stopped coming.

Sometimes, around this time of the evening, the wooden angel reminds me of her.

And I begin to work.

The first part's covering the gaps in her side. As gently as I can, I unroll her bark skin from the wound's edges and unlatch her rib cage. It slides easily on its hinge; when I first made her, I made sure that I'd be able to adjust her heartstrings whenever I needed to. Ceille taught me that much. Then the work begins, and one by one I knot each of her roots and twigs back into place in the weave of her body. The tremor and the fall knocked whole tissues of her loose and distorted what was left. This will take awhile, but it distracts me from how hurt she is.

It's a complicated trade, making things, making people, but it's what we Pardoners do. Every one of her now-frayed threads needs to be laced by hand, woven back into the fabric of my Angel, coerced to follow the pattern on its own. Most of these roots and things in here have been dead for a long time, and they've gotten dry and stiff. The dry parts don't go out of their way to help you, especially if they're old bits of the weave that have come loose in an earthquake. They need to be coaxed, one by one, gently bent back and ever so slowly re-knotted about one another in the corset of her small Angel's body.

Pardoners. Pardon me. When I was younger, I was always apologizing. I took responsibility for everything. Taking the weather personally. It got to be a habit, then a responsibility by itself, even when, really, I wasn't sorry at all. Ceille always used to poke me when I did that. What did she say? "There's a difference between truth and manners," was that it? It doesn't matter. I work for Manners, for the pale ghosts up in the Presidio, and not for not truth.

As the day goes on, the wind picks up outside, and the sky never recovers from being cold and white. Funny, these ghosts of absent weather. When you sit still for a bit and listen closely, the wind blows up off the ocean, and no matter how hard it shakes the houses and old, jagged trees it can't blow the fog away. The sky has faultlines, too, and every so often it stumbles up there on the tightrope: ghosts of absent weather.

Finally, her insides are all back in place and I tie the laces of her ribcage tight. Not even scars remain to embarrass her. I owe her that much at least. I crumple up some newspaper headlines I've been saving and fill her empty corners with them, assassinations and wedding attempts. No time for hugs; the most I can manage is to trail my fingers across the memory of her wound. Arm comes next.

She was wrong, that girl Ceille. It's the weather that takes me personally. As I wind the vegetable tendons in her graceful pianist forearm, I can hear this dry ocean wind pour down the streets in gusts, shearing what's left of the seeing, hearing leaves of the elm trees. All around me out there wooden giants are going blind, and the isolation of winter's starting again. Unless they sleep with their roots twined, every one of them is alone now. I'd almost feel sorry for them.

I caught one in the air once. A falling leaf. I just put out my hand and it fell right into my fingers. I'd never caught a leaf on the fall before. I felt so proud, turning it over in my fingers to look at it and marvel.

And it was all diseased. Infested. There was some kind of fungus in its side that had made it grow a patch of little, tiny centipede legs. A leaf with legs, or hair, or tentacles. That was the leaf that I managed to catch in the air, before it even hit the ground.

I braid the tender, new-sprouted roots of her open wrist as carefully as I can, holding every tendril of her flesh between my fingers as if it were something living, and I look at her face. Her veins, her nerves, the tendons of a cheek muscle to let her smile and sob. When I first made her, I had to weave every thread of angel separately. I worked without rest breaks. I worked without slowing. When I got too exhausted to touch her anymore with my hands, I held her roots between my teeth and nudged them into place with my face, kissing her to perfection.

Other people in my age cohort were always making visits to see their families, their loved ones, anything they'd left behind. I had my wooden angel for all of that. I wove her out of the wooden thoughts of plants, and the others struggled and despaired, and now they are all gone and only I remain. But I am a Master Pardoner, and I have perfected my trade. Everything a Pardoner can teach you is woven in my angel's hair.

The wind's picking up. You can always tell when the weak joints in the houses begin to rock, slowly and gently, and underneath your brain you think you're at sea. Strong weather tends to follow earthquakes, which makes sense when you think about it. It's like this new science, ecology: everything's connected, and when you unbalance one piece of it, the others wobble too. I like to think of it as some kind of circus act, tightropes again. Once the seismic plates lose their balance, the tightrope swings wildly, disturbing the other acrobats. At the bottom of the world, everything's roots are connected. For better balancing.

I was going to be a writer, you know. In the style of Professor Tolkien at Oxford, and David Lindsay and Mervyn Peake, I was going to make worlds. She was going to be an actress. I never had anything perfect enough to publish before the accident. The Presidio crowd must be hating this weather, though. Especially Brannan; he's always going around saying, "When the wind blows, Cradle will rock." I can see him now, huddled in a packing crate with his money, trying to take it with him just in case. Not the best kind of boss I can think of, but there are worse.

The nice thing about work is that it gives you something to do with your time. Every now and then, they send someone down from the Presidio with a work order: "This manacle seems to be fraying; this thrall's chains need to be let out a bit so it can sleep; could you work this line of thralls into the new buttresses for the Citadel; think about techniques for getting Beacons." Brannan thinks he needs to move his money into a smaller, tighter box. The Spaniard doesn't trust his harbingers any more so he sends a prerecorded oratorio, burning cold and whispery. He wants some pikes.

They all like my chains best, of course. I learned manacles when I was building my angel out of gathered roots. If you want the deepest secret of manacle-molding, it's there: gather the heartstrings of your thrall and put them in his mouth, and let your thrall chain himself for you. Chains have to work out from the inmost if they're going to work at all. They've got to start near the face. I chain all the new acquisitions.

I'm touching up the delicate roots of her face now. Reweaving a face is one of the hardest tricks of the trade, harder even than names. There are thousands of roots in any expression, and every single one has to speak with its own voice if you don't want to end up with just another death mask. Anyone can craft a still life. Anyone can map someone's scars and memories. What I do is make dead things that seem to move, to breathe when you're not paying attention.

It takes complete concentration over a period of several days to put a decent face on anything. I tend to charge extra for custom work: "brave" faces, "strong" faces. It's not that I mind the extra effort, but it's distracting, and the request usually goes against the grain of the material.

I love her face. It's my best work, only the best raw ingredients. She reminds me of Ceille. That's ingredients enough.

After awhile the day starts again, but the wind never stops. If anything, it's getting worse. Behind the familiar white of the sky, the clouds look like sore, black bruises forming. Looks like a storm coming soon. All the leaves have fallen.

I'm buried deep in her face, with roots knotted around both hands, vegetable rings on all my fingers. Every contour in her face matters. The way it used to get a little lopsided when she laughed late at night. The way her chin jutted when she talked about her parents. Her forehead. Every fiber is the most important thing in the world. You need absolute precision to fix a face, and complete concentration. You have to be able to close your eyes and rebuild it from memory. Faces are complicated, mysterious things. When I'm doing one, I don't notice the weather. I don't apologize. You can't afford it on facework.

I'm buried deep in her jawline, where everything comes together. Jaw, neck, earlobe. Hairline and the roots of her teeth. Suddenly, a noise. I turn slightly without realizing it and pull something loose from her throat. It sounds like a scream of some kind, but also like a police siren and like the call of large birds, and then it cries again.

Company?

When I pull out to get the door, I'm stuck in her and she won't let go. Her jaw's snarled around my fingers. I try to disentangle myself, but the roots of her face argue with me, and the siren screams again. Let me go, Angel. I'll be back soon. Please.

Something bangs downstairs, but my hands are stuck. Crazy thing. Before, all I could think about was how beautiful Ceille's face was, but I could never let myself get close enough to touch it. Now here I am, and her cheek won't let go. No matter how hard I try to slip out, she won't let go. Finally I'm reduced to yanking my fingers out of her face, one by one. I'm sorry. I'm sorry. I try not to look, but I know she's watching me with those red eyes. Masses of half-knitted root flesh rip out with my fingers.

Another bang. No time to cry, no time to fix things. I wedge the door open and it's one of Brannan's Greenback messengers, wearing his Crown of Thorns and Brannan's colors. The faded, almost-yellow green the shade of collector's paper dollars, trimmed in much darker green for Emerald Legion; the color of shadows cast by leaves in sunlight. He looks like he's in a hurry. Young. The house moans with the wind, but somehow he manages to stand tall. The weather doesn't affect him, but he's letting it into my house.

He touches a finger to the point of his Crown of Thorns in salute, and I tug at the Pardoners' banded chain on my arm in return, my fingers still a mass of knotted roots. I look like I'm sprouting. I wonder what they want in the Presidio now. Surgical tools? Bayonets?

He glances at me and into the house and gets a little skittish. All the Presidio errand boys do that. There seems to be something invisible on the walls that only he can see, and he develops a kind of tic, always darting his head about. Nod, jerk his head to check behind him, as if he's heard something. Smile, glance down in horror to check out his feet. Wasteful use of one's time. And energy. The harbingers always remind me of magpies.

He starts with the usual preamble and steals another minute of my working time. I wish he'd hurry up. He's stilted, pretentious, and even a bit arrogant around the mouth, but not in any way of which he's self-conscious. Of course.

Shoddy face-work. It looks like he did it himself. I could fix that around the mouth. All it needs is to pull his lip back a bit on this side, give him a little humility.

"Brannan the Shopkeeper, LXIVth Hegemon of the Legion of Thorns, Thane of the Inflators, Greenback Despot and True Founder of the Dominion of San Francisco, sends this message to Malone, Master in the Guild of Pardons. In Charon, all."

In what must have become a sleepwalker habit, he pulls the black leather collar of his uniform open and shows me the brands on his throat. I've seen it before and nod, go ahead. He gives his message. Apparently a party of old-time Temperance wrackers managed to escape from the Winchester House up in San Jose and got caught trying to hook up with Lo Ma Cameron's people near Chinatown. Needless to say, "Greenback" Brannan wants only the best manacles to graft onto his new "investments." The best for his money.

None of this matters to me. Brannan and the others get their toys, and they leave me alone. But now, I've got an angel's face drying in my fingers, and the errand boy goes on, listing the members of the Winchester group, their marks, visible signs of child-bearing on one of the females, and I catch myself noticing that none of this matters to me. Is this a bad thing? I think it used to bother me when things like this didn't matter. He seems to be winding down so I force myself to pay attention. ". . . Terms of payment satisfactory. I can't ask you to labor on the Sabbath of course, so you can start measuring for the bridles tomorrow night, or as it suits you. Yrs, Samuel Brannan, Hegemon so on, so forth. Message ends."

Sabbath? I look for my voice, trying to remember where I'd last heard it, how it worked. For a moment or two I experiment with what sounds like wheezing. Finally, I come close enough to make myself heard, and I ask him. "Sabbath? A holiday soon, I take it. We won the war?"

He pauses for the smallest moment and reaches up to tip his Crown of Thorns to a slightly different and probably more comfortable angle. Finding his off-duty face, I imagine. His posture shifts slightly and he nods again, a little taller, a bit relaxed. "Halloween! Not even Brannan can ask you to work on Halloween, and he knows that."

"Oh, yes," I say.

His mouth twitches. "You do remember that it's tonight, don't you? The big one. Halloween."

I try to remember what comes next in conversations

like this. "Halloween. Um. October. Trick or treat. I'm sure you're excited."

He nods, and you'd almost think there was more to him than the uniform, winged shoes, ears that hear and mouth that talks. I say "Well, hurry up. Message receipt acknowledge. Close to sundown. Get going." He's gone before I finish.

Halloween. I'm back in the Angel's room, through my darkened windows watching the boy flicker as he darts back up to the citadel. I catch myself hoping I'm his last duty of the day so he can get to whatever it is he wants to do.

He's probably going to spend the night tracking down the "mystery" of his death. Stupid to wear your heart on your uniform like that, but that's the way those guys are, so confident that the world is holding its breath just because they died without knowing why.

I miss Ceille. I wonder what she's doing.

It's getting dark out again. Halloween, mm?

When we were younger, we had this game where we'd call up all the radio stations and dedicate songs to each other. Any song. It got to where we'd have to make up fake voices to trick the DJs, or bribe them, or whatever it took.

I still remember the phone numbers. Funny. I push my voice in the direction of next door, where my phone is. Push. Tip the table, knock the earpiece off. Turn the dial, one number at a time. I don't even notice how hard this is. The other end rings. Someone, a woman, says "KOTO Request Line."

I push my voice over the telephone. "Could I make a dedication? The Fairports, 'Meet on the Ledge'? From Andrew to Ceille?"

She asks, "Could you turn your radio down, please? We're getting a lot of feedback and I can't hear you."

I push harder to make myself heard. "Could you play 'Meet on the Ledge'? By the Fairport Convention."

My voice is starting to get heavy, and I have to sit down, very slowly to keep the connection. She comes back. "No, we don't have it. It's either too new or stolen or something. Got an alternate?"

Push. It's heavy, and I can't make it very loud. "Also by them, 'Who Knows Where the Time Goes'?"

She says, "Also by them? Sorry, but they said we don't have anything by the Fairport Convention down here. To tell the truth, I don't think I've ever heard of them. Must be too obscure or too new for the station."

Pause. "Hello? Must be a bad connection. Hang up and try again."

The phone clicks and I drop my connection too. I'm too tired to dial again.

It's still very dark in here with my Angel. I look at her for a second or two before I remember what I'm looking at. She doesn't return the favor, but stares at the ceiling with her dried-blood heartwood eyes. Angel, angel. Have you forgotten me, Celatia? I know, it happens to me when I just wake up, too. It's me, though. Andrew. Every day in school I wrote you letters, and you wrote me back. Do you remember now?

It's me, Angel. We talked a lot about being perfect. About living life as a work of art, with every breath counting, every move of your head a gesture for the finished product. You wanted everything you did to be perfect. Whenever anyone wanted you to compromise, you'd do something extreme instead. I just wanted to be perfect, and that meant never doing anything too extreme.

We talked. About mind games, about life, about trust and about truth. We promised each other we'd never lie to each other. You showed me your scars and I showed you mine.

Ceille? Something's gone wrong with your eyes.

I need to go back downstairs to get some fresh materials from the backyard. To replace what got wasted when the idiot from Thorn interrupted me. The nice thing about work is that it makes you forget that time is going by.

It's spooky out here now. The moon's out, glimmering in the fog. Is it still Halloween? I've lost track again. The weather's gotten past the point of a thunderstorm. It's heavy, like a cut that's been put off for too long and which has festered. Too much up in the air even to fall as rain, so we have wind without movement, fog without rain. Up above, the moon gives light but no heat.

I go to one of the overgrown flowerbeds and start digging, down through the dry husks, black and cloudy amber in the moonlight. Down through the piles of brown, blind leaves. Down between the jagged stumps of rotten poppies until I get to the depth of the soft, dark mud, where the roots are.

Odd how I don't dig up any bones. You see, this entire neighborhood used to be the big cemetery district. Blocks and blocks of boneyard, from the park to the other side of that hill over there where St. Ignatius' is, but they had to move the corpses to build houses for the living. I don't know what they did with the tombstones. Pardoners got hold of enough of them to build the seawall back in the '30s, but I don't know what happened to the others. I hear you can still read the names on that sea wall, if you know where to look at low tide.

In this neighborhood, you get used to digging up bones in your yard. Generations of hereditary gardening has mined out most of the deposits by now, but you always wonder if today will be the day you find someone's finger in your roses. Some people dig and they get treasure. Here, you dig up bones.

No bones this time, only roots. Nothing in my hole but the white, twisted roots of the dead flowers. Dad was right when he said there's nothing worse than a tree that's gotten its roots knotted, growing inward, slowly strangling itself. They grow underground, like a cannibal forest, all these vegetable worms crawling over each other with no room to stretch out, no time to stop and think. Feeding frenzy over not enough dust.

The dogwood trees that Dad brought in from back east look dead, so I bet they're rootbound too. It's hard to tell in autumn, of course, but I wouldn't be surprised if this whole yard wasn't a huge, petrified thicket of suffocated roots just under the surface. I bet they tried to get under the house, hitting their heads in vegetable blind slow-motion against the concrete foundations until they ran out of strength. Under the house.

It's almost funny, walking on roots. Every step I take, I'm walking on tightropes. A hundred, a million tightropes, all tangled back on themselves like a maze, without ever knowing when I took that first step out on the wire. Without knowing where the other end is, if there is one. Tightropes wound around skulls and tectonic fissures, and none of us can sleep at night. You either keep moving or you fall.

One of the last notes I ever wrote to Ceille had a tightrope in it. Maybe it was the last one. I don't remember that much, but I remember this one. I used to work on them for hours, writing and then rewriting to leave just enough hints but not enough to get myself in trouble. It was a balancing act, and I guess I was too careful up there, didn't take enough risks. She should have figured it out. I made enough hints.

But because of all the rewriting I remember what I said, more or less, about tightropes.

> *It is possible, Ceille, to lead one's life with perfect circumspection. They tell you that nobody's perfect, that everyone makes mistakes. That's bogus. Every single tightrope walker now living is perfect.*

> *Balance is the secret. Being perfect means having total balance, being able to remain perfectly still. There are a lot of tightrope walkers out there in a lot of carnivals; if anyone ever tells you that everyone makes mistakes, point to the tightrope walkers, suspended alone between heaven and earth. The tightrope walkers. Happiness doesn't matter. It's a distraction. The wire cuts your feet up there, and your feet bleed, but it has to be tight if you're going to balance.*

There. Behold my only surviving work. Andrew P. Malone, R.I.P., survived by a pretentious fragment on tightropes, now probably also lost.

I remember the way your head would tilt when you were struck by something completely tangential to what people were actually trying to say. It was . . . it was as if someone invisible were talking to you, and you were trying very hard to listen, the way that dogs and cats listen. Looking at you listening, I always wondered what had struck you that was so terribly important that you would freeze like a forest animal. I wanted to touch your cheek then, every time. I remember the way you held a pencil, the way you ducked your chin when you'd swallow.

All the windows are still broken in the garage. I did that, right before my accident, broke them one by one. Funny how my hands never hurt.

I wish I'd told you sooner, Ceille. I wish I'd had the guts or the sense or the confidence to have told you sooner and then gotten on with it from there.

I wish my life had somehow been allowed to have more dialogue in it.

It's begun to rain.

It starts like it always does, with one drop falling for its own reasons, preparing the way, cooling the air as it falls. Then another drop falls, and another soon after, and then the sky loses control of itself. Before you know what's happening, drops are falling in sheets of water, running together in falling streams, and the clouds collapse into a vertical river falling to earth as they forget more and more of their balance.

Rain smells different now. Before the accident, it smelled fresher, more like lightning in the air. Now it smells like old newspapers in the gutter, or like inland, shut-in oceans, rain from the Dead Sea, whole lakes clotted with the white corpses of fish. I bring a hand up to cover my nose, but that only makes the rot worse, and the rain fills my eyes faster than I can blink it away. I'm running apart in the rain, like wax. There's a shape in the second-story window of the house and it looks at me with red eyes.

Rain-channels cut deep into the lawn, tracing strange calligraphy around flowerbeds and between blades of grass. Wherever they go, the channels unbury the roots of plants. In their tangles, the roots are their own maze, with the giants under the dogwood trees and the eyelashes of the dead poppies all together in knots. The roots are growing in secret, underground, an inverted garden of white flowers, a sea-anemone garden swaying underwater.

The storm and the thunder run together with the raindrops into a drone. Ohhh, says the voice behind the thunder. Looooow. Naaaay. Oh. Lo. Ne, and again. Does that sound familiar somehow? Is that you, Angel? No, it's someone else. Was it one of the voices buried deep in the earthquake, one of the teeth that ground? I don't remember. I don't remember. I wasn't paying attention.

It is easy, it is easy, someone says. I am fascinated by these trenches opening up like canyons, like the map of a battle or the human hand, forcing solid ground apart like wet paper. I feel like I'm on the only bit of firm land left in the world. I sway a little, almost falling.

It is easy, it is easy. I take a step onto the tightrope garden. Roots and rivulets. Step, then another. Balance.

Oh low ne.

There are other people here, men and women and children with olive skin and long dark hair, just standing still, dressed in loincloths, all of them crying. Some of them have seashells in their hair, and their alphabet is knots. Ohhhh, low nay. Oh. Lonely. Oh lo ne.

Everything is blooming upside down. I can't see straight with eyes full of rain. I forgot the important things like eyelashes. I stagger a little, it's thrown my balance off. The mud is slippery and I have to go slow to keep from falling.

There's something just ahead. The dogwoods are bursting into rootbound bloom.

Here I am, and you are walking very slowly against the gray sky, the yellow haze. She is going away again.

On the other end of the strand between the rising water she is there. Ceille, I missed you. How've you been? She smiles. The smile I remember best. I've been well, Ceille. I've been dead, but otherwise no complaints. She nods.

We're in a scene now, the ghost of her and I. Both of us have our lines perfectly. It's like we've been doing this dialogue every night for years. We're old pros.

"Ceille, I was wondering if we could maybe get married," I say, reading from the script in my head. I wanted to write.

She tilts her head and looks sad. As if it comes as any surprise, but she was always an actress. "Andrew?" she says.

I nod sadly, going over the lines one more time. "I mean," I say, quoting myself, "we could wait until after school, but I think it would be nice. We could wait, or maybe even just get an apartment or something somewhere for awhile."

She flashes a small smile. There's a nervous giggle

in her voice that makes me want to break something. "Andrew, this is a joke, right? We haven't even really dated or anything."

"But. . . ." I say. "I don't know any couples closer than we are. None of them really talk. We're great together, and I love you."

The smallest pause in the rain. The ghost twitch of a smile. "I love you too, Andrew, but just not like that. I never knew you were interested.

"You're my favorite person in the world, but I just never thought about you that way. Romantically."

"Why?" I say, losing interest in keeping up my part. I just want to leave.

"You can't explain these things, Andrew. I just never did. Maybe if you'd made some sign, given me some kind of hint, I would have had some time to think about this. It wouldn't be so much of a surprise." She looks somehow different from what I remember. Not nearly as fragile, but nicer somehow. More solid?

"I can change. C'mon. Just give me a hint. What have I been doing wrong?"

"Nothing, Andrew. You're fine, I'm sure. I just . . . oh, Andrew, don't be sad. It'd kill me if you were sad over this."

I think of reasons, then. She doesn't want to talk about them. I say some other things. She walks away, back into the rainstorm. She writes, but I never read the letters. And then I'm dead.

This time, I change the scene. When she turns away, I follow.

It's hard in the rain to keep track of her and keep my footing both. I wish she'd turn around and notice me. Between the roots and the mud trying to make me stumble I'm not making much ground. None of the tightropes in the lawn lead to where I need to go. Tracing their dead ends and knots wears me out, and I can barely see her in the rain now.

There's something in my way. Is it her? It looks like her. It has her eyes and her hair the color of cinnamon, and her height and her wrists and her neck. I'm so grateful she noticed I was following her.

I start to apologize for what I said when I notice that it has wings, and it isn't her. I'm too tired to go around the angel, so I stop. I can't go around. I might trip on a bone. I might get tangled in roots. I'd fall off my wire. But she's in my way and I can't see Ceille anymore.

"Pardon me," I say to my angel, hoping she will move so I can catch up with Ceille.

The angel doesn't say anything.

"Move over," I say. "I have to catch her."

The angel doesn't move. I shouldn't be surprised. When did she ever move, what did she ever say?

"Please get out of the way," I say, almost sobbing. Every word takes an entire breath. I can't see where Ceille's gone. Talking to the statue only kills valuable time that I need. I need it so much to meet up with her one last time.

I'm tired.

I scream at the angel. "You're just a doll! Get out of the way!" I try to push past it, but the rain makes me lose my balance and we both fall together in the mud. I dart my head up to try and see Ceille, but it's too late. The statue lies there, unblinking, with red wooden eyes in the rainstorm.

I call, but I've lost sight of her. "I miss you," I yell. "I love you." No one answers. She's gone. All the people are gone. After awhile, my voice breaks and I start to cry and it goes on for a long time with the rain.

After awhile I notice that I'm still here, facedown in the mud. The storm has tapered off into a sort of warm drizzle. The thunder has stopped talking. I am alone again in the yard.

No allegories, no angels, wooden or otherwise. This is what is true. I am in my backyard, in San

Francisco, after the rain. The grass has gone wild over the years, and the dogwood tree I used to play in when I was small has gone to thorns and knotted, mazy branches. In the moonlight, the grass is silvery black against the fence, and the last of the dogwood flowers are fragile, ghost-white, caught in the thorns. My father planted the dogwoods and he made that fence. Here, behind it, the yard is tangled and overgrown with weeds, rootbound and dry, but it is alive. And I am here, dry and dead, but I can still move, and maybe move to somewhere better.

There is a woman with the improbable, searing name of Celatia Thompson, and she was a girl who breathed and who was wonderful. There was a statue made of dry tinder and many, many gathered roots, and it cast a shadow that resembled the woman and blocked the sight of her until she was gone.

It's too late. Again.

It would be easy to die here, to breathe mud and run downstream with it. It would be easy to linger and dry out here with my roots exposed, turning red and dusty. But on the other hand, it's just as easy to drink the rain. I stand up and step off the tightrope and I'm on solid ground.

Time goes by. It's day, now night again, with a million small stars blinking in space and no one but a few specialists knows their names. From time to time one of them loses its balance, sparks, goes out. Time goes on. I'm not going to chain the Winchester ghosts for Brannan. Or anyone else. No more chains, not for awhile, if ever. Starting now, I resign all my commissions. When I turn back from the sky, I see my Angel staring up at me from her place. She can stay there. I don't think I'll go back to working on her, at least for awhile.

The Art of Dying

by Lawrence Watt-Evans

The lights came up in a sudden blaze, driving the darkness away from the easel, back to the studio loft's furthest corners, confining the night's gloom to the shadowy spaces behind the sparse furnishings—and of course, to the world outside.

Bethany suppressed her displeasure and discomfort at this abrupt, unexpected brightness; she would have thought that Anton would have chosen softer, more romantic light, but apparently he was sincere in wanting her to *see* his work.

She glanced at the canvas, not expecting much—not expecting anything, in truth, but to not even look would have been rude, and she liked to think that she was never unintentionally rude. Anton seemed so very intense about his artistic efforts; she really had to at least pretend to take them seriously.

The casual glance lengthened, and turned into a stare. She took a step toward the painting, her gaze fixed on the bright image.

A moment ago Bethany had been concerned only with the dark burning of the Hunger and the delicious anticipation of feeding, with the almost painful teasing she had been subjecting herself to as she let Anton babble. She had been caught up in the perverse enjoyment of delaying the moment when she would taste Anton's blood, in increasing the tension between need and satisfaction so as to heighten the eventual pleasure.

Now, though, that tension had vanished; the Hunger itself was nothing but a minor distraction as she studied the intense colors, the textured surfaces of the painting.

It was a cityscape, San Francisco at dawn, knives of sunlight cutting between the gleaming towers and shattering to jeweled shards on the waters of the Pacific.

It was utterly beautiful.

She stared at it, drinking it in with her eyes, wanting to absorb every detail.

"Glare," she said, her eyes still fixed on the painting. "Too bright."

Instantly, Anton twisted a knob and the light dimmed. "I had the lights way up so I could work on it," he said. "It was bright, but I didn't see any glare. I guess your eyes are more sensitive than mine."

Bethany smiled to herself. "Yes," she said.

"You like it?" Anton asked.

Bethany struggled for a long moment, and at last managed to tear her gaze from the picture and look at the artist's intense bearded face, at his black hair and guileless eyes.

That man had created this beauty.

She shouldn't have been so surprised, she told herself. After all, she had met Anton when that earthquake, earlier this evening, had startled them into bumping against one another at an artists' reception at the Palace of the Legion of Honors. Why should it come as a shock to learn that he, too, was an artist? Who else would she expect to meet at an artists' reception? She had gone mostly because it was a pleasant diversion on a quiet Friday evening, and what made it pleasant was the art, and the artists.

Of course, the surprise wasn't that he was one of the hundreds of kine in the Bay Area who put brush to canvas; the surprise was that he was a true artist—in Bethany's opinion, an artist of real genius.

That opinion might not carry the weight of some, after a mere forty years of undeath, but Bethany was confident of her conclusion. If this painting was not a work of genius, Bethany told herself, then she was no true Toreador, she was as bad as those poseurs of Serata's.

No, even those fools with their fads and flash, even the youngest Childe in the Clan, would see Anton's brilliance in an instant.

"It's wonderful," she said, smiling at Anton.

He smiled back, a smile of pleased relief. "Would you like to see some others?" He gestured at a dozen other canvases, leaning face-in against the east wall of the studio.

"Very much," she replied, thrusting away, for a moment more, the pulsing Hunger that drove her.

One by one, he lifted the canvases and displayed them, while Bethany stared in wonder at street scenes, sunsets, still life, each with that distinctive hard-edged, brittle light, like nothing she had seen before. While none of the other paintings were quite as magnificent as his most recent work, it was clear that that new creation was merely a continuation of ongoing artistic development, not a wild, one-time fluke.

Anton was a genius, the most brilliant painter Bethany had ever met in the flesh.

"Why haven't I *heard* of you?" she asked.

He shrugged. "I haven't exhibited anywhere yet. Haven't tried. I have an inheritance I live on, and I wanted to build up a body of work, my family always said my work wasn't good enough . . . do you *really* like them?"

"I *love* them—and I love *you!* Come here!" She meant it—she loved him, as he would love a fine wine. She threw out her arms to him.

She would have to be careful. She was very hungry, but she must not drink too deeply.

Not yet.

This one must be saved, must be made one of the

Kindred, not given to useless, ungrateful death—but she could not do that without permission of the Prince. She was no anarch.

She would have to speak to Vannevar Thomas as soon as she could; she could not allow Anton to face the everyday risks of mortal existence a moment longer than absolutely necessary. Such talent must be saved for the ages.

As his arms went around her, as her lips neared his throat, she took one more glance at the painting.

V*ery* careful.

"Bethany!" The voice was deep and penetrating.

Bethany paused, startled; she lowered her bulky parcel, then turned and peered through the dimness and smoke of the Alexandrian Club's main lounge.

She saw a figure approaching, and recognized it. "Stefan," she said in flat acknowledgment.

"I almost didn't see you," Stefan said as he squeezed his way through the crowd; the black leather of his tight pants brushed audibly against someone's clothing, and the silver pendants on his chest jingled.

Bethany had not particularly wanted to be seen, but she saw no reason to state the obvious; she simply waited.

"I didn't expect to see you tonight," Stefan said. "Weren't you going to some sort of event? Our host said you were."

"Over hours ago," Bethany replied.

"Oh, but . . . surely you didn't leave alone!"

"Is there something you want, Stefan?" she asked, already tired of the pretense of friendship. Stefan was one of the trend-following fools in Serata's circle, and there was no love lost between that group and Bethany's own, more traditional faction of the vampiric Clan.

"No, no—not at all! I was just surprised to see you." He smiled. "Pleasantly surprised," he hastened to add.

"I don't know why," Bethany said. "I come here often. If either of us should be surprised, Stefan, I would think it would be I. You are scarcely a regular here."

"Ah, Bethany, you misjudge me. While I can scarcely tolerate the self-proclaimed artistes who run the place, I must admit that this is a fine place to meet with others of our kind, and when I return to the City to pay my respects to my Sire I often stop in here afterward."

Bethany bristled at the slighting description of the club's management—both Cainen, who ran the Alexandrian Club upstairs, and Melmoth, who ran the secret club beneath, were *her* own kind, and kindred spirits, as it were.

"You come here, even though you don't like the management, and yet you ask what I'*m* doing here?"

"No, no, sweet Bethany," Stefan protested. "I merely express my pleased surprise at my good fortune, that our visits should thus coincide! I had resigned myself to missing the pleasure of your countenance."

She turned away from this flattery, picked up her parcel, and took another step toward the alcove beneath the stairs.

"Oh, don't hurry off!" Stefan protested, stepping quickly beside her.

"Stefan, I have business elsewhere." She pushed past him and ducked into the alcove.

He followed her as she opened the heavy oaken door and hurried down the thirteen steps into the stagnant gloom of the Vampire Club.

At the bottom she paused in the tiny foyer, and Stefan joined her. The foyer was small enough that the two of them, and Bethany's package, made an uncomfortable crowd.

"Aren't you going to knock?" Stefan asked, reaching for the massive brass ring.

Bethany brushed his hand aside.

"Stefan," she said, "I am here on business, to see the Prince, who I'm told is visiting my Grandsire. *You have no business here!*"

Stefan smiled, his long, white teeth a flicker of light in the darkness. "All the Kindred are welcome here, Bethany. I would not *dream* of interfering with your business, whatever it is—but I'm as welcome here as you are."

She glared at him; untroubled, he reached past and lifted the heavy knocker. Three times he let it fall against the carved oak while Bethany simply stood, her gaze hostile.

As the door swung open, Stefan remarked, "Besides, I hardly see what the great secret is—it's obvious that that thing you're carrying is a painting, and I presume it's a gift for the Prince. Why should the presentation be private? Afraid he'll see just how poor your work is?"

"It's not *my* work!"

"Ah, then your artistic judgment."

"At least I have some artistic judgment, you bloody *poseur!*" Bethany snapped, pushing past Stefan into the main lounge of the Vampire Club.

His laughter trailed after her as she descended through gloom and stale air to the lower deck.

In this place nothing lived, nothing breathed—but the undead moved in their semblance of life, past paintings that mocked the living, glorying in their own darkness. Here, Bethany met with her Prince.

Twenty minutes later, the preliminary formalities out of the way and the situation explained, Bethany carried the painting into the library, where the light was best, and carefully unwrapped it. A nude's oil-paint eyes looked on from one wall, while Vannevar

Thomas, vampire prince of San Francisco, and Sebastian Melmoth, master of the Vampire Club, watched with interest.

"The mission of the Toreador Clan is to preserve great art," Bethany said, talking to cover her nervousness, "and great artists, through the Embrace." She saw Melmoth's lips quirk with amusement at her presumption, and realized that she was telling her elders things they had known for longer than she had existed. "While of course I am still young by the standards of our kind, I have faith in my own opinions—I would never have been taken into the Clan myself, were I no judge of art. And in my opinion, Anton Prihar is truly a great artist." She pulled the last of the wrappings away, and held up the painting she had borrowed.

For a moment there was utter silence as Bethany's audience took in the painting—the towers cut by golden glory, the water spattered with diamonds of light. Then Stefan, standing in the doorway, began applauding. Bethany almost dropped the painting; she had been so intent on the two elders that she had not seen Stefan's arrival. "Superb!" Stefan called.

Thomas turned. "And by what right, whelp, do you dare intrude on this discussion?" the Prince snapped.

Stefan's hands dropped, and he bowed respectfully. "Your pardon, sir; I am here as the representative of Allanyan Serata, Primogen of the Toreador Clan in your city. It seems plain to me that this matter concerns her."

"Ah," Thomas said. "And how is it that Mistress Serata was aware of this meeting?"

Stefan looked suddenly uncomfortable.

"She isn't!" Bethany shouted. "Stefan just followed me! He's just trying to make trouble; he's hated me for decades!"

"Oh, Bethany, I don't hate you," Stefan protested. "I am simply drawn irresistibly to save you from your own fo—"

"Silence!" Thomas said.

Stefan stopped in mid word.

"I asked you a question, Stefan," Thomas said quietly. "And I did not ask you, Bethany."

Bethany cast her eyes downward as Stefan admitted, "Bethany spoke the truth, O Prince: I met her upstairs by chance, and followed her here. I did so, however, because my Sire has charged all of us who curry her favor to keep an eye on the actions of those who would deny her authority as the eldest Toreador in the city—this Melmoth, the one who calls himself Tex R. Cainen, and all their descendants, all their followers in the . . . shall we say, the aesthetic disagreement that divides our Clan? You know they call us mere poseurs, that they're so caught up in past glories that they can't see . . ."

"*We* can't see! You're so dazzled by flash and glitter that you throw away all aesthetic judgment . . ." Bethany began.

"I need no speeches," Thomas interrupted. "You may dispute art theory elsewhere, not in my presence."

"My apologies," Stefan said, smiling ingratiatingly. "But I truly am here as Serata's representative."

Thomas smiled back. "I see," he said. "And as Serata's representative, would you agree that this Anton Prihar should become one of the Kindred, that his skill might be preserved?"

"Oh, absolutely!" Stefan said. "Bethany's stumbled on a real gem this time, no question about it!"

"You are, of course, an irrefutable authority," Melmoth murmured quietly. Stefan ignored the sarcasm.

"And if I say that San Francisco is overpopulated, that there are to be no more Kindred created at this time?" Thomas asked.

"Then we would have no choice but to obey," Stefan said with a cruel smile.

"Yes, sir," Bethany said, ignoring Stefan's obvious

pleasure in her discomfiture. "But please, don't say that."

"The work is quite remarkable," Melmoth said, to no one in particular.

Thomas threw a quick glance at Melmoth, then at Bethany. "You all agree, then, that this painter should be Embraced?" The three Toreadors all indicated silent assent.

"Very well," Thomas said. "I will permit it."

"Oh, *thank* you!" Bethany said.

Stefan bowed. "I will inform Serata at once," he said. "I have no doubt that she will wish to Embrace this artist herself."

Bethany turned, shocked.

"But I found him!" she said. "His blood is *mine!*"

"And if Serata says he is hers?" Stefan asked, smiling. Bethany, wordless with fury, turned to the Prince.

Stefan quickly said, "Surely, the Prince will not deny the rights and privileges of the Primogen, to favor this foolish young creature? Allanyan Serata is an elder of the Fifth Generation; Bethany is what, Ninth?"

"Eighth," she said coldly. "I *found him!*"

"And would you refuse him a chance at greater power than your own?" Stefan asked her. "Is it, perhaps, your own power, your own ambition, that interests you, rather than this human's art?"

Bethany's hands came up, curved into claws.

"And pray, sir," Melmoth interjected, "What is *your* interest in denying this young lady her treasure?"

"Spite," Bethany snarled. "It's just spite."

Melmoth cast an expressive glance at the ceiling, then at the Prince.

Thomas gazed contemplatively back.

"Sebastian," he said, "you see my predicament. These two have pitted the authority of the Primogen and the natural respect for one's elders against proprietary rights. I feel like Solomon confronted by the two mothers disputing over a child; how to resolve this, save by refusing this man the Embrace, and thereby letting his talent die in a few short years?" He started to turn back to the others, not expecting a reply.

Melmoth surprised him by murmuring, "I always wondered why Solomon didn't ask the child which was its true mother. Surely even an infant knows that much—and this Anton Prihar is no infant, as his painting makes plain."

Startled, Thomas paused. A slow, thoughtful smile spread across his face.

"Indeed," he said. "Indeed!"

The two vampires stood side by side before Anton Prihar, their dark clothing and black hair islands of night's darkness in the brightly lit studio, their pale faces colorless blanks against the vivid hues Anton had chosen for the walls. To the artist they appeared an intrusion from some hostile, washed-out other world.

As, of course, they were—they belonged to the world of eternal night, the world of the Kindred, a world he had never known existed until meeting Bethany the night before, a world whose intrusion he had tried to stave off.

"Choose!" Stefan demanded. "We bring you eternal life, centuries in which to create beauty; you need merely tell us which you would prefer to escort you into immortality, little Bethany, or the great Serata."

"What does it matter?" Anton asked despairingly, the useless silver cross dangling from his hand. "Why should I care?"

"Your power would be greater as Serata's Childe," Bethany explained. "I can't deny that; it's a fact of our existence. But she and her followers have no true understanding of art, Anton; they're mere poseurs, dabblers, prone to trends and fashions, with no appreciation of lasting greatness."

"Ha!" Stefan said. "We aren't afraid of change, if that's what you mean—we appreciate innovation and originality, we aren't caught in the outmoded patterns of the past."

Anton paid no attention to Stefan; he looked at Bethany, then down at the cross, then back at the vampire.

"When we met at the museum," he said, "I thought it was fate. I thought the earthquake was destiny at work, throwing us together that way. But I thought you were a woman, not a bloodsucking monster."

"I am a woman," Bethany protested. "But I'm *more* than that. And you can be, too."

"You drank my blood last night," he accused her.

"Yes," Bethany said.

"You're a vampire."

"Yes."

"But the cross doesn't affect you." He jingled the silver chain.

When Bethany and Stefan had arrived at the studio door, returning the borrowed painting, Anton had confronted them with the talisman, thrusting it in their faces; they had ignored it as Bethany asked, "May we come in?"

Anton had admitted them, and listened as they explained the choice the Prince had set before him. Now the artist was asking questions, and Bethany did her best to answer—she did not want to deceive him. She wanted him to know what lay before him, to understand that he need never die.

"No," she said, "crosses and silver don't affect us. Nor garlic, nor the rest of it. All myths."

"And you don't sleep in coffins all day, and come out at night?"

Stefan smiled sardonically as Bethany admitted, "We don't necessarily use coffins, but that part is basically true. Sunlight burns us, can destroy us."

Anton glanced at the painting, at the knives of sunlight cutting through the city streets.

"You give up something, yes," Bethany said, "but you'll be free of age and death forever."

"And you drink blood. You prey on other people." Anton put a hand to the bandage on his throat.

"But you don't need to hurt them," Bethany insisted. "It can be pleasurable. You saw that."

Anton nodded. "In the stories, vampires can hypnotize their victims," he said.

"Yes," Bethany said.

"So I couldn't resist if you just came in here and attacked me again."

"No, you couldn't, not for long," Bethany agreed. "But the Prince has ordered us to offer you a choice between Serata and myself."

Stefan, bored by this, growled, "Choose, mortal. Bethany or Serata?"

"I need time," Anton said. "I need time to think about it."

"What is there to think about?" Stefan demanded. "We offer you eternity, and you have a choice between more power or less—choose now!"

"I need time," Anton said, "to put my affairs in order."

"No one needs to know you've crossed over," Bethany pointed out.

"Still, I need time," Anton insisted. "You're asking me to choose between a total stranger and a woman who is nearly so, between power and something that might be love—or might not. You two claim to be eternal—what does one day matter?"

Bethany smiled wryly. "It doesn't," she agreed. "Tomorrow night, then?"

"Serata will not be pleased," Stefan warned.

"Come on," Bethany told him. She took Stefan's arm and pulled him toward the door; he shook her off and marched out, Bethany close on his heels.

The fog was thick the following night, spilling through the streets in opaque billows, cutting off all vision and blurring all light; perhaps, Bethany thought, that was why Stefan was late, why she had arrived alone and found the door of the studio standing open.

When she saw the door open, for a moment she feared that someone had broken in, that Anton had fallen prey to human avarice—or Serata's.

There had been no robbery, and Serata had not disobeyed the Prince; a dozen paintings were set out on display, untouched. The one that Bethany had borrowed had a place of honor in the center. The note was pinned to that last finished canvas, and addressed to her—not to Stefan, only to her.

"Dear Bethany," she read, "I have made my choice."

She looked up for a moment, then continued reading.

"I had thought that you understood and appreciated my work," the note said. "You certainly praised it highly, and in your own way, I suppose you did appreciate it—but it's plain that you didn't understand it, nor did that other person, Stefan, who you brought here."

Bethany glanced at the painting, momentarily puzzled. "Perhaps I could have explained it to you," Anton's words continued, "but I don't think that Stefan or the creature he serves could ever have accepted it. All my life, other people have made my decisions for me—sent me to the best schools, found me the right jobs, always acting for my own good—until I inherited my grandmother's money and could finally do what I pleased.

"And now, I've succeeded too well, and Stefan's mistress would act for my own good, and destroy what she seeks to control. I can never be what you are, what you want me to be, any more than I could be what my parents wanted me to be.

"Goodbye, Bethany. I know you meant well."

Bethany dropped the note and looked up again, at Anton's body dangling from the noose, turning slowly, limbs stiff—he had obviously died hours before, perhaps just minutes after she had last seen him alive, and there was no hope of revival to either life or a vampiric approximation of life.

Even had revival been possible, Bethany thought, she would have respected this final artistic decision—or at least, she hoped she would have. Her gaze fell back from Anton's remains to his works.

His body hung below the broad studio window, below the row of too-bright lights, and the corpse's black shadow twisted across a dozen paintings, paintings that, one and all, showed bright sunlight slanting across the sky, illuminating fields, forests, streets, and spires, sunlight gleaming from whitewashed walls, sunlight scattered by dancing water, sunrises, sunsets—everywhere, on all sides, in every painting, the sun that Bethany had not seen with her own eyes for more than forty years, the sun she had asked Anton to give up forever, the sun he could not live without.

The Waters of Lethe

by Bill Bridges

Doctor Murry F. Bruckner scribbled more notes onto his pad, put his pen down, and looked over at his patient. The man was lying on the couch looking uncomfortable and nervous. It was only the patient's second therapy, and he was still unsure of the process. Doctor Bruckner cleared his throat.

"Ahem. Are you ready, Mr. Barnes?" he asked.

Mr. Barnes breathed deeply. "Yes. Go ahead. We might as well start now."

"All right. It really is for the best, Mr. Barnes. I'm sorry: Charles."

"That's not my real name, you know. I just pulled it from a phone book."

"Yes, I know. But let's use it for now, as if it had meaning. All right?"

Mr. Barnes was silent for a moment, then responded in a low voice. "Okay."

"Charles, have you thought more about your dream from last time?"

"Yes. But I've had another, stranger, dream."

"Oh? Does this one seem more important to you than the last one?"

"Yeah. I guess so."

"Then let's talk about it. What happened in this dream?"

"I—I was standing on the street, outside the hospital. The hospital was dark, evil. There was no light. I . . . knew that . . . *things* moved in there. I had to get away. So I ran. I ran all the way here, to your office. But this building was dark also. I was worried. Something was behind the door. I didn't want to go in."

"Something? What kind of thing?"

"I don't know. It was evil."

"Was it an animal? A lizard or mammal? A person?"

"It was all three, I don't know."

"Did any of it seem familiar to you?"

"Yes. The *things*. I've met them before."

"In other dreams? You remember these dreams?"

"No, not in dreams. In real life."

"Hmm. I think perhaps your memories of dreams and actual events is somewhat confused. But it's a good sign. At least some memories are coming back."

"No. I'm sure it was real. It wasn't a dream before."

"Charles, dreams can have an amazing pull on our psyches, especially upon a wounded psyche such as yours. You're suffering an advanced case of amnesia. You are desperate to have your memories—your life, your identity—back. In such an instance, I'm not surprised fantastic dreams seem so real, as if they actually happened."

"Then how do you explain the weird shit in every dream I've had for the past three weeks?!"

"Calm down. As I said before, it's either a reaction to whatever caused your traumatic amnesia, the psyche's attempt to make you deal with it by veiling it in symbols and mythic images, or perhaps you were a science fiction writer, and these images are things from your stories."

"Wait—that seems close. I almost remembered something when you said stories. Maybe that's it. Maybe I do write stories."

"You see. No cause for alarm. Our session is almost over. I want to see you again this Friday. Realize that our task in these sessions is to awaken the memory. You've drunk from the waters of Lethe, to use a classical metaphor for amnesia. But nothing is ever really forgotten; it's all in there somewhere." Bruckner tapped his head as he said this. "In the meantime, I recommend you go to the library or bookstore, to see if anything seems familiar. Who knows? Maybe you'll find a book or two you wrote."

Charles tried to fake a smile, but Bruckner wasn't fooled.

"Now," said the psychologist. "Tell me what happened in your dream last night."

Charles stared up at the ceiling as he spoke. "They're killing me: the dreams. I wake up every night sweating and shaking. I swear they're real—or at least they seem to be."

"Have you seen the 'things' yet, or do they still lurk outside your vision?"

"No. I haven't seen them. But I heard something new: a bark—a dog barking somewhere in the distance."

"From what direction?"

"Huh? I don't know. It was just far off."

Bruckner wrote something down on his pad. "Anything else?"

"No, just the same dream for a week now—except for the bark."

"Yes, the bark. Interesting. Do you recall ever owning a dog?"

"I don't remember. Maybe I did. I do like dogs."

"Oh? How do you know?"

"Well, I pet them when I see them. They seem to like me too."

"Good. Good. I like them too. I have a few myself. A setter and a beagle. What about the fiction? Have you looked in any stores to see if you recognize any books?"

"Yes. But I don't recognize anything. I don't think I've read anything in those stores."

"Really? Not even Huck Finn?"

"What?"

"*The Adventures of* Huckleberry *Finn* by Mark Twain. Ring any bells?"

"No. Is it a bestseller?"

"Sort of. Just about all American schoolboys are required to read it sometime in their education. So, either you did not have conventional schooling or your memory loss is still chronic."

"I guess so. I still don't remember anything."

"Well, just try those exercises I gave you; the memory tests. Perhaps by next week we'll have seen some progress."

"Okay. Thanks." Charles rose from the couch and headed for the door.

"Goodbye, Mr. Barnes," Bruckner said.

"Oh, God. I don't know what's going on anymore!" Charles cried.

"Get ahold of yourself," Bruckner said, sitting Charles on the couch. "Let me get you some water. Just sit down and tell me what happened."

Charles buried his head in his hands as Bruckner poured some water from a decanter into a glass and brought it over to him. He looked up and accepted the water. "Thanks."

"All right. From the beginning," Bruckner said, sitting in his chair and arranging his notebook.

"One of those things attacked me. And it wasn't a dream."

"What? When was this? Where?"

"Outside the hospital. Last night. I was walking to the market when it jumped out of the bushes. God, it had huge teeth and claws, like a bear's. It was dripping pus and screaming at me! Oh, God, I—"

"Stop it! Don't let yourself get carried away by this. It was obviously a hallucination. Brought on, perhaps, by the stress of your situation. Maybe you shouldn't go near the hospital any—"

"Doctor, it wasn't a hallucination! Look . . ." Charles pulled back his right sleeve, revealing three huge, closely spaced gashes across his arm. They appeared to be infected.

"Good God! Have you seen a doctor about this?"

"No. I was afraid. I just ran. I couldn't go back there. It's waiting for me."

Bruckner got out of his chair, moving over to look at the arm more closely. The injury appeared to be claw marks from some animal. The wound was too jagged, too irregular for a knife injury.

"I've got to get you some help," Bruckner said.

"Doctor, it's not my arm I need help with. It's my sanity. What's happening to me? You said the thing was just a dream, but it attacked me."

"Nonsense! Don't fall into that pit! You've been attacked by a wild animal, perhaps escaped from the zoo. Certainly not by a creature from your dreams!"

"But, it was so real."

"Of course it was. You're in the grip of an archetypal image, perhaps even your shadow. We must change our tactics somewhat. I hadn't thought your condition was so severe. I think we should try hypnotism."

"Will that work? I thought that was just hocus pocus."

"It can be a very effective tool when used with skill and understanding. It is a tool of discovery, not control. May we try it?"

"I've got nothing to lose. Why not? When should we start?"

"Right away. I see no reason to delay. If it can help calm you and release you from the grip of whatever unconscious content holds you in its sway, it can only help us now. Now, lie back and breath deeply."

Charles did as Bruckner told him and immediately

calmed down. Bruckner pulled his watch and chain from his vest—an old, but effective standard in hypnotism. "All right. Stare closely at the watch. As it swings, you will be getting very sleepy."

Bruckner went through the whole routine. In minutes, Charles was in a deep hypnotic state. "Now, Charles, when I snap my fingers, you will awaken. You will remember only what is good from our talk, not what is bad. Only what is good, what you want to remember, not what is bad, not what hurts to remember. Nod if you understand."

Charles nodded.

"Good. Now, let's go into your memories, your deep memories, the ones you have not been able to access recently. Can you do that? Nod if you can."

Charles nodded.

"Good. Now, Charles, what is your real name?"

Charles thrashed on the couch, but then calmed down. "Holds-Their-Songs," he replied.

"Holds-Their-Songs? Is that your name, Charles, or what you were told to do?"

"My name," Charles said. "And what I was told to do."

Bruckner looked perplexed and wrote some things down on his pad.

"Let's go farther back, to your childhood. Do you remember your name then?"

"Yes."

"What was it?"

"Daniel."

"Daniel? Was that your full name? Did you have a last name also?"

"Robertson."

"Did you have a happy childhood, Daniel?"

"No."

"Oh? Why not? What was bad about it?"

Daniel began to thrash about on the couch again, still hypnotized. He began to growl low and menacing.

"Why are you growling, Daniel?"

"Angry! Like a dog!"

"Why like a dog, Daniel?"

"I am a dog!"

"I thought you were a boy?"

Charles wrinkled his brow in confusion and squirmed on the couch.

"Aren't you a boy, Daniel, not a dog, but a boy?"

Silence for a moment. "Yes."

"What made you angry?"

"Hurt. Pain. Nobody understands."

"How old are you now, Daniel, when you feel this pain?"

"Thirteen."

"Don't the other kids feel the same, Daniel? Why is your pain special?"

"They don't! They don't understand! They hate me!"

"Why? Why do they hate you? Tell me why, Daniel."

Charles began swinging his arms about, contorting his face into a mask of animal menace. He growled loud and angrily.

"Stop! You are no longer Daniel but Charles, who does not remember the pain."

Charles was immediately still.

"All right, Charles. When did you get the name Holds-Their-Songs? How old were you then?"

"Twenty."

"Who gave you this name?"

"Celeste."

"Who is she? Your girlfriend?"

Charles growled threateningly.

"Stop. Be calm. Who was she?"

"Leader. Sept leader."

"Sept? What is that?"

"All of us."

"Who do you mean by us?"

"The other wolves."

"Wolves? Are you a wolf now?"

"Yes. No."

Bruckner scribbled more notes. "Why did Celeste give you this name?"

"So I would remember."

Bruckner was silent for a moment. "But you didn't remember. You don't remember their songs."

A tear ran down Charles's face, and he began crying.

"Why not? Why did you forget?" Bruckner asked.

"They are dead! All of them dead!"

"Who? Who are dead?"

"My pack. My pack."

"Your fellow wolves?"

"My fellow Garou."

"Garou? What does that mean?"

"The People."

"What kind of people?"

"Werewolves."

Bruckner didn't say anything for awhile. He looked down at his notes and over at his patient. He snapped his fingers. Charles blinked and looked around, as if coming out of a nap. He craned his neck around to look at the psychologist.

"Well? Did you find out anything?" Charles asked.

"Yes," Bruckner replied, looking out the window, not meeting Charles' eyes. "But . . . I need to think about it. Would you please come back at your usual time?"

"All right. Thank you, doctor," Charles said and headed for the door.

"Oh, Charles?" Bruckner said, not looking away from the window.

"Yes?"

"Get that wound looked at, will you? It's very bad. You never know what type of infection could get into it."

* * *

"Charles, I want to hypnotize you again. Is that all right?" Bruckner said.

"If you feel it's best, all right. But what did I say last time?" Charles asked, sitting in the couch again.

"Why don't we talk about that at the end of the session? I still have some unanswered questions."

Charles shrugged.

"Let's begin then." In a few minutes, Bruckner had Charles in a deep trance. He sat back in his chair and reached into his pocket, pulling out a small tape recorder. He pushed the record button and set it down with the microphone facing Charles.

"You are not Charles now, but Holds-Their-Songs. Who am I speaking to?"

"Holds-Their-Songs," Charles replied woodenly.

"Good. You said your pack was dead. How did they die?"

"The Wyrm killed them."

"Wyrm? What is that?"

"Dragon. Corruption."

Bruckner smiled and wrote something down on his pad.

"What do you mean by corruption? Have you done something corrupt?"

"No. The Wyrm is corrupt. I fight the corruption. Protect Gaia."

"Who is Gaia?"

"The Mother."

Bruckner smiled again. He wrote a small note in his pad. "This Wyrm. It tries to harm the Mother?"

"Yes. It tries to destroy Her."

"And you stand against it? You alone?"

"No. All Garou fight. My pack fought."

"They died in the fight. Where did they die?"

"Near oil factory. Gasoline smell. Foulness."

Bruckner wrinkled his brow. "When did they die?"

"One moon ago."

"One moon? One month?"

"Yes."

"Why didn't you die also?"

"Last standing. Escaped to spirit."

"What do you mean, 'escaped to spirit'?"

"Reached. Step sideways into spirit world."

Bruckner smiled once more. "So you retreated to a spirit world where they couldn't get you?"

"No. Retreated and ran. They are there also. Blights."

"So the corruption is in the spirit world also?"

"Yes."

"I want you to go back farther in your memories, to your childhood. I'm speaking to Daniel now. Daniel?"

"Yes?" Charles said, in a childish voice.

"When did your mother die, Daniel?"

"She's not dead."

"What about your father?"

"He's not dead."

"Daniel, did your father ever hit your mother?"

"No."

"Are you sure?"

"Yes. Why?"

Bruckner looked a bit annoyed. "Never mind. Daniel, have you ever done anything bad? Anything you wanted to forget and never remember?"

"Yes."

"What is that? Can you tell me?"

"I let my pack die," Charles said, in a deeper voice.

Bruckner looked annoyed again. "Is this Holds-Their-Songs now? Can you think of anything else? Any other bad things?"

"No."

"Tell me about the spirit world. Have you been there recently?"

"Yes, in my dreams."

"What about now, under hypnosis?"

"Yes. I'm here now. You are too."

"I am? Where am I? Where are we?"

"In a Chimera. A dream realm."

"Why? Why are we here? Why am I here with you?"

"You created it. The hypnosis."

"But I thought you went here in your dreams? They happened before I hypnotized you."

"Those were different places."

"Is there anything else here with us?"

Charles was quiet for a moment, as if thinking. Then he let out a low growl. "Yes—*it's* here. It followed me."

"Here? In the dream realm with us? Can you see it?"

"No. Sense it. Smell of Wyrm." Charles' voice was deeper, more menacing.

Bruckner squinted and stared at the couch and reached over to the lamp on his desk, which he pivoted and pointed toward Charles. Bruckner's eyes widened; Charles had grown larger. He was bulking his muscles up, stretching out, his feet hanging over the edge of the couch. Bruckner had seen contortionists before, but never this convincing. Charles was growling and thrashing his head about.

Bruckner began writing notes. He stopped for a moment, confused when a shadow moved across the wall. A shadow cast from behind him. He turned around and barely suppressed a scream.

Shuffling across the room on all fours, toward the couch, was a hideous beast, a slimy thing with spiked fur and huge fangs. Its fingers were razor-sharp talons and it eyes gleamed with a greenish light. It ignored Bruckner and appeared to be sneaking up on Charles.

Bruckner stared in shock and dismay. As it got closer to Charles it drew back, about to strike. Bruckner shook his head, trying to clear it, and snapped his fingers.

Instantly, Charles woke up—but the thing was still there. It leapt at him, screaming. Bruckner yelled in horror as it landed on Charles and began to claw chunks of flesh from his torso. Charles screamed—and the scream became an animal howl of rage as his body instantly grew to almost twice its size, now covered in fur. His head was that of a wolf.

Bruckner sunk low in his chair, trying not to be noticed.

The werewolf and the shambling thing tore into each other. The thing seemed at a disadvantage now, no match for the towering werewolf and its jaws. In seconds, it screamed and disappeared, like wisps of smoke in a breezy room.

Charles—Holds-Their-Songs—stood panting and catching his breath. He turned to look at Bruckner; the psychologist was whimpering in the chair, curled up in a fetal position. Holds-Their-Songs shifted back into human form and walked over to him. Bruckner didn't seem to notice him; he just stared at the wall.

"I'm sorry," Holds-Their-Songs said. "But thank you. I know who I am now. I had forgotten. The pain of my loss drove me to forsake my birthright. But I am a Galliard, and it is my duty to remember the songs of those who fall in the battle against the Wyrm. You have helped me remember them today."

Bruckner showed no response whatsoever.

"Don't worry; I know you won't remember this yourself. The Chimera is gone now. It was only a temporary creation. The Banes won't bother you anymore. It was me they wanted."

Bruckner began to slowly rock back and forth in the chair, still not responding.

Holds-Their-Songs took the tape recorder and removed the tape, putting it into his pocket. He took the doctor's notepad and tore out the pages with the session's notes. He looked at them for a moment and shook his head.

"Possible Oedipus Complex? Is that all the Wyrm

is? I'm afraid not, doctor." He crumpled the notes, putting them in his pocket, then walked out the door, closing it quietly behind him.

Five hours passed, and it was dark before Bruckner finally came to his senses. He looked about, confused, stood up and stretched. He looked at his notepad for a clue as to why he fell asleep so early, but there were no notes for today; only the last notes he had taken when his patient Charles had claimed to be a werewolf. Bruckner couldn't suppress a strange shudder. He shook his head and walked over to his desk.

He should probably go ahead and file commitment papers for Charles, just in case. His problem was obviously deeper than amnesia. Any fool who thought he was a werewolf certainly had bigger troubles than a small-time psychoanalyst like Murry Bruckner could fix. Perhaps Edward Gorrel, over in Utah, could handle this. Bruckner recalled he had mentioned a case with a supposed "wolfman" once.

Christ, Bruckner thought, what if this was becoming a common psychosis? What could possibly trigger such a wide-scale derangement in modern society? It doesn't matter, Bruckner decided. That's for the experts to determine. I'll just take the small cases, thank you.

He walked over to the window and looked out. On the street below a man was walking a large dog, which began barking as it passed the building. Bruckner shuddered again. He hated dogs.

Damned smelly, dangerous brutes.

Power

by Don Bassingthwaite

The telephone's shrill scream startled Emily enough that the scalpel she wielded with delicate precision skipped wildly. The cold blood of the dead man on the table trickled out over her fingers. She pursed her lips with frustration and reached for something with a broader mouth than the simple, institutional water glass that stood ready on the edge of the table.

Her fingers closed on a stainless steel basin. The falling blood struck the metal with a sharp, almost musical patter as she stripped off her latex gloves and strode across the room. She got the phone on the third ring.

"Morgue."

"Miss Grange . . ."

"Doctor."

"Sorry, Dr. Grange. This is John, upstairs. There's someone here to see you."

"What does he want?" She glared at the dead man on the autopsy table. The flow of blood was slowing already—he had been dead almost too long. She picked up the phone and walked back toward the body, the extension cable slithering over other sheet-draped tables. "I'm not expecting anybody."

"He says it's family business."

Emily cradled the telephone receiver between her head and shoulder and used her free hand to press down on the corpse's belly. Under the pressure, more blood spurted into the basin. "Tell him to use the usual door."

She heard John repeat the information. There was a

new voice in the background, one with a French accent. John spoke into the phone again. "He doesn't know where it is. He's a distant cousin."

A grimace struck her face. "Is he tall, black hair, gold-rimmed sunglasses? Wearing a jacket with an orchid in the button-hole?"

"I don't know what kind of flower he's got . . ."

Of course not, Emily thought. She moved her hand to the body's chest and pressed again.

". . . but that sounds like him."

Damn. "Tell him where the usual entrance is. I'll be waiting for him." She hung up without waiting for a response. Leaving the telephone balanced on a nearby body, she picked up the basin and carefully poured its contents into her glass. Then she settled down to wait.

It had been twelve years since Emily's Embrace, and her abrupt reassignment to night-shift forensic pathologist in the San Francisco Medical Examiner's Office. Twelve years as a vampire, and in that time, she had gotten to know almost all of the Kindred in San Francisco. There weren't that many vampires in the city who had French accents. Only one would have the nerve to identify himself as a "distant cousin," a member of one of the Clans that lingered on the fringe of the Camarilla. And he had come himself—his "business" must be important. The visit was almost welcome. Very few Kindred regularly came to the Medical Examiner's Office in the Hall of Justice. Even fewer came to her domain in the basement of the north wing. Most vampires sent their retainers when they had business with Emily, and the business was always the same.

Cover up the mistakes. Hide the stray evidence that popped up from time to time when a vampire lost control and killed someone. Provide death certificates that listed a more mundane cause of death, and make sure the body was disposed of cleanly. She was an important link in the Masquerade. The Prince had praised her work.

Her fingers tensed on the glass and she had to set it down before she broke it. The Prince's words were empty. She deserved more than this! Her domain was the Medical Examiner's Office, her subjects the Medical Examiner, the other forensic pathologists, and a few of the regular police. No one respected what she did. She was a lackey, a convenient service to be used when it was necessary and ignored the rest of the time. The other Kindred shunned her. Some important link! This was not the future a bright, ambitious medical school graduate had seen for herself. It wasn't even the future a more mature forensic pathologist, forty-eight but still ambitious, had seen in the first weeks after her Embrace by Clan Ventrue.

The sudden sound of the door buzzer wasn't enough to surprise her this time. "Come in, Jean-Claude, the door's unlocked."

"Can't you come out?"

Emily ground her teeth in frustration. "My equipment is in here." She pushed herself to her feet and began preparing another autopsy table. There was a burst of obscene French from the corridor. She smiled coldly. "I'm waiting."

The door burst open. Two large men staggered into the room. Between them, they bore a bundle wrapped in a blood-stained sheet. She motioned them to put it on the table. "Jean-Claude?" she called.

The vampire rushed into the room as though passing through the doorway was some kind of torture. He had a handkerchief over his nose and mouth, as if he smelled something bad, and his eyes darted wildly around the room. He dismissed his servants with a curt gesture. They filed silently out of the room and closed the door behind them. Only when they were out of the room did he remove the handkerchief from his face. "How can you stand this place?"

"It's necessary. And you get used to it," she replied tightly. "If it bothers you so much, don't breathe."

"I'm not. But the smell is still . . . everywhere! It sticks to everything. I'm going to smell like a corpse when I leave!"

"You get used to it," she murmured. More loudly, she said, "You're the first Setite I've had come to me."

Jean-Claude frowned, the expression creating deep furrows in his handsome face. "The Followers of Set," he muttered with something that sounded like shame, "do not normally seek out the services of others."

"Not normally?"

"I would prefer you to keep my visit here to yourself." He pulled back the sheet to expose the corpse he had brought. "He was one of my followers."

It was the body of a young man, perhaps in his early twenties, the ragged remains of his clothing plastered to his body with blood. He had been handsome, she supposed. His skin was deeply tanned, his muscles tightly defined, his remaining features clean and classical. But his death had been ugly. His body was almost a tatter of slashes, scratches, and bites. One of the deeper puncture wounds had probably destroyed something vital before he could die from loss of blood. Blood still seeped from some of the cuts. The body was fresh. The blood would be fresh, barely cold, still with the tang of life . . .

Emily realized that she was licking her lips. The glass of blood she had drained earlier stood nearby. She grabbed it and drank deeply. The blood was stale, the death older, but it would serve to keep her mind on the task at hand. Jean-Claude was staring at her with a look of disgust on his face when she lowered the glass.

"That was revolting. How can you drink dead blood?"

He looked as if he might throw up. Emily considered

taking another drink to see if he would but thought better of it. She set the glass down before turning back to the corpse. "You didn't come here to discuss my feeding habits. What happened to him?"

"A . . . ceremony got out of control at the temple." He shrugged. "My other followers attacked him."

"What with?"

"Knives. Pieces of broken glass. Their teeth and nails. It happens occasionally. With some drugs, a group can turn ugly like that." Jean-Claude snapped his fingers for emphasis.

Emily pulled the blood-soaked sheet away from the body completely. "If this happens 'occasionally,' I'm surprised I haven't seen you in here before."

"Most times it doesn't end in death. I try to make sure of that. A dead follower is of no use to me. This time it happened too quickly. He was dead in seconds." He shrugged again. "What can you do with him?"

She picked up a clipboard and pen. "Usually, I can list the death as a suicide, but I don't think that's going to work this time. I'll have to call in the next-of-kin, have them identify the body, then convince them it was a mugging or something. We'll cremate the body afterwards." She tapped the pen against her teeth in thought and nodded to herself. "That should work. What was his name?"

Jean-Claude glanced down at the bloody body. "Does it matter?"

"Yes, it does. I have to put a name on the death certificate and I have to find his next-of-kin. Who is he?"

"I don't know."

"I find that difficult to believe."

"He was a new recruit to the Temple." He picked up a flask of distilled water. Emily was surprised to see that his hand was shaking. "Someone brought him in for the first time last week. A lot of my followers try to maintain their anonymity. I usually let them for a while."

"Did he have any ID on him?"

"Someone stole his wallet."

Emily was tempted to throw the clipboard down in frustration. She held on to it. Jean-Claude was nervous, desperate for her help. She might be able to gain something useful out of this transaction. "Then who did he come with?"

"I don't know. All my followers ran. They're loyal to the temple, though. They won't tell anybody about it."

"I don't care about your followers! Isn't there anything you can tell me about him?"

"No!" Jean-Claude snapped back. "That's why I need your help! I don't know who he is, I don't know who brought him, but if anyone is looking for him and can connect him with the temple, I'm in trouble! I need you to cover for me, you blue blood . . . "

"That's enough." Emily straightened and glared at him coldly. Internally, she glowed warmly with victory. "Don't forget that you do need me. It's going to be a little more tricky, but we can still do it. You'll owe me, though. There's going to be a little bit of confusion tomorrow morning. We have an unidentified body next door ready to be cremated. One body under a sheet looks a lot like another body under a sheet, especially when the toe tags have been mixed up."

"And the death certificate? The next-of-kin?"

"The death certificate will be very ordinary. It will say that he died from a stabbing during a mugging." She shrugged exaggeratedly. "The body is found on the street and brought in late. I make some preliminary notes and then leave the autopsy for the day crew. Some idiot cremates the wrong body, we sack him, and I'm forced to fill out a death certificate based on my notes. The next-of-kin won't matter at all, although I'm sure they'll turn up eventually."

"Someone could still trace him to my temple."

"We say that the body was found somewhere dark and nasty but not too far from somewhere with lots of people. Somewhere he could have wandered or been lured away from. A night-club strip. I have some influence with the officers who patrol a suitable area. They'll remember finding the body and they'll have the reports to prove it." She smiled reassuringly.

"But what if he wasn't the type to go to a night club?"

The smile wavered but didn't disappear. "Jean-Claude, if he was the type to go to your temple, he was probably the type to go to a night club occasionally. Even if he wasn't, I suspect that he would have lied about where he was going anyway. If he told anybody at all. Relax. It will work."

Jean-Claude looked relieved. "This stays quiet?"

"It's foolproof. No one will ever find out. Just remember—you owe me a favor."

"Absolutely! Emily, I could kiss you!"

"A favor is fine."

"Anything! My temple is at your disposal!" He virtually danced out the door.

Emily watched him go. When he was out of sight, she permitted her smile to grow wider and more predatory. Jean-Claude was not the most powerful or widely respected vampire in San Francisco. Most of the Kindred loathed him, in fact, but he did have connections. And a favor owed was a favor owed. This was her chance to reach for a bit more respect from the other Kindred. This was what she deserved!

Her eye fell on the corpse Jean-Claude had brought, and she smiled again. If she was only going to incinerate it, she would be a fool to let the blood go to waste. She dipped her finger in the blood and touched it gingerly to her tongue, testing for the taint of vampire vitae. Not long after her Embrace, another vampire had tried to trick her into a Blood Bond by putting his own blood into a corpse. She certainly wouldn't have placed Jean-Claude above suspicion of doing the same thing.

The corpse, however, was clean. Emily whistled with happy expectation as she picked up her scalpel. She had fresh blood and, more importantly, she had Jean-Claude.

"What happened, Barr?" Emily reached back into the car and pulled out the black bag she carried to crime scenes. The flashing lights of a multitude of police cars and ambulances tinted the entire scene red. She hated field calls, but at least she got to the bodies quickly.

"Drug gang mostly, Dr. Grange." The lieutenant squirmed under the weight of the bulletproof vest he carried, then set it down altogether. "Might have been some cult activity—I heard chanting or something. Some gangs are like that. You felt that big quake a while ago? That happened while we were going in." He opened the door into the gang's warehouse hideout for her. "After you."

Emily stepped past him. It was surprisingly quiet inside. Barr fell into step beside her, his face grim. An ambulance crew was taking a wounded officer out on a stretcher. He murmured weakly and reached out for Barr as they passed. Barr held on to his hand for a moment, then let him go. One of the ambulance attendants caught Emily's eye and shook her head with resignation. The man on the stretcher had lost a lot of blood. It was obvious that he would be dead before morning. The smell of the dying man's blood, the smell of a great deal of blood, was heavy in the air. She was glad she had fed before coming.

The center of the warehouse was clear of crates. This had been the scene of a gun battle, dirty and brutal, in the close quarters. Barr dismissed the two constables who stood guard. Emily knelt to examine one of the several bodies lying scattered around the area. "How many of them were there?" she asked.

"These ones and about ten more that got away down into the sewers." Barr indicated an open trap door nearby. "We're looking for them now. They were tough bastards—just stood right up to it."

"How many wounded?"

"On their side? Not a one. They only left the dead behind."

She looked up at him. "And on ours?"

"Just Long." He struggled to maintain a stolid face. "Everyone else got off lucky, but Long took one in the chest. Cop-killer bullet, must have been. Cut through his vest like butter."

"Wasn't he under some sort of cover?" Emily opened her bag and pulled out a syringe.

"He was being a damned hero. Said he was going to take out the big man. I was near him. He pumped four good shots into that son of a bitch but they took him down anyways." He regarded the bodies of the gang members sourly, then cursed loudly and slammed his fist into the side of crate.

Emily turned to look at him evenly. "Barr, why don't you go back outside. I only have to get some blood samples. You don't have to stay."

"I have to . . ."

"Go." She locked eyes with him. His will was strong, but hardly strong enough to resist her. His mouth moved on its own for a moment, then he smiled and laughed.

"Sure, why not!" He turned to leave. "I'll just send the Forensics crew on in when they get here."

"Oh, I'll probably be finished before that." She almost smiled herself. It was so much simpler to do what she had to without the idiots from Forensics fumbling around in her way. It was fairly standard to take blood samples at the scene, but not her usual two or three from each body. One of the first things she had done after her Embrace was condition the Forensics crew to arrive on the crime scene a good thirty minutes late. Forensics had since become legendary on the police force for their tardiness. And no one else really wanted to be around when a forensic pathologist was working.

Emily took a syringe of blood from the first body, transferred it into a capped plastic vial, labeled it, and placed it carefully in her bag. She filled another and then moved on to the next body. Each gang member could provide her easily with two vials of blood. Three was greedy, and Forensics, for all their stupidity, might notice. Once the bodies were in the Medical Examiner's Office, she could take as much blood from them as she wanted.

At least the cause of their deaths was obvious. All of the gang members had come down in a hail of police bullets. Most lay in a cluster near the trap door to the sewers. She ran her hands through their clothing quickly, then stared in surprise at the ring she pulled from the pocket of one gang member.

The head of a cobra with exaggerated fangs stared back at her. The symbol of a Follower of Set. She double-checked the other bodies. Two others wore similar rings on their fingers, the third wore one beside a St. Christopher medal on a chain around his neck. All Followers of Set, but mortals.

"Emily . . ."

She whirled. The voice came from nearby, from a narrow gap between two large crates. There didn't seem to be anyone there, but even as her eyes wandered away there was a flicker of movement. Jean-Claude appeared from out of the shadows, propping himself upright against the cases. He was bleeding from a number of gunshot wounds. Four, she realized. The blood that fell from the wounds turned to dust before it hit the floor.

"Help me," he begged her. "Take me out of here." He stepped out away from the crates and managed a few steps before he fell. Even so, he continued to drag himself toward her.

Emily kept her distance from him. He desperately needed blood, and a desperate vampire wasn't picky about where he got it. She tried to think as she moved away. He was virtually at her mercy. If she wanted to, she could probably capture him easily. The Prince had been unsuccessfully hunting for the Setite temple since the first rumors of Jean-Claude's arrival in San Francisco had begun to circulate. If she presented Jean-Claude to Vannevar Thomas at his court, she could become the toast of Kindred society.

However . . . she bit her lip in thought. Vannevar Thomas knew about Jean-Claude himself. He hated him in fact. Even the most accidental encounter between the two of them inevitably resulted in harsh and icy words, though nothing more. The Prince had never moved against Jean-Claude personally. Rumor in the Kindred community had it that he regarded it as simply too dangerous. Was presenting the Setite to him likely to change that? And what if Jean-Claude escaped or was set free? Emily had no illusions about the treatment she would receive from him. She had already invested in him by covering up for him. If she saved him now, he would be very firmly in her debt.

She pulled two vials of blood from her bag. "Drink these." She rolled the vials carefully across the floor to him. Jean-Claude pounced on them like a cat, although the coordination necessary to open the vials seemed to have eluded him. He simply put the ends of the vials in his mouth and bit down until the plastic shattered. The fact that this caused more damage to his abused body didn't appear to matter to him. He swallowed the blood and the bits of plastic together. The worst of his wounds began to close.

"More!" he gasped, "Please, Emily! Give me more!"

Reluctantly, she pulled out two more vials and rolled them to him. This time he got the caps off and drank more neatly. When he finished, he was still gaunt from lack of blood, but his wounds had healed. Emily risked coming closer. She almost panicked when he jumped at her and wrapped his arms around her, but then she realized he was hugging her.

"I never thought I would be so happy to see a Ventrue. We were conducting a ceremony and the cops came . . ."

"Quiet!" She pushed him away. "Tell me later—I don't have you out of here yet."

"I'll go through the sewers!"

"No! They're searching them already, and they're armed. You aren't strong enough to fight them. I have a better idea. Don't go away!" She pushed another vial of blood into his hands. "Try to leave the bodies alone."

She walked quickly back out of the warehouse. Most of the ambulances were gone now. A few waited behind to carry the bodies back to the morgue. Forensics had finally arrived as well and was chatting with the remaining police officers as they unpacked their equipment. She picked one of the ambulance attendants at random. "You. Get a stretcher and a body bag and come with me."

"My partner . . ."

"Can warm up the ambulance. You don't need him. Come with me." Emily let a trace of ire creep into her voice. "Now." The attendant didn't question her again. Once they were back inside the warehouse, she stopped and made sure that he wouldn't remember anything about what was going to happen.

Jean-Claude was pacing nervously when they returned. When he first saw the attendant, he stiffened.

She realized that the hungry vampire probably only saw the man as a source of warm blood and hastily stepped between them. "He's your escape, not your supper." She pulled the body bag off the stretcher and unfolded it. "Get in."

"You must be joking." Jean-Claude regarded the heavy black plastic with undisguised loathing and poorly hidden fear.

Emily crossed her arms and shook her head sternly. "It's the only way you're going to get out of here without arousing suspicion about where you came from. I can control one or two mortals, but not the ten or twelve that you would have to walk past outside. You barely have the strength to walk anyway."

The Setite crouched down beside the bag. "It stinks like a corpse," he muttered resignedly.

"It should."

"Isn't there any other way to do this?"

"No. Besides, you'll only be in it for a few blocks. I'll follow in my car. The ambulance will stop once we're away from here and I'll take you the rest of the way with me."

He slid his foot inside as if stepping into a sleeping bag. "Where are we going?"

"Back to the morgue. I have blood there."

"Marvelous." He wriggled down into the bag and stared up at Emily as she tugged the zipper closed. "More corpses."

"Be thankful—you could have been one yourself." She gestured for the attendant to help her. Together they lifted the bag onto the stretcher. "Be quiet and hold still once we get outside. We'll go out the side door to avoid everyone."

"You're a wonder, Emily." Jean-Claude's voice was muffled. "You are wasted working alone with the dead."

She grimaced, though she knew he couldn't see it. "Tell me about it!"

"No vampire has helped me this way before."

"It's not coming free." She nodded for the attendant to start forward. She didn't want to run into the Forensics crew on the way out.

"I know, but . . . I mean, I'm almost sorry for dragging you into this thing with Doc Michaels."

Emily stopped, stunned. A cold chill ran through her body. The attendant kept going, and she had to take several quick steps to catch up to him. "What thing?"

"You don't know?" He sounded surprised. "Doc was blackmailing me. Turns out the young man I brought you last week was a favorite vessel of his. He wanted revenge and a cut into my drug deals. He said he knew where the temple was and that you helped me. I didn't believe him. He must have tipped off the police. He said he was blackmailing you, too." He paused, then added, "Until Doc said that, I was wondering if you had betrayed me." There was the hint of an edge to his voice.

If Emily hadn't already been dead, her heart would have stopped. She reached out and touched Jean-Claude through the bag. "No. I didn't. You're going to be coming out now, so be quiet. I'll be right back—I'm going to take the ambulance with you."

She felt numb inside as she ran around the building to the ambulances. "Doc" Michaels was a vampire of her Sire's generation. One of her Sire's blood siblings, in fact. One of the Prince's brood. He had his fingers in virtually every hospital and large clinic in the city, and she was the only other vampire in San Francisco with the medical training to understand how potentially powerful that made him. Her little domain in the Medical Examiner's Office brushed up against the bulk of his empire. Every time Doc stirred, Emily got shaken by it. If he knew about her dealings with Jean-Claude . . . she swallowed, abruptly aware that she might be playing right into his hands. Jean-Claude might not know it, but Doc Michaels' long fingers even extended into some of the ambulance companies. It was the only way out of the warehouse, though. She crossed her fingers and prayed that this ambulance crew was nothing more than what they seemed.

It wasn't hard to spot the ambulance attendant's partner. As she had suggested, he had the ambulance running, ready to leave. He sat in the driver's seat, hands tapping the wheel in time to music on the radio. Emily walked purposefully up to the passenger door and opened it. When he glanced up, she caught his gaze and held it. "Go to the side door," she instructed him, climbing into the passenger seat, "then help load the body there into the back."

She leaned her head against the cool glass of the window, letting the ambulance driver carry out her commands. How could Doc have found out about her? One of Jean-Claude's followers? No, he had sworn they wouldn't talk about the murder. Except that Doc could be very persuasive, especially when he had a scalpel in his hand. Jean-Claude? The Setites were devious. But why? He was in the same trouble as her. Could Doc have discovered his dead vessel and somehow Embraced him? Not likely. The body had been cremated right on schedule the morning after Jean-Claude had brought it to her.

At least she knew why Doc hadn't actually contacted her with a blackmail threat like the one he had delivered to Jean-Claude, Emily realized bitterly. It was Jean-Claude he was after. He would have little to gain from blackmailing her. There was no prestige in running the Medical Examiner's Office, even though it was the only large medical-related institution in the city that he didn't control. There was no power either, really. It was without status and without power, just like her. She was beneath his notice. She choked back tears of blood. No Kindred, except Jean-Claude, took any notice of her at all. Yet if Doc Michaels were suddenly to disappear, she would be the only one in the city who would really be able to replace him effectively. And he didn't even think she was worth blackmailing . . .

The plan seemed to spring fully formed into her head, jerking her upright with the force of its entry. Emily pursed her lips tightly as she thought. Doc had played himself into a losing position. She turned to look at the ambulance attendants as they loaded Jean-Claude into the rear of the ambulance. "Take me to a phone booth."

A dog skittered out of the way as the ambulance accelerated.

"Emily?" Doc Michaels called as he stepped into the morgue. "Are you here?"

Emily was pleased to note that his nose wrinkled in distaste at the odor in the room. She had turned the ventilation system off when she arrived several hours ago. "I'm here," she said quietly, in her smallest voice. She stood up from her desk and came around in front of it to greet him. Sitting behind a desk was a position of power—she wanted him to perceive her as weak. "Please. Come in."

He continued to stand in the doorway. "Perhaps it would be better if we went somewhere more comfortable?"

"I don't want any of the others to know about this. I can't go out." She stepped back as if she were nervous, and accidentally bumped into a corpse on a gurney. The room was packed with them. "Does anyone know now?"

"I haven't told anyone about your call." He started to step away from the door, then stopped. Emily wondered if he was suspicious. "My car is just outside though—and very private."

"No!" She forced a note of panic into her voice.

"Very well then." He walked completely into the room, twitching violently as the cramped conditions forced him to edge between two more corpses. "I must admit, your message last night mystified me. You sounded frightened. It's no secret your Sire and I are not on the best of terms, but the Followers of Set? Why would you think I . . ."

Emily saw Jean-Claude appear from the shadows by the door only a second before he leaped at Doc. The Ventrue's words ended in a sudden grunt of surprise as Jean-Claude tackled him. "Now, Emily!" screamed the Setite. "Now!"

Her hand went almost automatically to the nearest sheet-draped corpse and felt for the sharp stake that was hidden there. There were several others like it around the room, since she had no idea exactly where she would be when the time came to act. She almost had the stake in her grasp when Jean-Claude and Doc Michaels crashed into the gurney and spun it aside. Emily was left with only a sheet in her hand. She dived for another stake.

Doc Michaels had been an old man when he was Embraced. He still looked like a kindly, grandfatherly family doctor. Unfortunately, physical appearances meant little among the Kindred. Jean-Claude seemed young and strong, but the old man was matching him blow for blow. Emily had suspected that would happen. The two vampires rolled over and over on the ground as they fought. She couldn't get a clear chance at Doc. At the same time, she didn't want to try to separate them physically for fear of being drawn into the fight. She saw only one thing to do. When their struggle brought them close to a gurney, she tipped its dead burden off and on top of them. The two sprang apart instantly, repulsed by the corpse. Jean-Claude actually retched. Doc snarled and coiled, preparing to leap at his distracted attacker.

The stake went into his back and through his heart with a kind of dry hiss, as if she were stabbing a desiccated mummy. Doc Michaels shrieked and tried to lash out behind him. His fingers caught at her clothing, then fell away loosely as paralysis spread through his body. He tumbled to the floor. A horrible expression of rage and shock was frozen on his face.

Emily bent down and lifted him, careful not to dislodge the stake. He was surprisingly light. She held him with one hand as she opened one of the drawers that lined the wall of the morgue. It almost felt as if she were tucking a child into bed when she laid him out on the cold metal. Doc Michaels made a very natural-looking corpse, as if he had only recently died. Suddenly, she felt her Hunger rising. Ventrue were very particular about the source of their nourishment. Emily had discovered quite early that her Embrace had left her with a cruel and ironic need for cold blood taken from dead bodies. The body of a vampire was as cold and as dead as a body could be. She brushed Doc Michaels' collar aside to reveal his neck. The temptation was strong to drain the life out of him, to make the transfer of power complete. Very strong. She bent down, lips drawing back from eager fangs.

Jean-Claude grabbed her from behind and pulled her away. "No!"

"Let me go!" She struggled against him, but he held her firmly. "I want his blood, Jean-Claude. I need it!"

He twisted her around so that she could no longer see Doc Michaels' body. "You need him more! What if you need something someday? Information? Kill him now and all you will have done is commit Diablerie! Is it worth it?"

Emily pressed her Hunger back down. He was right. She relaxed. "Let me go." He did. She walked purposefully over to the drawer and slid it shut with a resounding slam, then looked up at the Setite. "Thank you."

"It would have been foolish to destroy such a resource."

"As foolish as attacking him prematurely? You were only supposed to close the door and lock it from outside."

"He knew something was wrong."

"I could have dealt with it—the bodies in the room unnerved him. I could have had him staked before he did anything." She sighed and wiped the back of her hand across her mouth. The blood was hers and not Doc Michaels'. Somehow she had split her lip in the struggle. "It doesn't matter now anyway. Did you get your followers and servants gathered back together?"

"Yes. I was fortunate."

"Take your people back to his haven. Make it look like it was broken into. Make it look like a Sabbat raid. That should keep everyone paranoid for a while. It will take the heat off us. Take care of anybody in his car too. And remember, Jean-Claude, you owe me very big."

"What if someone comes looking for him?" Jean-Claude indicated the drawer that contained Doc Michaels.

Emily pulled a ring of keys from her pocket and locked it. Then, with a grunt, she broke the key off in the lock. The drawer was officially empty and they had no shortage of other drawers for real bodies. No one would worry about fixing that lock for a long, long time.

Emily picked up the telephone before the second ring. "Morgue."

"Congratulations! I understand the Prince has just confirmed you as guardian of Doc Michaels' affairs."

"That's the easy way of saying he doesn't understand which end of a hospital the patient goes in, Jean-Claude. But thank you. It's actually going to take several weeks before I have complete control."

"What are you doing now?"

"Paperwork. They just brought in the body of a suicide from earlier tonight on Montgomery. He jumped from halfway up the Russ Building. Very messy."

"Still hard at work. You don't have to do that anymore."

She laughed. "I'll let the day crew handle this one, but I do enjoy my work sometimes. And so do you. What do you want?"

"You know me too well. There are five coffins on a boat coming into harbor the day after tomorrow. Can you arrange to have them taken past customs without being opened?"

"You're racking up favors-owed, Jean-Claude. And you're not the only one now."

"Just the first. It's good to have friends in high places."

"Consider it done."

"Thank you, Emily. I owe you."

"You owe me a lot."

"Good night, Emily." Jean-Claude hung up the phone and leaned back in his chair. A slow, evil smile spread across his face as he picked up a serpent-head ring from his desk. He had sent flowers to Constable Long's funeral. He always liked to reward his followers for their loyalty, and Long's fatal self-sacrifice in shooting him right on cue had been invaluable. It lent an air of truth to his story about the "surprise raid." He wondered if poor, innocent Doc Michaels felt the same oblivion as Long. The old Ventrue had almost given away his ignorance before Jean-Claude had been able to silence him in the morgue. He kissed the ring, then addressed it as if he were addressing the follower who had so recently worn it.

"We have her, Long. We have her."